Rise of the Ancients

Annuna

JC De La Torre

Rise of the Ancients – Annuna

ISBN: 978-0-9785272-3-5

Library of Congress Control Number:

Cover art by Jeremy Robinson visit Jeremy at –

http://www.jeremyrobinsononline.com/.

Edited by Angela Hooper.

Visit JC De La Torre at http://www.jcdelatorre.com

Published by

This novel is dedicated to my lovely Rita who's not a meter maid, my mother Irene, my father David, and you — my fans.

Acknowledgments

I wanted to take the opportunity to thank the people whom without their invaluable assistance, this novel would have never been created. First, I must thank my wife, Rita, without her love and support I would be lost. I'd like to thank Jeremy Robinson, whose guidance and example have been an inspiration to me. Among Jeremy's talents is the ability to create awe inspiring covers, as he did for this work. As an author, I can only hope to come near the success he has enjoyed.

I'd also like to thank Angela Hooper, who did another excellent job on the edit of the novel and the folks at Absolute Write and Critter for helping me rediscover my voice.

I'd also like to thank the De La Torre, Cabrera, and Dawson families for their love and support.

Finally, I'd like to thank you – my beloved reader. Without your inquiries and interest in this series, this sequel may have never been completed. Thanks for your encouragement, dedication, your commitment of purchase and your support. Please know this isn't the end of the saga but only the beginning and I promise I won't take as long next time!

Other Books by this Author

Ancient Rising -Rise of the Ancients Book 1

Book Details:

Printed: Paperback, 320 pages, 5.0 x 8.0 in., Perfect-bound

ISBN-10: 0978527216

ISBN-13: 978-0978527211

Suggested Retail Price: $9.95

Copyright Year: © 2006 Luna Brillante Publishing

Short synopsis: A widower is set off on an amazing adventure by a man claiming to be a God. Like Indiana Jones meets Clash of the Titans, follow Dan Ryan through Egypt, Greece, and the Mexican jungle as he unlocks the keys to finding the lost continent of Atlantis and the Gods that are imprisoned there.

Available at Amazon in paperback and Kindle format as well as in paperback at most online retailers.

BOOK II

ANCIENT DESTRUCTION

Chapter 1 The Waves of the Past

It silently rose in the distance, dark and foreboding, toward an angry sky. Prometheus, the god, flexed his immense muscles, his eyelids clamped down and his face contorted in a grimace. His invisible power reinforced the structure of the ship, enabling the craft to remain whole as it was battered and bruised by the unforgiving sea. Despite his protection, the frigid spikes of rain assaulted my skin and jet engine howl of the wind penetrated my ears. Lightning, a ballerina dancing among the clouds, crackled to the sea and briefly illuminated the wave as it descended upon us. I held tightly to the mast of one of the alien ship's sails, praying for deliverance from the two gods unleashing their fury.

Down we went into the trough that was the mouth of the behemoth. Prometheus held tightly to the steering mechanism of the ship as it rose. As with previous challengers, its nose pointed skyward darting up the wall of water toward the crest - but this time it wouldn't make it. For a moment, I hung to the mast like a trapeze artist to his line, but I lost my grip and dropped. Instead of a net I was greeted by the ship's cabin door with a painful thud. Another wrenching twist flung me over the top of the cabin, continuing my descent until I hit the ocean - a concrete wall tearing the air from my lungs and sending a shockwave of pain cascading through my body.

I looked above me just in time to see the Atlantean ship keel over and come crashing toward me. As I mentally prepared for my surely fatal encounter with my former transportation, the force of the wave's current sucked me underneath the water. The sea intruded my nostrils, my eyes, finding its way inside my mouth and down my throat. Through the murky haze of my flaming vision I saw the white foam of the wave above me, its circular corona continuing as it passed over. A white shimmering shape replaced where the roll of the wave had been...through the blurred view I knew it was the hull of the ship. Prometheus managed to right it.

My lungs begged for the absent air and I could feel the cold chill of the darkness creeping in. The Grim Reaper's scythe was being sharpened for me now. I knew for fact there was an afterlife – Persephone, the half mortal-half god, told me as much. The gods fed off the life force of things that had passed on – but she didn't really go into detail about how it all worked. Death remained a mystery. *Would I just be a floating buffet with no consciousness? Would I see my wife and daughter in the afterlife?*

It wouldn't be long until I found the answers. Once the last bit of oxygen deprived my brain I'd likely lose consciousness, crap myself and it would be over. In a sense, I welcomed it as penance for my misdeeds.

Slimy hands grabbed my bare legs and tugged on the chiton I was wearing. I opened my eyes, allowing the acidity of the saltwater to assault them again just to get a glimpse of what had a hold of me. Pulling me downward like anchors were two female creatures with scaly faces and large fishy-looking eyes. Their thin heads connected to a coral adorned humanoid torso that led to an aquamarine fish tail where their legs would be. It was those tails that seemed to give them unbelievable strength in pulling me deeper.

Darkness invaded from the outer reaches of my vision, taking up territory like a hungry lava flow. I was ready to succumb to it, accepting the inevitability of the end - but before it completely took me a muscular arm wrapped around my waist. I weakly gazed at the face connected to the arm and saw it belonged to Prometheus.

At first my body was the rope in a vicious tug of war between beings that a year ago I couldn't have imagined existed. Finally, losing the battle, the mermaids released my legs, shrieked in anger, and tried to attack him, but a simple gesture from his hand sent them crying in pain. The lava flow took the remaining shreds of my consciousness and all went black.

***

As my face felt the sting of the rain propelled by the category five winds, my eyes opened to the swirling tempest above the mast of the ship. Another bolt of lightning struck across the sky, dancing from cloud to cloud until it found its home in the sea a few miles to the west of us. The wooden deck beneath me was hardened, water logged, and swayed as the waves of Poseidon continued their assault of our vessel. Spray from the conjoining of the ship and its assailants shot into the air and collapsed on me. My lungs were still searching for the air – I coughed, vomiting water and seaweed that spilled down my cheeks to the deck.

"You live?" Prometheus asked me, his deep voice penetrating my now waterlogged eardrums like a spike.

I managed to croak a yes.

"Good. You look like death."

I thought of telling him, "I was dead. You saved me."

"Indeed," he responded, as if I informed him directly.

"You just read my mind?"

"Of course."

"Does that go with the 'being a god' territory?" I asked.

"Yes. You'll learn."

"Riiiiiight."

"You mock me?" Prometheus looked confused.

"No, no, I meant no disrespect." I coughed again, wheezing more salty wetness.

"Oh, so you still are in denial of your lineage."

"If you say so."

Prometheus' normally blondish hair was soaked dark and tumbled down his face and broad shoulders. His smooth face and pronounced jaw grimaced. His thick neck connected to a chiseled body as his muscular frame slipped back into his golden Atlantean chest plate.

"Your mortal ignorance is insufferable." He griped, "Has the fact that you released the gods and set us into our current predicament shown you nothing?"

"Yeah, it showed me that I'm a mark."

"Daniel, Zeus and Poseidon wouldn't personally be attacking us unless you were a threat to them."

"Me? Come on, Prometheus. You don't see me doing that hocus pocus you do. I can't fly. I can't control weather – I'm just a guy who somehow got some good people and myself into the middle of this clusterf-"

"You are a son of Hercules, Daniel – it's the reason why you were chosen by Hermes to release the gods."

"I'm the son of Jimmy Ryan – a con man from Yonkers who is doing twenty in the pen for scamming old ladies out of their social security checks."

"Anyway..." He extended his hand to me and assisted me to my feet, "...the Naiads can pack a wallop. Are you sure you're alright?"

"The Naiads?" I was dumbfounded.

"The half-fish, half-women. They are daughters of Triton, Poseidon's son."

"Ah, the mermaids. What did he do? Score with a dolphin?"

Prometheus erupted into ferocious laughter.

"You are a strange half-breed, Dan Ryan," he said, finally composing himself. "A strange one indeed."

"What part of this are you not getting, Prometheus? I am no half breed. I don't even know what Hermes was talking about."

"Dan, you know the answer to this – you were the only remaining descendant of Hercules and only you could free the gods from their underwater Atlantean prison – for it was Hercules that put them there. Now, you can continue to deny that or accept th-"

Prometheus suddenly looked skyward. The sheets of rain dissipated to a light drizzle and the roaring wind subsided to a slight breeze as the furious clouds pulled back to reveal a billion stars. The violent rocking of the galleon had slipped to a gentle caress, like a mother easing her child into a slumber.

"This is not good," Prometheus grumbled, as he took the wheel of the vessel.

A tremor beneath our feet shook the deck, followed by smaller tremors that created bubbling near the starboard side of the ship.

"Dan, take the wheel."

Prometheus stood toward the fore of the ship, peering out into the black ocean. The bubbling continued to accumulate, first a few, then, as if in concert with the vibrations, more and more of the bubbles appeared until there was a large foamy vortex directly in front of the ship. At the center of the vortex, a head with a crown of coral emerge, framed by long white hair and a long beard. His large, naked torso would appear soon thereafter, followed by his seaweed-covered loins and his muscular legs. Around his neck, he wore a chain of seashells laced in gold. He floated above the water, his immense muscles seeming to glisten as the moonlight shone on his wet frame.

"Finally decided to stop being a coward, Poseidon?" Prometheus taunted the god of the sea.

"Be still your tongue, Prometheus," he returned. "You will pass no further with the seed of Hercules."

"Are you going to stop us?" Prometheus laughed. "You? The second-in-command? Your waves did nothing but annoy me, and you are blocking our way. Do you truly want to face me?"

"You overestimate your powers, Prometheus," Poseidon retorted. "You are not the god you once were."

"Let's see then, shall we?"

Prometheus levitated off the deck of the ship and into the air, cupped his hands in front of him, and then expelled a beam of red energy from them striking Poseidon in the chest. The sea god tumbled backward, a shriek of pain erupting from his lips.

Poseidon fired back with his own energy beam and it sent Prometheus flying backward. He regained his bearings, then sent another burst finding its mark, this time sending Poseidon into the sea. He immediately rose with a wet and furious look on his face. Poseidon made a gesture toward the water and large, geyser-like streams of water struck Prometheus on both sides of his body.

BREEEEOOOOOH…a strange sound erupted from Poseidon's lips.

Exploding from the sea, an orca chomped down on Prometheus, swallowing him whole like some bad remake of Moby Dick. The whale crashed back into the water - he was gone.

Poseidon floated toward the Atlantean ship.

"Dan Ryan, if you and your companions wish to live, you will turn this ship around and follow my directions back to Atlantis."

Beneath us, a great eruption occurred and suddenly, the head of the orca flew past Poseidon. Its tail tumbled over the ship and its dorsal fin plopped on the deck. With innards scattered across the sea, all manner of watery beasts began to take their fill as Prometheus arose from its muck.

"Poseidon, you did not seriously believe you could defeat me with your pets, did you?"

Poseidon inaudibly growled a response and another energy burst erupted from him, blasting into Prometheus with everything he had. I heard him cry out in pain.

"You will die now, insurrectionist." Poseidon screamed as he continued to put all of his might into the power of his next attack.

I saw a globe of blue energy surrounding Prometheus… he was no longer visible.

"Dissipate into the abyss!" Poseidon cried.

"No…" I whispered.

Poseidon released the charge and the blue ball at the other end began to disappear, revealing a figure with long light brown hair, bulging biceps, and an annoyed look on his face.

"What?" An exhausted Poseidon wheezed in anguish.

"Was that truly the best you have?" Prometheus mocked. "I mean, really. I would get more of a challenge from Aphrodite."

"You… could not have survived that."

"Poseidon, for a god of your stature, you are particularly dense," Prometheus told him, smiling. "Of course I survived. Gods cannot die – and you cannot destroy me. I am a Titan – a higher order than you. I will always be stronger than you, Zeus, or any of the Dodekatheons you send my way."

"What is your profit in all of this?" Poseidon asked, "Do you aim to rule the mortals? We can give you that role once more."

"Are we to bargaining now?"

"What else is there? I cannot defeat you and you cannot defeat me. We are at an impasse."

"Wrong, king of the sea." Prometheus growled, and a blinding white light erupted from his outstretched hands, looking like two bolts of lightning. The bolts swirled around Poseidon, striking him over and over, drawing cries of agony.

Prometheus continued his torment, a wild, angry look appearing on his face. He was determined to end Poseidon's existence. As Poseidon writhed in pain, the stars disappeared, the wind picked up and rapidly the wall of rain pelted us.

"Well, Zeus," Prometheus called out as he continued his barrage on Poseidon, "Have you come for the same treatment as your brother?"

"Release him," a booming voice stereoed from the clouds. "Release him - now."

Prometheus ignored Zeus' request, continuing his attack against what now appeared to be an unconscious Poseidon.

"RELEASE HIM!" Zeus cried out again.

"Come take his place!" Prometheus called back. "Or withdraw this storm, the waves, and trouble our journey no more."

"Agreed," Zeus' voice boomed. "If you release him – you will not feel the wrath of the wind, rain or waves the remainder of your journey."

"So be it." Prometheus replied, as his hands dropped to his side, releasing Poseidon, who simply slipped into the sea, no sign of life emanating from him.

Once more, the rain stopped, the wind died down, and the skies retreated back to reveal the moon and its heavenly companions.

Prometheus returned to the deck of the stilled ship and fell to one knee.

"Are you alright?" I asked.

"The battle took a lot more out of me than I let on," Prometheus rasped in obvious pain. "I need to rest."

"You need me to pilot the ship for you? I'm no mariner but I used to have a small boat I took the family out into Tampa Bay."

"No, it will not be necessary."

Chapter 2 Genesis

Prometheus used his psychic ability to put the ship in a kind of autopilot and I helped him down into the crew's quarters where my companions, Doc, Mina, and Martin Jackson awaited. Doc led the Atlantis expedition and had been searching for the lost continent for decades. Marty was one of the leading Egyptologists in the world but the lure of Atlantis pulled him into being part of Doc's team. Mina was Doc's assistant and granddaughter – and much more than that to me.

"Jesus H. Christ," Marty said as we entered the room. "We felt like we were in a popcorn popper in here. What the f-"

"Everyone alright?" I asked.

"Yes, we're fine," Mina replied with a hypnotic smile, intoxicating me. I found myself longing to hold her, kiss her luscious lips, and stroke her silky brown hair. During our journey together we grew an unbreakable bond. I tried to resist it, believing it was disrespect to Annabelle, but the electricity between us was undeniable and irresistible.

"So do ya wanna get us up ta speed there, Dan?" Doc asked, snapping me out of my trance.

I relayed to them all that had occurred topside. Mina drew close to me and put her arms around me.

"I can't believe we almost lost you," she said.

"I'm fine. Prometheus here needs a little rest, though."

The crew quarters were spacious, with large bunks that could pass for king size beds at home. The bunks had a strange, soft material, nearly silk-like but a texture that I've never felt. It was thin and see-through – yet strong. The inner chamber of the quarters had unremarkable grey and white, no special fixtures, or decoration. It lacked the iridescence of the top side sails and painted exterior hull. We lay Prometheus down on one of the empty ones and he seemed to doze off.

"What are we doing here, Dan?" Marty asked, waiting a few extra minutes to be sure Prometheus was asleep.

"I don't know, Marty."

"Where are we going?"

"I have no clue."

"We're way over our heads here," Marty continued. "I never signed up for any of this."

"None of us did, Marty" Mina interjected.

"I don't understand – why did you free them?" Marty continued, "I mean, we could have left their asses there in sea world and billions of lives wouldn't be lost."

"I know that, Marty," I sighed, "I feel the burden of that every day."

"Then why did you do it?"

"I was told to – by Persephone."

"Right, how could I forget, the god bitch told you to free the gods, find this paluka and all would be good." Marty mocked as he pointed to Prometheus, "I hate to break it to you Dan, but her credibility is crap right now."

"She got us out of Hades realm, she helped us escape Atlantis, and we're on our way to try to save what's left of our kind."

"Yet, if you would have just let these bastards where they were our kind wouldn't need saving!" Marked barked, "You're a coward!"

"Back off, Marty," Mina said, "He did it for us."

"He did it for his own ass."

"I did it because I didn't have a choice," I added, "They would have made me do it either way – I chose the only option that gave us a chance to escape and try to stop this."

"And yet where are we, Dan?" Marty continued, "In the crosshairs of hell."

"That's quite enough there, Martin," Doc interjected.

"No, I don't think so," Marty replied, "He hid his contact with Hermes until the last possible minute. He put us on this trek – something none of us asked for – and cost us the lives of Noah, Roger, Mort…my Serenity – for what? My best friend and fiancé are dead because of you."

He took a swing at me but I dodged and slammed him into the wall of the crew cabin. Marty's glasses popped off the bridge of his nose and hit the floor.

"Marty," I replied, "I know you're upset. We're all upset. I don't know how the hell this happened. When my wife and little girl were killed, I was in desperate straits. Hermes came to me and he took advantage of my condition. He told me that the gods were all that stood in between us and annihilation – the gods would save us in return of their freedom. I was a mark, Marty, pure and simple."

"You were an ass."

"I was – but you know what? In the state of mind I was in – he could have told me Sonny and Cher were imprisoned on Atlantis and they could save us – I would have believed him. He led me to all of you, and you were more than willing to help me. You can't put this all on me – your zeal for finding Atlantis led you to this. Well, you found it Marty, what do you think of it?"

"Let go of me!" He barked and I complied

"We all wanted Atlantis, Marty," Doc added, "You know as much as anyone how much findin' tha lost contin-tah-nent meant ta me."

"To all of us," Mina concurred.

"You used that against us," Marty continued, "You preyed on us to continue your quest to screw us all. Is that what it was about? Is it about Annabelle? Jeanie? You hated your life – God – so much because of that drunk driver you decided – screw the human race – may you all go to hell!"

My fist connected forcefully to the bridge of his nose knocking him on his backside.

"Stop this now!" Mina cried.

"Don't bring them into this. He tricked all us by leaving little clues for us to follow – in Akrotiri, Alexandria – wherever we needed it. I didn't know what to expect when we got there, Marty. Hell – I wasn't sure if I even believed it – other than the fact that Hermes seemed to have crazy powers I couldn't explain. He wasn't human and if he said the gods were real and were going to deliver us from our own destruction – who was I to argue? I was a pawn, Marty, just like you."

"And so here we are, oh wise one," Marty continued, "We can't take on gods, Daniel. We're nothing to them. Flies on crap. Look how they have already annihilated most of our kind. Nukes, tank, armies – they're no defense. Any resistance has been obliterated. We may be the last of our kind – we don't even know if there's anything left to save. Perhaps if we accept the New World Order, Zeus will spare us…"

"The New World Order?" I was aghast. "Are you serious?"

"Come on, man, ya daft?" Doc added.

"Yeah. Maybe I am – but not as daft as trying to take on gods."

"Marty," I continued, growing more annoyed, "the New World Order means death to all humans. Our right to exist is at stake here, or have you forgotten that?"

"A king needs subjects, Dan. If we submit to his rule, he will spare us."

"Submit to his rule? Just like that?"

"Yeah, why not?"

"Because, Asshole," Prometheus' voice came from behind Marty, "You will not live to serve Zeus. You and your kind are being exterminated. Zeus wants to start over, with a new set of humanoids, more docile than your breed."

"I told you, my name is Marty." While searching for Prometheus on Atlantis and battling our way past the Sacrolites, a band of zombie-like creatures, Prometheus had once heard one of our fallen companions refer to Marty as an "asshole" and took it as his name.

"And I told you, it matters not."

"Why would Zeus recreate us? He's already conquered us – he doesn't need to do anything else."

"You lack the knowledge to make that assessment of Zeus."

"Then," I interjected, "Why not enlighten us? What are you people? How did you come to this world?"

"You know the answers," he replied strangely. "You only need to search your mind for them."

"What the hell does that mean?"

"You have power inside of you that you have not yet tapped, Daniel Ryan," Prometheus replied. "And to think you had resigned yourself to the lowly role of a scribe. So much power and you were going to waste it."

"Power?" I was lost. "What power? I'm no different from any other man."

"You are wrong," Prometheus retorted. "You have the blood of Hercules coursing through your veins. The power of a God held back by your mortal ignorance."

"I don't know what you're talking about."

"Have you ever had visions? Memories of the past? Visions of the future?"

"Déjà vu? Everyone has that."

"Not like you do."

I stopped for a moment, considering what he had said. My sense of déjà vu was strong. I remembered my visions well and when they came to pass, I was always a bit stunned. Further, I would get vivid memories of the past in my dreams- but none of that helped me save Annabelle and Jeanie.

"You are special, Dan," Prometheus continued. "You may not have realized it until now, but you are different."

"He must mean special as in short bus, right?" Marty interjected.

"Shaddup, Marty," I croaked. "Fine, I'm different. That doesn't mean I know what you're talking about. Spell it out for us."

"Very well," Prometheus sighed. "I will begin with the creation of your world."

"And please spare us the religious mumbo jumbo," I added. "We know you are not really gods."

"Oh? And what would you consider a God, Dan?" Prometheus asked, "Is a God not a sentient being more powerful than you; one that creates life throughout the universe? Would you not consider that a god?"

"Yes but…"

"Ah, you mean in the religious context of the word?" He had read my thoughts again. "But your belief in the one unilateral god is not unlike what we are."

"I'm sorry, I don't agree," I retorted. "Hermes tried to tell me the same thing. At least in my belief, my God created the universe. He is the Supreme Being, the Creator of all. He provides us the foundation for our civilization, the rules that govern our lives. I also believe that he sent his only son, Jesus, to save us and to purge our sins. I believe when I die, I will see my wife and my daughter in Heaven."

"Ah yes, this Jesus man," Prometheus replied. "I can see this being was powerful in your beliefs. I do not know him but I do know the things you speak of exist."

"You mean there is a God? There is a Heaven?"

"The God you refer to we call Thoth. He is the –"

"Did you say Thoth?" Marty asked.

"Indeed."

"Thoth was a minor god in Egyptian lore," Marty interjected. "Tantamount to Hermes in the Greek culture."

"Thoth, the same level of that worm, Hermes?" Prometheus erupted. "Be glad I do not annihilate you where you stand. Be careful, Martin Jackson, or you will feel my wrath."

"Okay, okay, I'm sorry," Marty backed off. "I'm just saying that among the Egyptian deities, Thoth was a very minor character."

"Obviously, these Egyptians were fools. They shouldn't even know his name."

"Thoth was a good god, though," Marty continued. "He was their god for wisdom and magic."

"Thoth is much, much more than that."

"And Heaven?" I had to ask.

"This Heaven you speak of is my realm, my home. The home of the Annuna."

"The Annuna?" Marty interjected.

"Yes."

"The Ancient Sumerians, one of the first known civilizations on Earth, that is before we discovered Atlantis, of course –"

"And Zu," Prometheus added.

"Zu...geezus....we haven't found that yet," Marty continued. "Anyway, the Annuna were the Ancient Sumerian deities. Those who 'came down from heaven'. Are you saying you are one and the same?"

"Indeed," Prometheus continued, "and in a sense, you are right. We did come down from heaven, so to speak. We originate from another plane of existence. Is your race familiar with the five dimensions?"

"We know of three for sure. We have hypothetical opinions on a fourth," Marty replied.

"There are five, and we come from that fifth dimension."

"How did you reach ours?" I asked.

"The body you see before you does not exist in the fifth dimension. In that existence, we are energy and consciousness."

"Why did you come here?"

"To create life, of course." He smiled. "Now be silent. Hold your questions for later, as for now, I am going to tell you the true story of the creation of life on your world."

Prometheus began to speak, and as his did, I felt my eyes droop. The hypnotic sound of his voice seemed to overtake me as visions began to appear in my consciousness, as if the TV of my mind had been flipped on. They were powerful, immersing me into time and space... as Prometheus' words left his lips I could no longer hear his voice, but could see what he was saying. I was there, a ghostly silent witness to the alien colonization of our world.

Chapter 3 Nibiru

I was in another world, their world, and its name was Nibiru. In the fifth dimension, it is a world much like Earth, with blue skies, green lands rife with vegetation, plus large oceans that fed the life system of the planet. Instead of animals, though, Nibiru is home to the strangest of creatures – the Annuna. They were beings of energy. They held the form of human beings, but they were not. They were visions, life force, a consciousness, souls, ghosts. A civilization of specters that were beyond death, disease, war, and at a stage of perfect evolution. They were a world of gods.

They fed off the life force of living things throughout the universe, including their homeworld. When a creature died, its life essence would be deposited in Tartarus, a realm between Nibiru and our dimension. There, they would be judged on their deeds in the life they had just completed. If they were deemed to be good and just, the dead's essence would be allowed to join with the Annuna and become one of them. Those who were evil would remain in Tartarus, their life force devoured by the Annuna until they were no more. Only higher, more advanced thinking beings were judged, as only they were worthy consideration to be among the Annuna. A species had to have some technological advancement, some conscious thought, or scientific learning.

While their food choice would make you might think the Annuna to be a warlike race, bent on killing to fulfill their hunger it was the exact opposite. Their idea of feeding was to create as much life as there could be throughout the universe. A life force wouldn't sustain them unless it had matured through a full, complete life. They detested war and pestilence, simply because it took life before the lives had completely matured. The power was also great, as it fed their ability to control weather patterns, the seas, objects, and create life where there was none.

The Annuna's leader and creator was Thoth. I couldn't see Thoth, he had no shape or form. It was as if he was a large ball of energy from which all life had sprung. Perhaps it meant that this being was a remnant or the cause of the big bang that created the universe. One thing I knew for sure was Thoth was a sentient being, and omnipotent. When he spoke, all of Nibiru shook. The Annuna, perhaps the greatest race in the universe, was subservient to this being. He was their God.

The world of the Annuna looked like an advanced society, with large buildings, stadiums, and gizmos of all electronic origin. Only, they weren't really there. The buildings themselves were simply ghostly images, perhaps there to give those who weren't born as Annuna some semblance of their former existence. They - like the beings that used and resided in them – were simply molecules held together by pure energy. If you looked closely, you could actually see an electric discharge flashing in them. The buildings themselves were silver with odd shapes. Since the Annuna did not fear gravity, they did not need to observe the typical laws of architecture, thus allowing the buildings to have strange angles and weird contortions.

There was an obvious hierarchy in their society. The servants and warriors of Thoth were definitely the elevated ones. They were the Angelus, or as we knew them, Angels – exactly as Jewish and Christian tradition had seen them. The rest of the society was made up of workers, similar to worker bees; they would search the stars for worlds that could sustain life and then bring this information to Thoth. He would then decide whether or not to populate the system.

This is what happened with Earth's sun, which they referred to as Sol. When a young Annuna, Cronus, discovered Sol and a primordial ten planets surrounding the relatively young sun, he sought council from Thoth. I'll call Cronus a man since he looked an awful lot like one of us, even though what appeared as flesh and bone was nothing but pure energy. As he entered the Great One's throne room, Cronus, who was a large being, came in front of Thoth in reverence, on hands and knees. He had dark hair with grey streaks down the sides, just above his tiny ears. His slender frame didn't command the respect of a god, nor did his light complexion and light blue eyes.

"My Lord," Cronus said to his God, "I have located a system I would like to attempt to seed."

"Young Cronus, I am happy to finally have you before me." Came Thoth's booming reply, "Yes, I know. Sol – a very young system."

"Y-y-yes, Lord," Cronus replied. "It is a strong system with large outer planets that should be able to protect the inner planets from comets, asteroids, and other space debris. I feel they are good cand-"

"Silence, Cronus!" Thoth boomed. "I know your beliefs before you even state them! You have interest in three of the inner worlds in the system."

My mind told me that Thoth was referring to Eden, a world previously unknown to us, Terra (Earth) and Marta (Mars).

"Y-y-yes, My Lord," Cronus replied. "You know all of course."

"Sol is a special star," Thoth said. "Those beings who evolve there may be worthy of becoming Annuna. I will take special interest in the development of that world. I would like for Uranus and Gaea to take the honor of polonizing there."

"Great Thoth," Cronus replied. "Your wisdom knows no bounds. However, my father and mother have gotten weak in their advancing age. They do not retain the life force as they once did, and they may not be up to such a monumental and important task."

"I agree with you Cronus, and I appreciate your candor – so few are brave enough to challenge my will." Thoth replied.

"My lord," Cronus backpedaled, "Your will shall always be done."

"Its fine, Cronus, you need not be concerned." Thoth continued, "You will go with your mother and father to the Sol system. They will assist you in your assignment. Bring your sister, Rhea as well – create life."

"Thank you, Lord!" Cronus replied excitedly, "Thank you!"

It would be only a short time later that Uranus, Gaea, and their two children, Cronus and Rhea, made their way to Sol. Uranus was nearly identical to Cronus, only his hair was completely grey and you could see small indentions on the energy that would be his face, almost simulating wrinkles. He wasn't as visually bright as Cronus, his essence was dimmer, perhaps revealing his age. Gaea looked slightly younger, with blond and grey hair intertwined, and trailing down her shapely body. She had a kind, gentle face with soft eyes. She too was brighter than Uranus. Rhea was the spitting image of Gaea, only younger, more vibrant. Her hair was completely blonde, and what we would see as her body was gorgeously and perfectly proportioned.

On Marta, they created life in the form of small reptilian and mammalian species, none that would reach any level of sophistication. On Terra, they created a world that would be ruled by the reptiles. On Eden, Adamus and Eva, the first humanoids in the Sol system were created, and the first great human race rose. It was a world of beauty and peace. There was no war, no evil. It was the perfect utopian society.

The civilization would mature rapidly, first from hunters-and-gatherers to engineers and architects. They would build gigantic monuments and temples to Uranus. Pyramids and cathedrals that rivaled Rome rose from the dust of the planet. Uranus and Gaea were kind rulers, viewing each of the three worlds as their own children. They did their best to foster life on each planet. Cronus and Rhea both supported their parents, and did much of the creation of the smaller life forms for the humans and reptiles to eat. They basically created the ecology of the world.

As they returned to Nibiru to recharge their powers, Cronus became jealous of the accolades his father received for making such a wonderful eco-system. Uranus would stand in the middle of a large stadium with thousands of Annuna chanting his name. He received awards, and the Annuna, who had their own form of news media, would go on and on about the greatness of the legendary Uranus. There were Uranus effigies lining what we would call streets, although they had no motorized vehicles to transport them – as energetic organisms, the Annuna possessed the ability to teleport wherever they liked. Glory belonged to Uranus, and it chapped Cronus.

"Father, why did you not mention Rhea's and my work during your honor acceptances?" Cronus asked his father as they entered their domicile.

"Son, do not be ridiculous," his father laughed. "Yes, you created the insects and the small protozoa that inhabit the oceans. Of course, you created the fish and other smaller creatures that are important to the ecology of each planet. But do not kid yourself. Any lower Annuna could have done the same. Not all can create the perfect humanoids."

"So are you saying Rhea and I do not deserve honor?"

"My ambitious son, the time will come when Thoth decides you are worthy of such honors. That time has not now."

"Thoth did decide I deserved the honor, but you took it from me. So it is yours now. You tell me my time will come, but when?" Cronus barked. "After your retirement? How long must I be in the shadow of the great Uranus and Gaea?"

"Fame, glory," Uranus replied to his upset son. "An Annuna does not crave these things. Son, you must channel these jealous urges into your creations."

"Thoth gave me the task, yet you stole it from me," Cronus repeated.

"Thoth called all of us, surely you misunderstood his intentions," Uranus replied to his furious son. "It is only natural the most experienced of our clan would be the primaries to create the higher life forms. These jealous urges of yours, my ambitious son, do not allow them to consume you, or you will not remain among the Annuna."

"I care not of my place among the Annuna," Cronus croaked. "I only care to receive what rewards I deserve. I have done great things for the Annuna, and I have yet to see the profit in it for me."

"The profit?" Uranus was shocked.

"Indeed, I have had my eyes opened to the deception that is the Annuna way. Thoth is blind."

"Silence" Uranus slapped his son across the energy that would be his face. A spark erupted from the contact point. "You will not defame Thoth in my presence! You will be silent now, insolent boy."

"I will not, Father," Cronus continued. "The Annuna project themselves under the guise of benevolent creators, but in truth, we are dictators, destructive dictators who take worlds and make them our own for our own designs, to feed our power. With that power comes the need to seek the approval and adulation of the other Annuna. Is this not why you became the best creator? Is that not the reason you stole the Sol system from me?"

"I became the best creator so that I could provide life to the cosmos, and life force to the Annuna."

"I saw you out there, Father, I could read your thoughts as the crowds chanted your name."

"My son, your ambitions are misguided. I will speak with Thoth about your thoughts and get his guidance. Perhaps we can get you a system of your own…once you've been reeducated."

"*I had a system of my own*," Cronus thought to himself, but kept silent. He knew what reeducated meant. He would have his consciousness wiped clean, and only the pleasant memories would remain. He didn't want to push his luck and have his parents force the issue immediately.

"Now, my son," Uranus continued. "Do you feel capable of assisting your parents in Sol or do we need to leave you behind?"

"I will do as you will, Father."

"Good, good, now rouse your sister," Uranus replied. "We will return to Sol at once."

As his father departed, Cronus looked at his sleeping sister.

"Sister, wife," he roused her, "it is time for you to rise."

"Yes, my husband," Rhea replied as they kissed. As when he was struck earlier by his father, a tiny little spark appeared between their lips as they met. Apparently, it was quite normal for the Annuna to keep it all in the family (of course, considering that they didn't really have bodies or DNA to corrupt, and their idea of procreation was seeding, it wasn't quite as backwoods hillbilly as one may imagine).

"The time has also come for us to end Uranus and Gaea's reign over us."

"I do not understand."

"You will, Sister." A strange look in his eyes developed. "You will."

Chapter 4 The Rebellion

Uranus worried about his son's threats but his attention would be distracted by the inhabitants of Eden. The world had to deal with dramatic climate changes because of its unusual orbit. He had to help his humanoid inhabitants evolve quickly so they could survive the harsh winters when Eden was furthest from the Sun. Eden's thick atmosphere allowed some protection and retained some of the heat, but the winters were long and Ice Age level harsh. Each Edenian year was equal to ten Earth years, but once it would pass, it would cost the lives of hundreds of thousands of the humanoids.

Meanwhile, Gaea would continue to focus on Terra and the reptiles who ruled it. Terra's winters were nothing to worry about, thus she didn't have to grant great intelligence to the beasts. Cronus and Rhea were given the frigid but still livable world of Marta to create small species. As each year passed, knowing that Uranus owned the advanced civilization, and Gaea had the fertile reptilian world, and they were only given the smallest and less hospitable of the three worlds, Cronus' jealousy of his father's respect and glory increased further until it couldn't be held back any further.

Cronus remembered a comet that would pass close to Eden every thousand years or so and searched the solar system for its current location. He found the gigantic celestial traveler making its turn around the sun. It wouldn't be long before it made its way around and give its spectacular light show to the Edenian inhabitants.

"*Excellent,*" Cronus thought to himself, "*I can change its course ever so slightly, he will never notice and when it hits, it will destroy all that my father has created. He will learn the cost of his theft and I will take over as the supreme ruler of this solar system."*

Cronus used his power to hurl asteroids at the hundred kilometer center of the comet. Its corona took the brunt and after several hits, the trajectory changed.

While Cronus made his treacherous preparations, the attentions of the family were diverted.

"Mother, I have to tell you something," Rhea said.

"Speak, my child, I have to make sure that my reptiles' food supply is in high demand. We had an unusually dry summer."

"Mother, I am with child."

"Oh Thoth be praised! Is it true?" Her mother exclaimed.

"Yes."

"Is Cronus pleased?"

"I hope so," Rhea replied.

"Why would he not?"

"Cronus seems to have his attention elsewhere."

As Uranus joined the two women, Cronus returned from his side project and Rhea made the announcement to all. Cronus feigned excitement but kept his eyes trained on his father, who was ecstatic with the news.

"I will teach him every secret I know!" Uranus exclaimed, "He will be the best creator among us!"

"You have made me wait a millennia before you provided me your secrets," Cronus growled at them. "And now you plan to bypass me and give it to my child?"

"No, no," Uranus replied, stunned at his son's anger. "You misunderstand. I will teach you together and you both will replace me as the top creators in the Annuna order."

"This is the final insult, father, I am no longer your son." Cronus barked in return. "You have treated me poorly for the final time."

"Cronus wait!" Uranus called after him but he was gone.

Cronus left for the end of the solar system hiding behind the planet that one day have his father's name and waited in frigid isolation. Uranus and Gaea searched for him but after a few hundred years, they gave up and helped Rhea prepare for the coming of the child. With his son gone, Uranus found a little peace. He knew his son was rebellious, but he hoped that some time alone in the outer reaches of space would help him mature into the father he needed to be.

Rhea discovered it wouldn't be that easy. Not only was she with child, but she would have six babies, which was unusual, even for the Annuna. Uranus told Rhea that she needed to take the children back to Nibiru. One child could be raised, taught what they were, and their role in the universe while in the depths of space, but six? It was unheard of. As they prepared to leave for Nibiru, the comet drew closer and Uranus noticed its placement in the heavens and its strange trajectory. As he drew close to the glowing globe and its massive ice-filled tail, he began to understand what was happening.

"So this is it, my fallen son?" Uranus called out.

Cronus emerged from the tail, indignant as ever.

"So, as I expected, you have discovered me," he smirked, "It matters not, as you will be part of its journey."

"You know I will not allow this."

"You have no choice, Father. Your world will die."

"But why? Why do you want to destroy the perfect eco-system? Thoth is pleased." Uranus pleaded with his son. "You know we were created to bring life. Not this."

"That is your problem, Father," Cronus smirked. "You fail to see our power. Not only can we create, but we can also annihilate and then remake as we wish."

"That is not what Thoth has taught us."

"Thoth is shortsighted and powerless against us. We are the power in the universe. I am only the first of our kind to attempt to seize our rightful place."

"My son," Uranus wept, "You are lost to us, you are no longer an Annuna."

"So be it," Cronus growled back. "I will cease to be of the Annuna, and I will be the first line of *the Titans* - rulers of the Third Universe."

A great battle ensued between the gods. These gods fought differently than Prometheus had with Poseidon. Instead of earthly elements like wind, water, and fire, Cronus and Uranus battled with cosmic powers – nuclear, dark matter and anti-matter explosions came from each attack as the two brutalized each other. The battle waged for yeara, drawing closer to Eden in the gravitational pull of the killer comet. Cronus finally would strike the final blow as his weakened father was no match for the younger Annuna.

"Thoth…Thoth will avenge me," Uranus said, "The Angelus will come down upon you if you do this, Cronus."

"Once my race has grown strong even the Angelus would dare not challenge me," Cronus replied, "You are finished old fool."

"You cannot kill me, Cronus," Uranus said.

"Perhaps not, but I can devour your essence and make your power mine."

"No! You cannot!"

"Yes…I can." Cronus approached his dying father and his hand dove into what would be Uranus' chest. A slight misty collection of particles appeared where Cronus' hand and Uranus' body met. His father began to dim as Cronus' drained him.

"You do not have to do this, my son," Uranus pleaded, "You can let us go back to Nibiru – let us live out our days in retirement before we return to Tartarus to be renewed."

"So you can send the Angelus after me before I am ready? I think not," His son replied, "Good bye, father – your teachings now belongs to me – your quickening enriches me and gives me all of your knowledge and power."

"Cronus…please…stop.." His father weakly replied, transparent and nearly invisible. As the last bit of his father disappeared Cronus retracted his hand, clinching it in a powerful fist.

"The Annuna no longer run this system. It belongs to the Titans."

The comet continued on its course and crashed into Eden, killing the planet's inhabitants, sending it out of orbit and hurling toward the sun. The inner-core of the large planet superheated and exploded, sending massive amounts of rock and debris into the solar system. One large piece of Eden struck Terra, ending the reign of the dinosaurs and changing the planet's climate by altering its orbital trajectory. Other remnants showered Marta in a red clay, destroying its atmosphere and ending what little life the planet had been able to produce. The rest of the debris took orbit around the sun between Marta and what we now know as the large gas giant, Jupiter, forming the asteroid belt.

Cronus' mother, Gaea, was devastated by her son's act.

"Thoth will destroy you for your treachery," she wept, as she saw the smoldering remains of Terra and the debris field that was once Eden.

"Mother, my battle has never been with you, I have always loved you as a son should love his mother."

"But your father…you took your own father's essence."

"I am the product of my father's gluttony," Cronus replied calmly. "Had he shared some of his glory, he would not be gone now."

"I…I must return to Nibiru."

"To warn Gabriel and the others? I think not, Mother."

"What will you do with me?"

Rhea appeared next to her mother and her brother. Three celestial sentient beings with no care for air, water, or any of the other building blocks we know of as life. Just pure energy, floating in space like any other heavenly body.

"Cronus," Rhea growled, "you have succeeded in destroying all of our work. Where is Father? He will be furious with you."

"He's here, would you like to say hello?" Cronus sneered, pointing to what would be his stomach.

"By Thoth, what have you done?"

"I am maximizing our power, my wife. For our children," he replied. "With the power of Uranus and Cronus combined, we will make a new world – a better world."

"You….you absorbed him?"

"Indeed. His power is my own and makes me all-powerful."

"You...you bastard," She turned her attention to their mother. "And what of Mother?"

"I have a special place for her."

Cronus imprisoned his mother at the center of the newly formed satellite that floated around Terra, a moon, surrounding her in an energy prison that in her weakened state, she would never be able to penetrate. She would dissipate from the lack of an energy source, and eventually disappear. Rhea didn't have the power to contest him, thus she became subservient. Once his children were born, and fearing they would overthrow him much like he had his own father, he immediately killed his sons, Hyperion, Mnemosyne, and Themis. Only Rhea's pleas for mercy stayed his drive for hunger, sparing the remaining boys, Oceanus and Iapetus, and their only daughter, Tethys. He had begun the line of the Titans.

Thoth and his warriors, the Angelus led by Gabriel, knew of Cronus' betrayal, but Thoth instructed them not to intervene in the public family dispute. Amongst themselves, they were upset with their God's decision but none would challenge him because it was something you just didn't do. The deity's reasoning was simple - he had made Cronus primary on the task of building a world for life in the Sol system. It was Uranus and Gaea who had interjected themselves as the primaries, taking it from their son's hand.

Thoth felt that Cronus was right, Uranus had begun to want the adulation of his fellow beings; it had been less about the creation and more about the glory. While Cronus' methods were deplorable, Thoth decided to see what became of Sol, and to let Cronus make his first creation.

Of course, Cronus didn't know any of this; he lived in constant fear of Thoth's vengeance for his actions. As Terra recreated itself and the mammals began to assume power on the world, Cronus watched closely as Oceanus and Iapateus created a climate more conducive to the mammalian rule. As his wife Rhea gave birth once again - this time to quadruplets Atlas, Epimetheus, Menoetius, and Prometheus - while Oceanus and Tethys joined, creating Clymene, Cronus finally began to soften his angry demeanor. He had surpassed his father. Uranus had only created worlds but Cronus not only created a world in his vision, he had also created a new version of the Annuna – the Titans.

Chapter 5 Daybreak

"I need rest," Prometheus said as he rose from his bed.

I was violently snapped back into the present, as if being fiercely awakened from a deep sleep. I yearned to return to the state, it called to me, but I knew Prometheus had had himself one trying day. It's not every day you defeat Poseidon and force Zeus into submission. The others also seemed worn out by Prometheus' yarn, and each sought the solitude of the crew's bunks.

"There is room for one more in mine." Mina smiled toward me as she climbed up into hers.

"Great, I thought you'd never ask," Marty quipped, as he jumped in with her, they laughed as she playfully punched and kicked him until he vacated it, creating a space that called my name.

"Not this time," I shocked myself in saying, "I really need to rest. I have a feeling tomorrow is going to be a lot worse than today."

"Hey, uh, Dan?" I heard Doc's voice behind me.

"Yeah, Doc."

"We've been on this vessel for nigh two days, and I'd have ta say with all tha excitement in just trying ta survive, none of us have had anything ta eat or drink."

"Yeah, I know. I'll talk to Prometheus once he has risen," I replied, as my stomach suddenly reminded me that Doc was absolutely right. In our haste to escape the zombie-like creatures called the Sacrolites, and flee Atlantis, we had had no time to pack provisions for this trip. It's funny, when you're fighting for your life, you forget the simplest things like finding appropriate resources for food, water, and a place for excreting waste. I still wasn't sure where we were going, but if we didn't get something in our stomachs soon, it wouldn't matter. Prometheus would pull the Atlantean Galleon into *Where The Hell Are We* harbor with four skeletons in the crew quarters.

I slept well… I think. My mind kept replaying Cronus' rebellion over and over. I couldn't wrap my head around the fact that Thoth had done nothing. He didn't care. *If Thoth was God, then didn't that mean that God didn't care? If God didn't care, then what chance did we have?* Until this moment, my faith had been waning, to say the least. Now, I wondered if my life had not been wasted. Praying, devoting time, and paying tribute to a God who could care less whether we lived or died – Why? *So we could get to Nibiru and not be food for these beings?*

Even before Atlantis had risen, wars were being fought over religion on this backward primitive rock. Psychos walked into the middle of malls and detonated bombs in the name of Allah. Why? For what? Countless number of people killed for nothing. It wasn't just the radical Muslims, though. So many died, tortured and persecuted by Christians, it made fanatical Islam look like a game of patty-cake. Jesus was supposed to come back and deliver us from all of this madness, but where was he now? *Was he just some crackpot with the gift of the gab and rabid followers, just as Hermes had said to me a year ago?* I refused to believe him then, but now…

Prometheus woke me just before daybreak and invited me to join him on the bridge of the galleon. I glanced at Doc, Mina, and Marty, each were sleeping soundly. It was good that they got their rest. I had a feeling things were going to be getting a lot worse. Once I reached Prometheus' side, he smiled slightly.

"There is food and water in the main galley, a few paces from the crew's quarters," he said quietly, almost in a whisper.

"I don't think my stomach could handle twelve-thousand-year-old bread," I joked.

He chuckled briefly.

"Did you see nothing while you were underwater?" He laughed. "You failed to see the large mechanical mechanism underneath this boat?"

"Sorry," I quipped, "a bit too busy drowning."

"Well, the mechanism is ingenious. A testament to the advancement of the Atlantean society." He seemed to beam with pride. "A large net combs beneath the ship, it swallows up all manners of fish and sea creatures. Once it scoops it up, it takes the beasts into the hull, where another machine sorts, cleans those suitable to be eaten, prepares, and divides it. You will never be hungry while you are on this ship."

"And the water?"

"Taken from the sea itself, the water is desalinated and sterilized, then placed in what you call a freezer and chilled to a pleasing temperature."

"Fascinating."

"Ah," he said, turning his vision out to the sea, "The rumble of your innards is not what is troubling you, though, is it?"

"No. It's not."

"Daniel," he began, "It is not that Thoth does not care for your kind. He cares for you like a shepherd cares about one of his sheep."

"Yes, Christians know the shepherd metaphor."

"And that is why I chose it."

"Reading my mind again," I sighed. I really didn't like that part of our relationship. He could read my thoughts, but I couldn't read his.

"Daniel," he continued, "Thoth is for the greater good. He cares about all species throughout the universe. He cares about all life. Not just the Annuna. Thoth is not an Annunan deity. He is everything to every life form in existence. From the largest beast to the smallest cell, to the very essence of the Annuna - their ascended power."

"Then why did he let Cronus destroy his father? Why does he allow Zeus to destroy this planet? And please don't give me the 'Thoth works in mysterious ways' line, because Christians have been overusing that one for centuries."

"Thoth is the Creator, the teacher," he replied. "He is not some warrior to come down and bring his judgment on his creations. He can only show the way, the guidelines. It is up to you and I to make the correct choices in our lives."

"And this is the Annuna way? The way of goodness?"

"It was…until Cronus changed things and created my race; the Titans. What I know of the Annuna, I can attribute to my mother, Rhea."

"And the other Annuna, they never challenged Cronus?"

"Daniel, you must understand," he sighed, "there are five dimensions of existence, in this dimension, the universe is teaming with life. There are hundreds of thousands, perhaps millions of planets like Terra, I'm sorry, Earth. Were there Annuna that wanted to destroy Cronus for his vile act? Of course. Thoth told them to stand down, they did, and it would not surprise me if Cronus has been forgotten. For your sake, you better hope they have not."

"What do you mean?"

"You will know when the time comes."

"Great," I replied, becoming frustrated, "More riddles. More mystery."

"I apologize for the lack of information, I just feel it is in your best interest to not weigh your mind down with what must be done."

"What he means," an awfully familiar voice preened from behind us, "is what your sacrifice will be."

"Hermes!" I exclaimed as I saw the young God, his boyish face with the tiny bit of forced blond stubble. His curly close-cropped hair hugged his head like a crown, and his well-proportioned frame filled his white chiton. His deep blue eyes peered into me.

"I thought I told you to stay off this ship, worm," Prometheus barked.

"Be still, Muscle-head," Hermes sneered. "I come with tidings from Lord Zeus himself."

"Zeus is powerless to stop us," Prometheus angrily retorted. "He knows it and nothing he has to offer interests us."

"Perhaps." Hermes sauntered toward me. "But it may interest our good little scribe here."

"Step another foot near him and I will not simply deposit you into the sea as I did the last time we met."

Hermes had a look of fear in his face and took a few steps backward.

"Fine, fine, let me get on with it then," he rattled off. "His Majesty, Lord Zeus offers truce in the war with the mortals on the condition that the one named Dan Ryan returns to Atlantis to answer for his forefather's transgressions against the Gods. We must ensure that the betrayer's seed is forever wiped from the face of this world. With no offspring, we know that the line ends with Ryan, and this will be sufficient in ending the war and ensuring Zeus' place as ruler of this world."

Silence. If I sacrificed myself, those who still remained in the world would live on, albeit as slaves to Zeus' new order, but it beat extinction. Since I lost Annabelle and Jeanie, death had not been a fear of mine. Sure, the adventure of going to Thera, Egypt, and eventually Atlantis had energized me and the love Mina Constantopolus filled the dark void that was my heart. Still, in a sense, I welcomed death. I knew that after accepting the eventuality of it when the Naiads had attempted to drag me down to Davey Jones' locker.

"I will accept the terms on the condit –"

"No, you will not!" Prometheus interrupted, "Hermes, I warn you one last time. Be gone from this vessel and tell your master he will get no such satisfaction from us. His time is over."

"I believe young Ryan has a mind of his own and can speak for himself."

"Prometheus, I can save my race."

"Silence Daniel! No more from you!" Prometheus boomed. "Hermes, you are wasting your energy here. Go clean the feces off of Zeus sandals, it is what you are best at."

"Is this what you wish, Danny-boy?"

"I trust Prometheus."

"Fine!" Hermes erupted in anger. "Your cowardice will doom your species and good riddance to them, you insolent fool!"

In a flash, Hermes was gone. I glanced over to Prometheus, who was still seething with anger from Zeus' proposal.

"Why didn't you let me accept the offer?" I barked at him a little more harshly than I intended.

"Daniel, do you not see?" he cried. "Zeus is terrified. He knows only you are capable of ending his reign here. Only you have the power to stop him."

"Me? What can I do?"

"You are mortal, yet you are a God! You may be the only being in this galaxy that can reach Nibiru – reach the Annuna. Reach Gabriel and the Seraphim."

"But how can I reach the Annuna?"

"I'll show you the way, but first there's something we must do."

"What's that?" I asked.

"Training. We may not have to deal with Zeus and Poseidon but if Hermes appearance is any indication – I believe we may face more challenges."

Chapter 6 The Ways

Prometheus floated above the ship, his Atlantean armor sparkling as the rays of the sun bounced off of it.

"Now Daniel," He ordered, "I want you to concentrate – clear your mind – focus on creating a barrier around the ship."

I tried to do what he asked, feeling a bit silly in the process. I thought of the shield of a Roman warrior and imagined it covering the entire ship.

"Good…nice…now brace for impact," Prometheus said.

Prometheus fired his energy beam, striking the ship but it didn't penetrate my invisible shield. Pain resonated through me as if his attack on the shield was an attack on me. I could feel the heat generated from his attack and the power it took to ward it off. Prometheus changed his tactics, firing his lightning bolt attack and that got through the shield, striking the hull and rocking the ship. I lost my balance and my concentration broke. The ship disapproved violently, rumbling and swaying in the calm seas. As I fell to the deck, Prometheus glided down, steadied the vessel and glared at me like a teacher catching his student reading comics in class.

"What was that?"

"I'm doing the best I can," I replied, drained.

"Hardly…you haven't even scratched the surface of what you can be," Prometheus said, "Now - concentrate harder – allow nothing to penetrate your thoughts but protecting this ship. Your life, the life of your woman and her companions depend on it. If I am defeated – you are their only protection."

"If you're defeated – we're screwed."

Prometheus glared that teacher stare again.

"Okay, sorry Obi-Won, please continue." I relented.

Prometheus launched off the deck and into the air once again. This time I pictured a knight in his armor, and then having that armor on every portion of the ship. Prometheus again began his attack and I repelled each one. For a half an hour he tried every attack in his arsenal – energy beams, lightning bolts, wind, waves, nothing penetrated the Dan Ryan Steel Fortress of Death. That was until…

Mina opened the cabin door and popped her head out.

"Danny, the guys wanted to know if there's anything we can do to help out topside?" She said, her voice commanding every ounce of my attention.

Prometheus was in the midst of his lightning attack and as my attention was no longer on the ship but on grabbing hold of the luscious creature before me and touching her, feeling her embrace and essence. Instead of her, I received a blast from Prometheus in the chest – it sent me across the deck of the ship, slammed me into the side of the cabin and knocked me dizzy. As my vision cleared I looked down at my chi ton and saw a dark black splotch where the bolt entered me. I reach to the top of my head, my short cropped hair stood up like I put my finger in a socket.

"Thoth save me!" Prometheus said, "What were you thinking?"

I looked at Mina and Prometheus gave me *the stare*.

"Woman, what do you want?" Prometheus barked at her.

"I just wanted to see if there was anything we can do to help?"

"Yes! Stay below and stop distracting Daniel!" Prometheus retorted, "I nearly killed him."

"Sorry!" Mina looked like a scolded puppy that just doodled on the carpet.

"Are you okay?" She said as she moved quickly over to me and helped me up.

"Yeah…I think," I said, "You know…you're very pretty…what day is it?"

I didn't have my faculties yet.

Prometheus reached the deck and placed his hand on my chest. Immediately the dizziness dissipated and the pain across my body went away.

"You were not too badly damaged," He said, "But I believe the lesson was well taken."

"Yeah, when I'm in a fight, hot chicks are not allowed."

Mina giggled.

"Well, if that is your weakness, let us hope they do not send Aphrodite." Prometheus laughed, "Okay, we've done defense for a while – let us try some attacks."

"Mina, you may not want to be up here for this," I said.

She kissed me on the cheek and headed back down the cabin deck. For a few hours, we tried unsuccessfully for me to generate an energy beam. I just couldn't do it.

"Visualize the power in your hands."

"I am."

"Then why is there no power?"

"Because I don't have any." I replied.

"If you can provide a shield, you can perform an attack." Prometheus sounded annoyed.

Try as I might, the only thing between my hands was the sea breeze. As the sun began to set, Prometheus finally gave up.

"I do not expect you to learn everything in one day," He sighed, "At least we got some defense down. Let us head below so you can enjoy some nourishment."

"What will you eat?"

"Oh, do not worry about me – my reserves are full – I just need to rest."

We went below and Prometheus retired to the crew quarters while I joined Mina, Doc, and Marty in the mess hall.

It was good to be with them again – they were my only connection to sanity.

Chapter 7 History Knocks

I was greeted in the Mess by the strong smell of fish. The Mess, like the rest of the ship was larger than a typical ship's eating area, grey with white tables and chairs. Doc sat at the end of one of the many tables, Marty and Mina flanking him. He looked like the patriarch of a family. He was a bit worn by the events that got us to this point. When I found him, digging away in the Greek Isle of Thera he was full of life and excitement. He had been a renowned archaeologist until his quest for Atlantis made him a joke in the academic community. Still, the Greek-born Scot attracted some of the brightest minds in the field.

Mort Collins, a marine archaeologist, who led the underwater portions of the expedition, Serenity Archibald, Marty's fiancé and the top of her field in ancient or dead languages. Noah Deveaux, who gave up a professorship at Cambridge to join their exploits. For years they toiled finding endless clues that led to other clues that led to dead ends. That was until I walked into their lives.

"Dan, come sit with us," Doc said as I approached their table.

"Hey Dan," Marty extended his hand, "No hard feelings, right?"

"Not at all Marty," I replied, "Sorry about the…"

"The shiner? I deserved it."

I took a seat next to Mina, who smiled a little as I brushed by her. The plate of fish in the middle of the table called to me and I quickly searched for a plate, locating an empty one, I quickly filled it with the catch of the day – gargantuan grouper. The plate wouldn't stay full for long.

Mina slipped her hand on to mine and squeezed. We did that from time to time, there wasn't anything sexual about it for me, I just enjoyed feeling her touch – the spark that jumped between us each time our fingers interlaced.

"I just dunt know how we coulda ended up here," Doc broke the silence, "Where did it all go sideways?"

"I don't know, Doc, I really don't."

"It was when you met Hermes, Dan." Marty interjected.

"Marty, don't start up again!" Mina warned.

"No, no, I'm not," Marty continued, "But that's really where this all began, right?"

"Yeah, your right," I agreed, "If Hermes doesn't come to me in that little chapel after I buried Annie and Jeanie – I wouldn't have come to Thera to seek you out and we wouldn't have gotten here."

"You were quite convincing when you came," Mina said, "I remember I almost had you taking off in handcuffs by our security."

"I knew there was somethin' about cha, Dan," Doc added, "That's why I believed in ya - and I don't regret that decision."

"None of us do." Mina continued, "For so many years we searched for Atlantis – you gave us the final pieces to find the continent."

"And fulfill an old man's dream." Doc smiled.

"Yeah, but the cost…" I replied.

"No, I was wrong to put that on you." Marty said, "We had no idea what we were getting ourselves into. You didn't kill Seren – Grahame Solitaire's men did."

Mina's hand shuddered at the name. I helped her escape him, but even after so much time had passed from Solitaire's demise, she still feared him. She married the billionaire adventurer in London when she was young and foolish. At first he was debonair – a James Bond or Bruce Wayne, sweeping her off her feet – but once he had her he treated her like a possession, as if she was his new Ferrari or yacht. Mina had always had an independent spirit but Solitaire found a way to strip her of that freedom, turning her into a shell of what she was.

"You're an insignificant little bitch," he'd say, among other less flattering characterizations. He showed his dominance, beating her on several occasions. When she left him, he tried to have her killed – sending henchmen to run her down as she crossed the street, take shots at her. In fear for her life, she fled the country and joined her grandfather at Akrotiri but by then, Solitaire was no longer consumed with her but another addiction – the pursuit of Atlantis.

While Doc's ambitions were for scholarly consumption, Solitaire saw dollar signs. He wanted to create an aquatic theme park around the find and have the wealthy pay thousands for the right to go down to the ruins of the lost continent.

Hermes led us to clues that eventually brought us to Egypt in the port city of Alexandria. We needed to find the lost Library of Alexandria, believed to have been burned to the ground by Caesar, Hermes told us that the main section of the library actually had been submerged in a mighty earthquake and remained intact, protected by an air bubble.

While we were searching for the library, Solitaire's henchmen snuck onto our ship and killed most aboard, including Serenity Archibald. They beat up Doc and took Mina. I attempted to rescue her but managed getting caught myself. We were about to be tortured before Marty and Noah came in guns blazing to save the day. Solitaire was cut down in the crossfire but we learned that it wouldn't be the last we'd see of him.

"It's okay," I whispered to her and she placed her head on my shoulder.

"When we got ta Atlantis and saw the ruins," Doc continued, "It was validation for my life's work. Years of ridicule and mockery, washed away in one instant. It was tha greatest and worst day of meh life."

"How we managed to get out of there, I'll never know," Marty added.

"It was our desire to make things right," I replied, "We had to do something about the gods. If I didn't free them, they would have found another way – that was pretty evident. Maybe Hermes would have found a way to get my dad out of prison or raise Jeanie from the dead. Who knows?"

"I think it was meant to be you, Dan," Mina said, "You were meant to find us, we were meant to find Atlantis, and you were meant to stop this."

"We'll find a way." I agreed, "As long as we have Prometheus we have a chance."

A large explosion rocked the boat, shaking the room and knocking the plates and utensils to the floor.

Chapter 8 Apollo's Attack

Prometheus raced from the crews quarters and joined me at the top deck. A large explosion came from above us, sounding like a huge bomb detonating overhead. Out of the bright light appeared a large man with dark skin, wild, wavy orange hair, and wearing an all white chiton with a circle of golden suns around the neckline.

"Prometheus," the god Apollo's voice was deep and gravely, "the time has come to lay down this fruitless venture and return to Atlantis for judgment."

A large bow appeared in Apollo's right hand and his left reached from behind him into his quiver to grab a flaming arrow.

"Prepare yourself, Daniel," Prometheus whispered.

Apollo floated to the deck of the bobbing Atlantean vessel.

"I am having difficulty understanding why it is that you continuously must disobey my father," he sighed. "I have no desire to destroy you."

"Apollo, you know full well you lack the power to defeat me. I have already defeated Poseidon, what do you think you can possibly do against me?"

Apollo shook his orange curled covered head slightly in disgust.

"My teacher, my friend," he sighed, "Have you learned nothing from the last time you opposed Zeus? Io was destroyed as a result of your disobedience."

A quick flash, like a memory, fleeted through my mind of Prometheus, in love with the half-mortal, half-god, Io, a love forbidden by Zeus. They ran away together, to another land on

Earth. Zeus found them and imprisoned her on a lonely mountain; doomed to an eternity of solitude for disobeying the king of the Gods. It wouldn't be enough to stop Prometheus, he found her and freed her from their prison. While Zeus could never defeat Prometheus, he could destroy Io, and he did so without prejudice.

"You were my best student, Apollo," Prometheus replied. "But you have learned nothing. We are not meant to be on this world. This world belongs to the mortals."

"Belongs to the mortals? Are you daft?" Apollo gaffed. "They have been in control of this world for twelve thousand years, and what have they done? Constantly bicker about land and differences of culture, destroy one another, and pollute the air and the seas? This world was teaming with life, but like a disease, the human infestation has destroyed countless species and plant life, and they are killing this planet."

"Maybe so, but it is their world to destroy, not ours. We are the Annuna. We are the creators, not the rulers."

"I am not Annuna and you are not either. I am a Dodekatheon and I was born to rule this measly little rock alongside my father."

"You are a good boy, Apollo, but misguided," Prometheus groaned in frustration. "If you attack us, I will destroy you."

Apollo flew off the deck into the cloudless blue celestial above.

"You do not comprehend the anger my father has right now," he moaned. "I wish there was another way to resolve this... but you give us no choice. I will miss you, my mentor."

Prometheus turned to me, a look of concern seeming to splash over his face.

"Daniel," he said hurriedly, "listen to me carefully, I will need your assistance in protecting the ship. Clear your mind of all things, of all fear you may have and concentrate on one thing – a barrier."

"Okay," I mumbled, and tried to do what he commanded. I closed my eyes and completely emptied my mind of all thought except one; protection of the ship, an invisible barrier between what Apollo threw at us and our salvation.

"Good, no matter what happens – you must hold."

I felt myself extend my arms from each side of my body as if I was Moses parting the Red Sea, and it felt like there was an energy exploding out of my body. My muscles locked and I seemed to go into some sort of trance. As if I was controlled by another being, I could feel my head turn toward Prometheus, who had his eyes trained on Apollo. I looked up toward the sun god and could see him gesture toward the sky. Right on cue, I suddenly felt a searing heat grip my mind and could feel my skin burn. A blue-ish colored flame seemed to surround the ship. It was excruciatingly hot; I was a shrimp on the barbie, sautéed just right. My skin's pores seemed to gush fluid.

The blue flame surrounding the ship turned a bright burnt orange. My eyes caught Prometheus, leaving the sanctity of the shield and he began his barrage on Apollo. My mythology was rusty, but Apollo was one of the most beloved of the Greek gods. While he was often referred to as a sun god in today's literature, he was also a god of prophecy, healing, and music, archery, light, and truth. This was not an evil God. Seeing him pulling fiery arrow after fiery arrow, pointing them at Prometheus and sending them flying like ballistic missiles didn't make him evil. It just made him an enemy, an obstacle from our goal – whatever that may be. He was putting up a surprisingly good fight, considering what Prometheus had done to Poseidon. In addition to his heat attack on me and the ship, Apollo peppered Prometheus with one shot after another. It was all Prometheus could do to ward them off. His luck would finally run out; one of Apollo's arrows found their mark, embedding in the golden chest of the handsome god, sending him sprawling backward, dropping until finally crashing onto the deck of the ship with a thunderous thud.

I looked toward the sky and saw Apollo make a signal with his hands – a circular motion with his index finger extended. He stared at me, his eyes suddenly emitting an red, sparkling, frightening glow. His orange locks seemed to rise, as if filled by an unseen energy. Apollo closed his glowing orbs, shrieked a hideous, monstrous scream and when he opened them, a blinding blue-white energy burst seemed to release from every pore of his essence.

I felt it instantly, searing, unimaginable heat, a hundred-fold worse than the attacks before. I fell to my knees as the ship began to rock, the sea around us bubbling and gurgling, evaporating before my eyes. I felt ill, queasy, but it wasn't from the rapid descent of the ship in the ocean, or the violent rocking motion caused by the boiling soup below us; it was from the radiation that was surrounding us. I knew that if the heat didn't kill us, the radiation would. We were in a large microwave and we were about to become the Jiffy Pop.

"Daniel, what is the opposite of fire?" Prometheus, seemingly helpless now, called out to me from the deck.

"Water."

"Exactly."

I understood immediately. I closed my eyes, concentrated on the raging ocean underneath Apollo, and in my mind I pictured the water underneath him spiraling upward, an upside-down aquatic tornado. The vortex swallowed Apollo whole, breaking his spell and stunning him momentarily.

It gave Prometheus time to pull the arrow from his chest and rise to his feet.

"I will finish this," he growled.

"Hold, Prometheus," an unfamiliar voice said from behind us. "You are weakened and you cannot take the both of us on at the same time."

"Hephaestus?"

Prometheus had a look of betrayal - an *et tu, Brute* vision of contempt.

"Yes, my friend," Hephaestus replied. "You have fought well but your little insurgency is at an end."

Chapter 9 Sea of Fire

I saw fear in Prometheus' eyes for the first time. He was badly weakened and was in no shape to face the wrath of two Gods while protecting the ship.

"Daniel," he wheezed, "I must face them."

"You can't –"

"Whatever happens to me, you must not allow them to capture this vessel. You must continue on."

"But how can I –"

"I cannot battle them and maintain the shield. I have been trying to help you, but now it is up to you to save this ship. You must concentrate every single ounce of energy in your soul to protect it. If you fail, the ship and all you care about will be lost. DO NOT FAIL."

Exhaustion was coming over me as well, but I didn't dare whine to Prometheus. He had been through hell and back protecting us. Yet there he still was, facing odds that were formidable in his present state. He was the last of the Titans – and if he fell, the race begun by Cronus would be no more. Zeus would be victorious, and mankind as we knew it would end.

He couldn't protect us any longer. It was up to me and me alone. But what could I do? Sure, I could manage a few little parlor tricks but I was no god. How could I stand up to two deities if a Titan himself couldn't? It was folly. If the ship went down, if Prometheus fell, all would be lost. I knew it. I couldn't allow that to happen – so I had to let him focus his energy on Apollo and Hephaestus.

"Lay down your sword," I heard Apollo calmly whisper. He was drenched, looking like a cat that had fallen into a toilet bowl.

Hephaestus took residence beside him. He had dark brown skin, and little facial hair covering his beautiful and well-curved face. His body was as chiseled as Prometheus', bulging muscles and biceps accenting his mocha, foreboding frame. It was truly amazing how each of the Gods were beings of such allurement – each more stunning than the next.

Prometheus rose from deck of the ship, he seemed to care nothing for the odds.

"Stop, Prometheus." Hephaestus waved his hand through his closely cropped hair that adorned his furrowed brow. "Look at you. You are wounded. You are weak. I do not wish to end you. Surrender, my friend, the battle is lost."

"I surrendered once to you, Hephaestus," Prometheus wheezed, "and it cost me Io. I will not make that mistake again."

Hephaestus' mouth pinched like a child scolded by his mother and about to throw a temper tantrum. Then he frowned, a tear escaping from his right eye and dropping off his unusually large lashes.

"Forgive me," he whimpered.

"I do." Prometheus smiled.

I closed my eyes as it began, trying to focus on the ship and creating a protective shield around it. I envisioned an ironclad shield, like a knight would carry into battle, and pictured it surrounding the ship in a cocoon of protection. I could hear screams and carnage above me, but I dared not look up and take my mind off the ship for a moment.

My mind did wander… but it didn't journey to the battle raging aloft, but to Mina Constantopolus. My mind could see her, holding close to her grandfather, Theo. Marty clutched a nearby wall, listening intently. My mind's eye focused on Mina, her lengthy legs were crossed, Indian-style, as she leaned back against Doc. She was beautiful, even when terrified, her creamy white skin with not a blemish on it. Her dark silken hair was down, and trickled across her back and expansive chest. Her lips, thick and rose-colored, seemed to beg to be kissed.

She had struck me like a thunderbolt that day I saw her for the first time, chasing after me, believing I was a lost tourist who had gone into an unrestricted area of their dig site in Akrotiri. As our adventure unfolded and I discovered my destiny lay in Atlantis, she was there every step of the way. I never intended to fall in love with her, especially so soon after the death of Annabelle and Jeanie. At first, I was ashamed of it and I pushed her away. Yet we had to work with each other, piecing together a puzzle that was the location of Atlantis, and in that time, the love we developed was undeniable.

We would just spend days together in a little café chatting about nothing important for hours and hours. We, of course, would talk about what wonders we might find in Atlantis, and how it would affect the world (we had no idea). I would talk some about Annie and Jeanie, but I consciously tried to stay away from that subject. She talked about Grahame Solitaire. He found a device, a golden rod that looked an awful lot like a shiny penis, that the Mayans called the Rod of Destruction. It wielded tremendous power – its combination with another rod of similar make, and several skulls made of crystal and stone formed a type of superconductor that generated all the power in Atlantis.

The Rod also had a dark secret for Solitaire… the person invoking the ancient incantation written on its shaft would become immortal – so to speak. Solitaire loved this idea, but failed to read the fine print. While he would indeed become immortal, he wouldn't be indestructible; so if he was "killed", he wouldn't die, but transform into something different; a creature that only has one thing on its mind – eating humans and other animals. This was Grahame's fate.

Mina always trembled and I always tried to guide the conversation away from him by telling her a funny story about Jeanie or Annie, and that seemed to make her feel better. Still, I could almost feel her wince when bringing him up. I tried to avoid him at all costs.

Mina and I had made love several times over the past year we were together. It was, without question, an incredibly erotic, sensual experience, and I always found myself longing for the next encounter. The first time's intensity scared me a bit and at first I shunned her. The longing to return to her arms and connect with her on a spiritual level overcame those fears and eventually I accepted it.

It was troubling for me, only because I had just put my wife and daughter in the ground. After time passed and we grew closer, I didn't care what anyone thought. I buried the guilt with my wife, and didn't let it touch me anymore. As cruel as it seemed, my wife was dead. She wasn't coming back. I didn't believe she would want me to spend the rest of however many days I had left pining over what I no longer had. I needed to live my life. Finding Atlantis was therapeutic in that sense. My whole life, I had written fictional characters who experienced amazing adventures in their lives. Most had to go on quests to discover the truths about themselves and life itself. I now found myself on my own quest for truth.

I believe that's why I took Hermes' barbs. His constant harping on our twentieth century religious beliefs in a young carpenter's son from Galilee. I knew he wasn't telling the truth – and I wondered if Atlantis would give me an answer. It gave me some answers, all right, answers that led me straight to this place, this moment, with the fate of the human race riding on my ability to do things I never dreamed possible. If I failed, I would be responsible for the extinction of my kind.

I wondered had Annie and Jeanie not been killed, had I never come to Akrotiri or Egypt or Atlantis, would all of those millions of souls who perished not have been extinguished like the flame of a match? The world would have kept on, I would have lived my normal life, and eventually, I would have died. My legacy would have fallen to Jeanie and then her children, and her children's children. We would have lasted another few generations and then the window of opportunity would have opened again... or would it have?

Hermes didn't believe so. He said he came to me because I may have been the final chance the Gods had to be free, and save the human race from the environmental Armageddon coming for us. It sounded good. Little did I know that the fixing of the Earth included our extermination. A *How To Serve Man* conundrum if there ever was one.

No, what had happened had to happen. I knew that now. Annabelle and Jeanie had to die. Hermes had to see his opportunity to get his claws into me when I was at my lowest point. I had to meet Mina, Doc, and the others. I had to find Atlantis. I had to free the Gods. Then I had to find the true God – be it the one I believe in or the alien God that Prometheus said controlled the universe – to put a stop to Zeus' reign of terror once and for all.

"DANIEL – SNAP OUT OF IT!" A familiar voice drew me out of my deep trance. It was Prometheus. He had hold of Apollo by the neck, while Hephaestus attacked him from behind with bursts of flame emitting from his hands, directing their way to the small of Prometheus' back.

I glanced back down to the deck – it was a fiery inferno, the flames were like rabid dogs after a piece of meat, chasing up the sails and down the railings toward me. While I was in my little daydream, Hephaestus had surrounded the ship in a sea of fire, and it made its jump to the ship, underneath my weakened shield. I was failing again.

I closed my eyes and envisioned a huge wave hurling toward the ship. I grabbed hold of the wheel and held on as the wave crashed into the bow, violently rocking the small Atlantean vessel, threatening to capsize us once again. I turned the ship into the blow as much as I could, and felt the ferocity of the water as it burrowed its way through the boat, slamming into me and threatening to rip me from the wheel. Where the fire had been, dripping charred black Atlantean metal remained, its translucency robbed by the conflagration.

I once again felt the salt water stinging my eyes and burning my scrapes. I was weary of the sea.

The ship was saved – at least for now. The sea of fire was gone and the focus of Hephaestus and Apollo weren't on us, but on the final destruction of Prometheus. They were winning. I could see with each blast of radiation, fire, and Apollo's simple bow, mankind's champion was growing weaker. It wouldn't be much longer now.

Suddenly, an image darted into my head: Hermes, in the crew's quarters of the ship – battling Doc and Marty trying to get to… MINA! He's after Mina! I let go of the steering and sped below. The wave had flooded the cabin so I was knee-deep in water when I forced the door to the crew's quarters open. I found Doc collapsed and dazed, while Marty floated unconscious, face down in the water. I pulled him out, checked his pulse and breathing – he was alive. Mina was nowhere to be found.

"Hermes you goddamned bastard!" I cried out. "Bring her back! Bring her back damn you!"

***

I collapsed to my knees in despair as the water approached the center of my chest. If my suspicions were true, Mina would be the second woman I loved that would die because of me.

<BOOOOOOOM>

The sound was thundering, like the sonic boom of a stealth bomber, exploding its way to supersonic speed… but right over our heads. I collected myself and raced top deck.

Prometheus had collapsed near the main mast. I looked toward the sky but didn't see Apollo and Hephaestus. In their place was Ares – the god of war. He was a hulking figure. His head was cleanly shaven, which was quite unlike his chin that bore a large, full black beard, and his skin, the color of dark mocha, was covered by red and blue battle armor that was extenuated by large spikes protruding from the shoulders. In his hand, he wielded a large battleaxe, with colors matching his armor. Even in his beauty, he was frighteningly hideous.

"Mortal," he called down to me a deep rusty voice, "Know this – you are on borrowed time. Give up this ridiculous folly and your woman might be spared."

Suddenly, the sky grew red and Ares seemed to explode, yet I knew he hadn't. He had simply disappeared.

I raced over to Prometheus' side and turned him over. A large gash, like that of a strike from a battleaxe, had dented his golden armor and pierced his chest.

"Prometheus, are you alive?" I said to him, without quite contemplating the question.

"Yes, I believe I still breathe," he wheezed.

"What happened?"

"The battle waged on as you went to save your woman," Prometheus replied weakly. "I was choking out both Hephaestus and Apollo when Ares appeared and struck me down."

"Why did they stop?"

"I do not know," he wheezed. "But I believe they were never truly interested in defeating me. They knew they could not – not without the power of Zeus and the other gods behind them. They were a diversion to take your woman."

"But for what purpose?"

"Is it not obvious?"

"No."

"Each fears the power you possess, thus none want to challenge you directly. They want to force you to surrender."

"Will they kill her?"

"Whether you surrender or not – yes."

"Then I can't surrender," I replied. "But we must return to Atlantis – to save her."

"No, we will not be going back."

"BUT WE HAV-"

"We will not be going back!" Prometheus coughed. "There is much more at stake here than your lover."

I was fuming; I had no control over my life. Every single pore in my body said, *Go to her, save her*. This being stood in my way. He made the choice for me.

"On the positive side," he continued, as I lifted him to his feet and he gingerly moved toward the entrance to the crew's quarters, "I doubt we will be challenged again until we reach land."

Chapter 10 Mutiny

"I have had enough!" I screamed as I followed Prometheus below deck.

The floors that had previously been filled with spillage from the angry brine seemed to be only damp with the evidence of what had come before it. I assumed there was some sort of drainage system within the vessel. Not being a seafaring man, I didn't know if that was standard fare for ocean-going ships. It must be. I had seen enough of those Discovery Channel reality TV episodes about the ice fishermen – the one that had Bon Jovi's *Wanted: Dead or Alive* music in the background during the commercial that the station played five trillion times - to know those ships had to deal with some pretty crazy water and weather.

Prometheus weakly entered where Doc and Marty were now on their feet, their long troubled faces protruding.

"Did you hear me? I've had enough!" I repeated.

"Enough of what, mortal?" Prometheus replied fragilely.

"Enough of you telling me what I can and cannot do. Enough of Hermes' tricks, the gods attacking me, enough of not being able to save the people I love."

"You would trade saving her life for the extinction of your entire species?"

"Of course not," I angrily retorted. "But we shouldn't forfeit it when we have the power to save her."

"If I may?" Doc interjected in his heavy Scottish brogue. "Prometheus, friend of man, wise Titan among gods, my Lord, I humbly beg of ye ta join in tha retrieval of ma granddaughter. Sire, she's all I gawt left."

"We've battled all of these frickin' gods as we go to who the hell knows where," Marty added. "What difference does it make if we go back for her?"

"Every second we are delayed," Prometheus wheezed, "every moment we waste, another million of your kind is destroyed. The population of your kind is already at a critically low number. By the end of the week, your species will be no more. We are almost at our journey's end – to turn back now and return to Atlantis will end with Zeus being the victor."

"My Lord," Doc continued, "my granddaughter lost her parents when she was but a wee child. I lost my daughter and son-in-law, but gained a new daughter. Mina is all I have left. Is there anything… anything ta be done?"

"Prometheus," I added, "when we made our escape from Atlantis – you flew us up to the next land mass of the interior of Atlantis – the next ring, where we found this ship. Why not fly us back to Atlantis, we'll get Mina, then fly back. One of us can stay behind to keep the ship going."

"Flying is too dangerous," Prometheus again resisted. "If we could have simply flown to our destination, I would have already taken us there. But you have seen what we have had to face. Do you believe I could have battled those other Gods, including Zeus himself, while flying us in the air? Impossible. You would all be dead, and I cannot allow that."

"Then Mina is lost ta me," Doc sobbed. I grabbed his shoulder.

"I got her back once," I consoled. "I'll get her back again."

"I must retire," Prometheus said weakly. "Worry not about the steering of the ship. I have it controlled and it will take us where we need to go. If the direction of the ship suddenly changes, it will simply correct itself and return to the appropriate course."

***

We were all exhausted and I recommended we all rested. I was certain Doc and Marty wouldn't sleep much, but I found myself in the deepest sleep I had ever known. I dreamt of Atlantis, the risen beauty of it. I could see Zeus' palace, golden, shining as the sun kissed the metal and caressed the stone. My mind took me to inside the massive chambers of the main hall. Gargantuan statues surrounded by the most beautiful works of art I had ever seen, leading to an immense throne room where the twelve thrones of the Dodekatheon gods resided.

I saw Zeus perched on his, the largest of all of the thrones, his brother Poseidon sitting next to him. Zeus' hair was completely white, and his slightly wrinkled face sported a beard down to his midsection. Next to him was a golden scepter embedded with large diamonds and emeralds.

Before them was my Mina; naked and lying unconscious on the floor. She lay on her side, her dark hair strung across the floor, her arms and legs contorted into a fetal position, covering her exorbitant breasts. Her arms and legs were covered with scratches and scars.

"Mina Constantopolus," Zeus calmly called to her. "I want you to know that the one you love, Dan Ryan, had the opportunity to end this."

Mina weakly looked up and then her head returned to the floor.

"Yet he cowardly decided to hide from his crimes. He refused to return to Atlantis to face judgment for Hercules' and his own betrayal. He was offered safe passage for his return to Atlantis by my subject, Hermes, and he refused. His recreant nature has sentenced you to this torture. It saddens me to see a creature such as yourself tormented in this way. Deny him, submit allegiance to your god Zeus, and I will end your pain."

Mina lay motionless.

"I will ask no more. What say you?"

"Zeus," I heard Mina's voice weakly protest from the mass of hair covering her face, "go… go screw yourself."

Zeus smiled, as if he took pleasure in her defiance.

"Yes," he muttered, "a splendid creature indeed."

Zeus rose from his throne.

"HADES, COME FORTH."

Out of the shadows came a hideous beast about twelve feet tall. Huge dark red horns protruded from what looked like a black helmet. His face was dark black except for his eyes, which were red, glowing bulbs. His body had a red pigment to it. He had a human's torso, but extremely large with immense muscles, without an ounce of fat on his body. His shaggy legs were shaped like goat's and his tail was like a serpent's. Huge long nails protruded from his claw-like fingers.

"Yes, sire." Hades' dark voice boomed in the hall.

"The mortal has chosen to endure more. Release the furies upon her."

"By your command." Hades replied, turned toward Mina, clapping his claw-like hands and then pointing a long, importunate digit toward her.

From the ground escaped a red mist, like steam absconding from a broken pipe. Inside the haze, there were small demon-like creatures; their color matching the haze. I could barely make out their gold-colored glowing eyes, small jagged teeth, and tiny dagger-like claws, but they were there. The mist floated toward Mina and enveloped her. She screamed a hellish, gory shriek as the beasts attacked her, digging their claws and teeth into her undraped derma.

***

I rose so fast, my head blasted into the top bunk, waking Marty.

"What? WHAT HAPPENED?" he cried out, a little more terrified then the situation dictated.

"We're fine," I quickly retorted, as I rubbed the area of my head that had its untimely joining with the metal above me.

"You okay?"

"Yeah, bad dream."

"Was it about, Mina?" Doc's voice came from the shadows.

"Yeah, it was."

"It wasn't a dream," Doc replied.

"I know."

"We have ta get ta her."

"What if we refuse to go any further?" Marty asked. "What if we just demand to that big lunkhead that we won't step one foot on land until he takes us back to save Mina?"

"Why canna we just get him ta go?" Doc added, "We don't need him right now – we have you. You can protect tha ship while he's gone."

"Because the moment I am gone," Prometheus' voice came from behind us, "Ares would have all the Gods descend on this vessel and obliterate you. Dan and my powers combined are the only things preventing them from doing this."

"Well, we refuse to go one step off of this ship until you take us all back to Atlantis to save Mina," Marty demanded.

"You are inconsequential – Dan is all that matters," Prometheus replied. "Had I any evil within me, I would have left you all to die at the hands of the Sacrolites, and only taken Dan."

"I would have never left without them," I disagreed.

"You would not have had a choice in the matter, as you do not now."

"And if I refuse to do whatever it is you want me to do?"

"Then you kill your race."

I cursed and kicked the side of the bunk, causing more damage to myself then the object that absorbed my rage.

"Then let us go back," Doc replied.

"An old man and a weakling?" Prometheus scoffed. "You wouldn't make it *to Atlantis*, none the less inside Zeus' castle."

"We got ta try, damn ya!"

"No, you do not," Prometheus replied calmly. "She is already dead."

"You don't know that," I shot back sharply.

"I can tell you exactly why this cannot be," Prometheus continued, "I can finish the story of the Gods. I can tell you why you cannot go back to save Mina Constantopolus."

"Then do it."

Prometheus raised his head as if sensing something. "Now is not the time, for we have reached land."

Chapter 11 Dawn of Man

The ship lurched heavily, striking something solid and knocking all of us to our knees. Well, all of us but Prometheus, who steadied himself against the entryway of the crew's quarters. He smiled as we all struggled to find our bearings.

"Quickly, mortals!" he barked. "Ares' beasts will descend upon us quickly if we remain."

"Beasts?" I managed to question back as we moved toward the doorway.

"Indeed," he answered as he made room for us to pass. "All manner of foul-minded monstrosities."

As we reached the deck of the ship, the sun greeted us with a bright white, warm glow. I looked back as Doc struggled up the stairway, finally reaching my side.

"I was beginnin' ta think I may never see the like again," he wheezed.

"Yeah," Marty added, "I think I may kiss the ground when we get off this thing."

"Let me help you with that," Prometheus boomed from behind us.

Suddenly, we were all airborne, levitating off of the deck, above the masts and the sails, which I now knew were made of a similar strange fiberglass-like material the ship's hull consisted of, and finally on to the sandy beach about a hundred yards away from where the ship was grounded on a reef. The ship itself had begun to list back and forth. The tide was coming up and battering it against its coral trap. Even an alien ship like this Atlantean vessel stood little chance against Mother Nature.

"Mother who?" Prometheus asked as he walked past to scan the immediate area.

"Mother Nature."

"Ah, you must be referring to Gaea."

"No, no, humans refer to the elements – wind, rain, all sorts of weather as the acts of Mother Nature."

"Not your God?" He looked puzzled.

"Well, God too, but – ah hell, never mind. It's just a figure of speech. Stop reading my mind."

"Prometheus," Doc interjected, "what of Mina?"

"There is nothing further to discuss," Prometheus replied. "If she lives, your only way to save her is to press on."

"Where are we?" Doc asked.

"New Aztlan," he quickly replied. "Silence and follow."

Prometheus looked worn out, haggard. He had been through some hellacious battles to get us to this point, and it was obviously wearing on him. I began to wonder about his motivation. *Why help us? We were an inferior race. We couldn't defend ourselves even if we fought with every powerful weapon we had. The gods ruled this world. We were no longer the dominant species on Earth. So why align himself with a dying race – one that perhaps deserved its fate considering the atrocities it had transacted on nature and animals alike?*

"It is the will of Thoth," he replied.

"Thoth, God, whatever name ya choose, I think he cares little for our plight," Doc called from behind us.

"Thoth cares."

"If you say Thoth works in mysterious ways, I swear…" I couldn't help myself and giggled at my suggestion.

"I am afraid I know none of the answers you seek," Prometheus admitted, as he again read my thoughts. "I live my existence in the rules of the Annuna as they were taught to me by my mother, as most of the Titans did. The Dodekatheons, however, held ambitions more like my father. I do not know how to explain these things to you in a way your mortal minds can comprehend, however, I can tell you how we have reached this pinnacle, and how you will be the savior of your kind."

Me? Dan Ryan? Hack author of apocalyptic fiction, the savior - the new deliverer from evil? Yeah, right.

Prometheus stopped on a ridge above the beach.

"There."

I joined him as the others struggled their way up the steep incline.

"Yes, good," he continued, "it seems well fortified and should be high enough to avoid any… I believe you refer to them as tsunamis."

His eyes were trained on a small cement blockhouse that had a cream colored exterior with large arches leading to the interior of the structure. Portions of the roof were flat while others seemed to jut upward like a pyramid. The roof was made of small circular red clay. Palm trees swayed near the little structure.

We approached cautiously, afraid to alert the owner to our presence and provoke an unwanted confrontation.

"Use your mind, Daniel," Prometheus commanded. "Can you sense anyone in the home?"

I closed my eyes and concentrated on the structure. I wasn't really sure what I was concentrating on. *Was there anyone there? I didn't know. I couldn't know. I'm not Superman - I don't have X-ray vision that removed the concrete from blocking my view of the contents, like a cataract.*

"I sense nothing."

"Good."

"No, I mean, I get no sense one way or the other. I have no idea if anyone is there."

Prometheus grimaced.

"Your mortal ignorance limits your true potential."

I felt Doc place his hand on my shoulder. He was amazingly still in relatively good shape, considering his advanced age and the sheer mental anguish he was going through. His face looked a little more weathered than I remembered from when we first met. The whiskers of his now week-old beard seemed to age him a few decades. Still, he seemed strong, determined. Marty stood next to him, looking tired. I didn't think his thin frame could get much more slender, but it had. He looked frail, weak, even weaker than Doc. I shuddered to think of my own reflection. If the house below had a mirror, what horror awaited?

"Come," Prometheus finally said, "the sun grows weary and is beginning the journey into the sea. Ares will most assuredly have his creatures of the night scouring the jungle for us. We will be safe in that small sanctuary."

The jungle. Perhaps for the first time, I looked past the small structure to see the huge rainforest that lay behind it. Dense brush and leaves seemed to fill the entire horizon.

"We must take our rest before we enter tomorrow."

"Enter what?" I asked.

"The jungle, of course."

"Have you gone completely insane?" Marty exclaimed.

Prometheus began his trek toward the home and we all reluctantly followed. A wave of his hand allowed us entry into the small domicile. It had definitely not been used in quite a while. As we entered the large living room area that seemed to double for a dining room, I noticed a white, powdered substance lightly scattered across a huge, long wooden table. Dark brown spots littered the grey cement flooring. Dust, grime, and cobwebs were the décor.

"This is a safe house for drug runners," Doc announced what we all had come to realize. "We're in South America."

"No, you are in New Aztlan – what I believe you now call Mexico," Prometheus corrected. "You have completed the same journey that the survivors of Atlantis made twelve thousand of your years ago."

"I knew I knew that name – Aztlan," Marty recalled.

"Of course, in all tha commotion, I had forgotten," Doc added. "I must be goin' senile in me old age."

"Aslan? The Lion in Narnia?" I asked.

"No," Marty laughed slightly. "AZT-LAN. Some obscure Toltec carvings refer to this place of origin – Aztlan… the water city."

"The Toltecs?"

"There's much debate on tha Toltecs, Daniel," Doc added, going into his professor mode. "Some think of them as an Aztec ethnic group, others tha society that remained from tha Maya, and became tha Aztecs, others don't believe they actually even existed as an empire. Mostly, I believe they were tha peace-loving ancestors of tha Maya and Olmec, and they were overrun by tha much more barbaric Aztec."

"Aztlan is Atlantis," Prometheus interrupted. "The primitives that lived in these jungles were taught by survivors of the disaster."

"How do you know this?" I asked.

"Atlantis was destroyed by the gods, not by Hercules." Prometheus replied. "Poseidia, the Atlantean capital, existed until Hercules sunk and imprisoned us."

"I don't understand."

"I know you do not," he sighed. "You will soon enough."

***

After a quick check of the house, we knew we were alone. Prometheus rested as we all took advantage of the running water taking what was probably our first shower in a week, and perhaps the last we would ever take. There was still some canned food stored in the pantry of the small, unimpressive kitchen. Peaches, beans, and corn mostly – but enough to fill a stomach that was upset and sick of fish. We were all still wearing the chitons provided us by Persephone on Atlantis, but we found clothing more suitable for jungle travel in the drawers in the bedroom. Luckily, some of these drug runners were just my size. I dressed in camouflage and even found boots that were the right fit.

Once clean, shaven, and appetites were satisfied, it was time to come to Prometheus. He rose from the small bed as we approached, and greeted us in the narrow walkway that separated the three bedrooms in the house. We followed as he made his way to the living room area and sat on the faux leather, tan-colored couch.

"As you remember," he began solemnly, "Cronus had disposed of his mother and father, Thoth had forbidden Uranus' fellow Annuna from exacting revenge, and Cronus was left to his own devices."

As his words trickled from his mouth, I once again felt as if I had been transported back in time - a shapeless form, floating among Cronus and his new race of Titans. The Earth, ravaged by the destruction of Eden, was plunged into an Ice Age. Life was struggling to survive on the barren ice world. The Titans worked feverishly to save the planet but were losing as many of the species were dying off. Rhea had once again become pregnant, with twins; Zeus and Poseidon. She had already given birth four other children and with each birth, she grew weaker and her children lacked the power of their earlier siblings.

"Again?" Cronus complained.

"Yes, it does not please you?" Rhea looked hurt.

"Do we not have enough? The first set of children were enough – and have helped us survive this ice age," Cronus replied, "But this new line – they're filled with jealousy and rage against their brothers and sisters. They lack their power and are resentful. It is causing unrest."

"It matters not, they are all our children."

"These two…I have a bad feeling about them," Cronus said, "I wish for them to not exist. You will not have them."

"I will have them!" Rhea cried, "You cannot prevent this."

"I cannot? Do you forget with whom you speak?"

"No, but you cannot harm me. The children will not stand for it."

"They will never know." Cronus replied.

Cronus forced Rhea into the same lunar prison that held his mother. Unknown to him, though, Rhea continued with the pregnancy despite her incarceration and Zeus and Poseidon were born in the center of the moon. Annuna pregnancy and the birthing process are vastly different from their human counterparts. First of all, there's no pain. There's no mess either. It's almost as if it's like a cell dividing. Once completed, the smaller Annuna begins to rapidly grow and expand, growing more and more powerful as he saps his mother's energy. The twins about drained their mother to naught, and then finished what had remained of the essence that was once their grandmother.

They easily broke out of their prison and found Hades, who Cronus had assigned to build a reservoir of the dead, the underworld known as Erebus. Hades was secretly creating a much more vile, evil place, Perdition, where the most destructive and evil souls would be sent until their final judgment. Hell, if you will. I knew Perdition well, as it was there that I would discover the meaning of fear and the zombified beasts that they call the Sacrolites.

In Perdition, Hades had a beast, a barbarous monstrosity that had one hundred arms and hands, looking like some freakish Hindu god – the Hekatonkheire. It was gargantuan in size, with no head. Its eyes and mouth were embedded into the torso that sported the arms. Hades also secretly created the giant Cyclops, as well. Minions of his own device. Zeus used these beasts to announce his presence to Cronus and the other siblings, attacking his father with all of his might. Lines were drawn. Most of the Titans sided with their father, Cronus, while Hades, Hera, Hestia, Demeter, Iapateus, and his three sons, Prometheus, Epimetheus, and Atlas joined Zeus.

The line had been drawn, the Titanomachy – the great war of the Titans, had begun.

Chapter 12 Titanomachy

"I grow weary of this place," Cronus exclaimed, as he freed his sister/wife from her lunar confinement.

"I care not what you grow weary of," Rhea barked back at him in defiance.

"Angry?" He seemed a little taken aback. "Ah yes, I guess you would be."

He took her by the hand and lifted her into a corporeal state.

"Your last two sons are devils," he continued on. "They have raised an army against me, trying to take my kingdom from me. I told you this would happen"

Rhea chuckled slightly, smiling slyly.

"So much like their father," she mused. "So much so that they left their mother for dead inside of Luna. Had they not believed they had completely devoured me, there would have been no one to release. If only our mother was strong enough to fool them as well..."

"I believe it is time for us to return to Nibiru," he ignored her jibes. "We should return and face Thoth's judgment."

"They have you beaten."

"Absolutely not!"

"No, you are beaten," she smiled. "You could never admit defeat, my love, my brother. But you would never contemplate such a return if there was even a sliver of hope that you could remain in power here in Terra."

"For eleven years, this war has waged. Eleven years that has already cost us so many of our children, Iapateus, as traitorous as he was, dead. Tethys, Clymene, Menotius. Gone."

"Perhaps if you hadn't destroyed so many of your own children, you would still have an army to defend you."

"Perhaps." His eyes drew dark and cold. "And perhaps if I had killed them all, along with their mother, I would not be concerned by this now."

"And you would be alone. So the truth is revealed. The great Cronus has truly been defeated. And what of Terra?"

"Terra is dead."

"Add that to the list of your failures."

"Woman," his voice grew deep and angry, "you test me. We will return to Nibiru at once."

"And why should I go? The children have no ill will toward their mother - I was not the one who betrayed my mother, and murdered my father."

"You are as guilty in this as I am, and they have already tried to finish you once."

"We shall see if Thoth agrees in your assessment."

"Then it is agreed, we shall return to Nibiru."

"Agreed."

Cronus summoned Zeus and the other rebels for a meeting on Terra. The Earth, as a result of the all-out war, had flooded and only life in the ocean seemed to survive. They met on a ship created by Poseidon, a great vessel that resembled one of our aircraft carriers today, only made of that same, strange Atlantean material that our shipwrecked galleon consisted of. Zeus, looking arrogant and stoic at the same time, sat on a golden throne as his disgraced father entered the chamber and knelt before him.

"I am finished," Cronus whispered in shame.

"Are you?" Zeus seemed to mock him. "It only takes eleven years to construct your demise?"

"Your contempt may be misplaced, my son," Cronus retorted. "It took me only one battle to dispose of my father, Uranus."

Zeus grew angry at Cronus' affront, rising off the throne, descending down the steps and backhanding his father across the face, embers exploding out from the contact.

"It is much easier to stab someone in the back, rather than face them," he barked.

"So it is," Cronus conceded.

"So you surrender to me then? What are your terms for this… generosity?"

"I do not surrender to you," Cronus replied. "However, I will accept a cessation in hostilities."

"And why would I do that when I have you defeated?"

"There is no need for you to destroy me, Son." Cronus looked up, trying to appear weak, frail, unworthy of fear. "Your mother and I will return to Nibiru and face Thoth's judgment."

"Ha, so that is your endgame?" Zeus pointed at him with a steely hand. "Flee in disgrace back into the loving arms of Thoth, so that he can avenge you by sending his Angelus after your rebellious offspring?"

"I will ask him for no vengeance, only forgiveness for my past transgressions."

"Preposterous."

"Had Thoth sought to inflict his wrath upon me for my acts, he would have surely done so by now, my son."

Zeus stroked his long brown beard – it was strange for me, seeing him before he had grayed.

"So your terms are to let you go free, return to Nibiru, never to come to the Sol System again."

"Yes."

"And what of Oceanus? Atlas and Prometheus, who traded sides like harlots trade their bed?"

"Kill them, exile them. They are yours."

"A fine leader you became," the son mocked the father. "It amazes me that it took this long for us to defeat you."

"We are all Titans, Zeus."

"No, Father, you were Titan. Your father was Annuna. We are the Dodekatheon. The Titans are dead."

"And what will you do with your new race, my son? Will you continue to rule a dead world?"

"No," Zeus laughed, "I will succeed where you failed. I will rebuild Terra in my image. All manner of beasts will worship me as king of the gods."

Zeus looked at his brother, Hades, and motioned for him to remove Cronus from his sight, and ensure that he indeed returned to Nibiru. Hades created a doorway on Terra, hidden deep in a dense forest. There, he watched as Cronus and Rhea stepped through the doorway and into a bright, white light. A trans-dimensional doorway, Prometheus' definition came into my mind.

With the war over, Zeus assumed control of Earth. Oceanus was imprisoned in the deepest trench of what would eventually become the Pacific. Epimetheus served Prometheus' sentence for his betrayal of Zeus during the war. His punishment would be an eternity of suffering in Perdition. Zeus forced Prometheus to swear allegiance or the same fate would befall Atlas as well.

Zeus gave the sea to his brother, Poseidon; to Demeter, the plant life. Hestia was to provide the moral framework of society. Hades would return to his duties as the king of the dead. To Hera, he professed his undying love, fidelity, and rule over the heavens. Prometheus was charged with the creation of man, while Atlas would create a large city for the gods to reside in. It would be an ocean city, like none ever seen before – and it would be named Atlantis.

Chapter 13 Only the Strong Survive

"You will need your strength for the continuing journey," Prometheus told me, ripping me out of my trance. "We will need to continue through the jungle."

"You can't just fly us where we need to go?" Marty asked.

"No, the jungle is too dense. It will be a three-day journey, and the trail will be fraught with danger."

"Man, everything always has to be *fraught with danger*." Marty slumped in his chair.

"You need not come," Prometheus added. "Dan is the only one who is required on this journey. It may be best – as a coward and an old man will undoubtedly slow our progress."

"Hey, I'm not coward, pal! I fought as bravely with the Sacrolites as anyone here."

My mind darted back to our escape from Atlantis. In our path stood an army of hideous creatures with ungodly large teeth, dark black shiny skin, and soulless eyes. They were the damned remnants of the Atlantean army who had used the ancient curse inscribed on the staff of the Rod of Destruction to gain immortality in the hopes of becoming an insurmountable force. Instead of living forever, they became the Sacrolites – zombie-like beasts with an uncontrollable need to feed. Each time they "died", a smaller piece of their humanity slipped away until there was nothing left - only the craving.

We were in the outer ring of Atlantis, where I had asked the gods to transport us when I freed them from their underwater penance. I was told Persephone to find the Champion of Man, Prometheus, as only he could help us save our race and that he served exile in the farthest ring from Poseidia, the capital city and home to Zeus' castle. Stumbling upon an ancient home that had been empty for nearly ten thousand years, I found a shield, golden armor, and a large broadsword that looked similar to a Scottish clan Chieftain sword. It came in useful, as we were ambushed by three Sacrolites that called the dwelling their home. I was able to dispose of them, but not before losing Roger Stanfield, our linguist and authority on ancient texts. We had already lost most of our team, with Persephone transporting the mortally injured Noah Deauveaux back to Poseidia and the death of Roger. All that remained of the band of brothers who had rediscovered the lost continent of Atlantis were Doc, Mina, Marty, and yours truly.

The first wave of Sacrolites came like locusts – with their claws and teeth gnashing, making an awful clicking sound as they approached. We battled our way to a clearing, where Prometheus airlifted us to the Atlantean shipyard and we followed him to the ship. The sun was setting and we would have the added benefit of nightfall to obscure our escape. Prometheus lifted us to the ship's main deck and we took our stations along the deck as he moved behind the wheel of the vessel. He inserted a small crystal he had in a pouch hidden inside of his armor into a slot on the steering console, and the ship hummed to life. The galleon eased itself into the canal and made for the outlet into the Atlantic. It brought us to here, this abandoned drug runner's safe house.

"Yes, yes, you fought well," Prometheus conceded. "I apologize for disparaging your courage. However, I still believe it best if you remain here. The old man does not look well, and you do not have the strength you will need to complete this."

"With all due respect, my Lord," Doc replied. "Tha have my Mina. I canna sit idly by while ya two traipse in tha there jungle going ta God knows where in search of God knows what. I canna do that."

"And I go where he goes," Marty pointed to Doc.

"You will die in that jungle."

"We accept that as a possibility," Marty answered.

"A probability," Prometheus corrected. "Very well."

Prometheus turned to me, shaking his head in disgust.

"And Mina?" I asked him.

"You have seen the visions. You know the answer."

"How do I save her? Where are we going?"

"You cannot save her," he sighed. "And there is another story I need to tell you before I reveal our destination. I need you to understand why we are going there, and what you will need to do when we get there."

"We have no time for stories – we have to get where we need to go before it's to frickin' late."

"It is critical you know these things."

"Fine, spill it then." I grew impatient.

"Not now, rest, we have many, many miles ahead of us. Plenty of time to relay the tale of the fall of Atlantis."

"We know that story," Marty replied. "We know that Hercules used the Rods of power and an ancient curse to sink Atlantis and imprison the gods for eternity."

"You know only what that worm, Hermes, has told you."

"I don't understand," I replied.

"You will. Consume. Rest."

I tried to do as he commanded. Prometheus retired to another room of the house, presumably to regenerate his own powers. The Greek god looked worn, tired. We had traveled thousands of miles, dealt with the fury of Poseidon and Zeus, the heat of Apollo, the fire of Hephaestus, Hermes' abduction of Mina, and of course – the Sacrolites. He said the worst was yet to come but I struggled to even comprehend what could possibly be worse than what we had already dealt with.

My mind drifted back to Thera, the beautiful, small Greek island where I first met the amazing team around me. Noah Deuveaux, the large, muscular African American Professor from Cambridge; Roger Stanfield, the amazing linguist, ancient texts expert, and - as we found out later on our journey - an MI-6 spy. Al Chisom, Stanfield's intelligent, but easily duped assistant; the unflappable Mort Collins, marine archaeologist, and my trainer for underwater exploration; Serenity Archibald, the brilliant Proto-historic archaeologist and lover of Marty. Exceptional minds – all gone.

I remember the team's excitement in Akrotiri, the thousand-year-old city discovered in Thera, when we found an Egyptian tablet that not only established that the Egyptians and Minoans exchanged in trade, but it proved the existence of the Pillars of Atlantis.

"Perhaps this was like a bargaining chip, or maybe they were letting the Akrotirians know that the history of the world was in Egypt," Marty had said. "I don't know. Essentially, in layman terms, the cartouche reads, *'In our possession are two Pillars made of gold. They are the history of your world. They are from your ancestors of the sunken land. The Pillars reside in our most sacred of places'.*"

The pillars had been more of a myth than Atlantis itself. Plato said the history of Atlantis was written on two great pillars made of gold that resided in the Temple of Poseidon in Atlantis. It was believed that during the cataclysm, those able to flee the disaster took these Pillars to Egypt.

That night, Hermes would drop another bombshell; that the Library of Alexandria wasn't destroyed by Caesar in fifty B.C. but fell into the sea and under the waves of Alexandria after an earthquake fifty years before he sacked the city, and in that library was a scroll with the location of the pillars.

Off we went to Alexandria, Egypt, and we did indeed discover the sunken library. It also cost us many lives. When Solitaire was killed, or at least we thought, I came into possession of his most precious item; a briefcase with the Rod of Destruction, a small golden cylindrical object that looked similar to an Egyptian obelisk, except there were no pointed ends – but rounded – with what looked like hieroglyphics etched on each side of the cylinder. A precursor to Minoan Linear A, Roger had said.

There was also a chronicle of their trip to a lost Mayan village in South Mexico; they called it *K'ak'nab Mam Atot*. Solitaire's archaeologists had been excavating for six months when they found the rod, along with other gold artifacts. The rod was set aside from the other gold pieces – placed on a stone pedestal as a sign of reverence.

While acquiring that information was important, our greatest discovery would be finding the Library of Alexandria. We found it in the Eastern Harbor, buried in an underwater sea cave. The library's main room had developed an air pocket that had stabilized for a remarkable two thousand years. None of the books and knowledge of the ancient world had been destroyed. It was, without question, the greatest archaeological discovery of all time – that was until we lost it all. An underwater earthquake ripped through the Eastern Harbor and shook the air pocket loose, flooding the final chamber of the library, and would have claimed me too if not for Hermes appearing at the right time.

Before the final destruction of the library and its precious contents, we managed (with a little intervention from Hermes) to find the six scrolls we needed.

The first, in Macedonian and from the time of Alexander the Great, stated that the Oracle granted sanctuary for the Pillars of Atlantis at the Shrine of Amun. Marty, who was our expert in Egyptian history, told us the Temple of the Oracle was in Aghurmi, in the Siwa Oasis, and was one of the most excavated sites in Egypt. He was certain they weren't there.

The second scroll was a description of one of the pillars themselves. Also written in Macedonian, the first scroll detailed one of the pillars, which it said was solid gold, standing as tall as a grown man, on it were strange markings that appeared to be ancient. One of the priests called its origins At-lan-tis.

The third scroll was the description of the second Pillar.

The fourth and fifth were short tales of Atlantean war history, and the final scroll was an ancient cartographical representation of the Atlantic Ocean, and an accurate representation of the Eastern coast of the Americas. In the middle of the Atlantic, a gigantic island just west of Spain stretched from the 30th to the 40th latitudes. The island was circular in nature, and seemed to stretch forever. It was nearly the size and shape of Australia, and broadly displayed Atlantis as its name. The position of the island placed it squarely on the junction between the

Caribbean, Eurasian, and African continental plates, and probably some of the worst seismic activity in the world. We had the location of Atlantis – but we still needed to find the pillars. After ten thousand years, there may not have been much of Atlantis left – the pillars would be final, incontrovertible proof of the existence of Atlantis.

We left for Aghurmi and discovered a previously un-known chamber under the sanctuary of the Oracle. It would be in this chamber we found them, and Grahame Solitaire would reveal himself for the final time. He had been trailing us, hoping we would discover Atlantis and a way to release him from the curse of the Rod of Destruction. He had already turned into a decom-posed, horrid-looking monstrosity of a human being – a Sacrolite. His features were not discernable, as where there should have been a face resided only decayed black flesh and bone, where his eyes were remained two white globes. He had few strands of hair on his head, and those few that were there were spread so far and thin, it was hard to see them. He wore human clothing, a safari outfit to be exact, but his arms and legs appeared to be nothing but a thin membrane of flesh over bone.

Hermes, for the first time revealing himself to the rest of the team, destroyed Solitaire by setting him on fire, and instructed us to find the secrets of the pillars, and in turn, the secret to raising Atlantis. Doc objected at first, stating that the pillars were enough validation, but Hermes has a way of convincing you to do his bidding.

We spent months pouring over the pillars, trying to deci-pher a language that had been dead for nearly twelve thousand years. Eventually, Roger and Noah scored a breakthrough, learning that the two Rods of power worked in conjunction with four mystical skulls as a sort of superconductor. Better yet, three of the four skulls had already turned up in antiquity – although some were believed to be middle-aged forgeries. The experts were wrong; they were the real deal. All that remained was to find the two most important pieces – the Golden Skull and the Rod of Creation.

We continued working on the translation of the pyramids and finally found a passage in early Egyptian that said the Great Menes, one of the first dynasty kings, commissioned a great statue to honor the dead Atlanteans. The statue was erected in Giza near a city called Athlanto, and the pillars, along with what they called Osiris' penis and head were placed in a sacred hidden chamber beneath it. Osiris' penis would be the Rod of Creation, the Head - the Skull. And the statue? The one and only Sphinx. A friend of Doc's with the Egyptian antiquity admitted they had discovered the items under the Sphinx, but the Egyptian authorities asked for him to destroy it, fearing what religious ramifications the discovery of Atlantis would have on the unstable world stage.

He hadn't followed their wishes, instead returning the items to the hidden chamber under the Sphinx, and sealing the room, hoping one day for the political climate to change enough for them to be revealed to the world. After retrieving the Rod of Creation and the golden skull, we headed off to find Atlantis. After a brief layover in Spain, where we were able to commission a naval research vessel, we headed out into the Atlantic to find our fantasy world. We were given an experimental deep-sea sub, capable of diving deeper than any sub in the world, and identified a deep trench that would undoubtedly have to be where Atlantis fell.

Down we went, deeper and deeper into the abyss, and like some kind of bad horror movie, we were attacked by a giant squid. It did a number on us, causing the sub to lose control and spiral down into the trench. We would have been finished, but Hermes once again came to our rescue and led us the rest of the way, putting some type of force field around the ship and gliding it as if it was on some type of autopilot.

I'll never forget the first time I laid eyes on the debris field of Atlantis. Jutting out into the sea and into our view was a statue that looked strangely similar to Hermes. Then another that depicted a figure with a large triton in his hand – Poseidon, I assumed. Each moment, the sub's lights and the illumination from Hermes' powers, or whatever it was, would reveal another statue, pottery, and then finally – columns and buildings – destroyed. More and more artifacts and edifices presented themselves in all their grandeur. A large dark pyramid-looking structure revealed itself out of the mist of blue.

My eyes were focused on a structure dead ahead – emitting the same strange light that Hermes had encircled us with. That was our destination, for sure.

The structure drew closer and you could make out tall skyscraper like obelisks that could have once been buildings, then deeper in, completely intact buildings and other structures. Further still, you could clearly make out a Mayan-looking pyramid – larger than any that could be found on Earth. At first, you could only faintly see it through the distortion of the saltwater, but as we drew to the edge of the city, its size became apparent.

Poseidia. We entered the city and could now clearly see what we were barely able to make out through the barrier or force field, or whatever the hell it was. The city was perfectly intact – it was the same as it was when it sank to the bottom of the ocean twelve thousand years ago. Clear canals separated each ring of the city. The outer ring was obviously where the mortal Atlanteans had lived. Tiny structures resembling houses and apartment-like dwellings littered the outer ring.

Ring two, the secondmost outer ring, had a huge wall surrounding the entire ring. The great wall of Atlantis. Here, I could see strange-looking vehicle-like machines. I could see boats that were built, or in the process of construction. They looked like Spanish galleons but were seemingly created out of some new element – as they glowed just like the other buildings in the city. Each building emitted the same white iridescence.

Ring three seemed to have temples, monuments, and something that looked similar to the Roman Coliseum, or a stadium.

Ring four – the innermost ring – housed the large pyramid, surrounded by much smaller temples. On the top of the pyramid sat another expansive structure that wasn't visible from outside the shield. It was a palace. It was made out of solid gold, with rubies, jewels, and crystals adorning the walls. In the front of the palace sat a solid gold statue of a figure with a large lightning bolt in his hand. Zeus, of course. Hermes set the sub down just in front of the statue – it thudded to a rest, shaking the floor beneath us slightly.

It would be here that Hermes would tell us of my lineage. I was a descendant of Hercules, the son of Zeus, and the man who brought an end to the Dodekatheons' reign on Earth. I was the only one in the world able to undo what he had done. And why would I? Well, to send me on the journey, Hermes had given me the spiel about how we, the human race, were destroying ourselves and the planet, and that only the return of the gods could make things right. I bought it at the time, but I wasn't buying it anymore. I refused to help. As a result, Hermes killed Mort, and Zeus sent us into Perdition.

If there was a hell, it had to be Hades' realm of the damned. It would be there that I would meet a truly developed Sacrolite for the first time. Evil, hideous beasts that wanted to rip and devour the flesh from my bones. Thankfully, I was spared such a horror as Persephone appeared just in time to rescue me.

Persephone, would tell me the story of the Annuna, confirming that Zeus and his cronies were not gods, but powerful, nigh unbeatable beings. But they could be stopped, and I was the only who could do it. She told me to seek out Prometheus, and he would take me where we needed to go but before that I had to raise Atlantis and free the Gods.

I had no reason to trust her, but did so anyway. There was something about her that seemed genuine. I knew Hermes was full of crap the first time I lay eyes on his feminine constitution, but Persephone – something was different with her. She honestly seemed to want to help us.

I did as she asked, but not without demands of my own. I had Zeus free Doc, Noah, Roger, Marty, and Mina. I had him swear not to harm us, or any of the human race, and to take me to the Outer Ring, where Prometheus had last been seen. Zeus agreed, and following Hermes' instructions, I reversed the curse. Zeus had tricked me – he agreed only to spare countries that didn't oppose him. Any who resisted would be annihilated. Well, my own U.S. of A. had never backed down from a fight, and they were the first to be massacred. Other countries who resisted also felt the Gods' wrath. He did at least hold up to his bargain of taking us to the Outer Ring to look for Prometheus – of course, they thought we would never make it because the Sacrolites would make short work of us.

But we had eventually escaped, and found ourselves on that godforsaken ship that deposited us into the jungles of Mexico.

Chapter 14 Kings of the Jungle

The next morning, we stood at the foot of the jungle. It shrieked, cajoled, and came alive as we approached the foot of the dense green foliage-filled landscape. Prometheus looked refreshed, like someone who had just woken from the deepest sleep of their life. Doc and Marty weren't in as good a shape. Obviously exhausted, malnourished, and basically at the end of their rope – they didn't look ready for the next leg of this journey. Prometheus sensed this, looking toward them with a little disdain.

Doc and Marty wore the same clothes they had acquired from the small Mexican house; Marty in his jeans, t-shirt, and a camouflaged windbreaker. Doc was in his explorer khakis that made him look like an Indiana Jones wannabe. Prometheus still wore his golden armor. It covered his immense torso like a warm hug. His legs seemed to explode from the small lambskin covering his midsection. His golden mane was matted down, tied at the back. He looked at Marty, then Doc, then back to me, shaking his head.

"This is your final opportunity," he said to them. "No one will think ill of you if you decide to stay in that house."

"My granddaughter is still out there," Doc replied, "I can't with good conscience sit idly by when tha's a chance she can be saved."

"You know my answer," Marty added.

"If you choose to go with us, know this," Prometheus relented, "our speed in crossing this jungle is of the essence. Every second, a thousand more of your kind is extinguished by Zeus and the others. There aren't many left. We will not stop. We will not wait if you fall behind. And yes, we will face many challenges. I only have the strength to protect Dan. I cannot protect you all."

"Understood," Doc replied, more determined than I had ever seen him.

"She may already be dead," Prometheus continued. "And I do not believe you will survive."

"So be it," Doc replied. "But she's not dead. I know she's not."

Prometheus nodded, perhaps with a little admiration for the old man's determination to remain by my side in the hopes we could somehow find a way to save Mina. Prometheus' muscles seemed to glisten as he drew his sword and swiped away some of the brush that obstructed our entrance into the dark chaparral. He hacked and gashed a passage; we followed slowly, cautiously taking in our surroundings.

A growl ripped through the air, feline in nature and an image of a black puma seemed to find its way into my mind's eye. The shrill of its prey gave us an answer to its fate. The jungle was a city at its highest action; moving, and swaying. With every step, another branch snapped, or an animal cried out in agony, anger, or angst. A small monkey flipped above us through the trees, wailing as if he had been impaled by one of the twigs he clung to. The humidity was causing the shirt I had found at the house to cling to my body. Perspiration dripped from my face, the dirt, grime, and filth seemed to join with my skin with every continuing step.

I tried to shallow my breathing and conserve some energy. It had been quite a while since I had hiked, and my last trek was in the Hillsborough County State Forest, hardly a dense South Mexican jungle. My arms, naked due to the shirt's short sleeves, took the brunt of the surrounding bristles, thorns, and brambles. Tiny scrapes and irritations itched incessantly, and were becoming more frequent across both arms.

The land was riddled with hazards. I found myself continuously losing my balance on fallen tree trunks, tiny rocks, and uneven land. I slipped once, scraping my leg. Doc and Marty both had their trials with the unwelcoming terrain as well;

tripping, sliding, and slipping repeatedly. Prometheus seemed undeterred by the forest, blasting through the foliage like a bulldozer creating food for the paper mills.

We proceeded deeper into the jungle for hours with no stops for rest. My leg muscles seemed to tear from my body in a relentless revolt against the exertion my body was placing upon them. My feet and ankles seemed poised to join the rebellion before finally, at long last, we reached a clearing near a lake and Prometheus stopped.

Doc and Marty collapsed on the ground behind me, both panting and dry heaving.

"Didn't work out much in Akrotiri, boys?" I quipped.

Marty flashed me a look telling me to go have carnal pleasure with myself, and I chuckled a bit. I glanced around the clearing. The flowers in the bushes were bright, vibrant with a brew of reds, yellows, and pinks caressing the leafy greens. In front of us lay a small lagoon and a picture perfect waterfall. I began to make my way toward the water when I heard Prometheus' bellowing voice.

"HOLD!"

I watched as he approached.

"Do not go in there," he commanded. "Carnivore fish- I believe you call them piranha."

"Oh," I gulped; thinking of my hand after a hundred hungry man-eating fish had had their way with it.

I took a swig from the canteen we had commandeered from the house, the water felt refreshing as it made its way down my throat, touching each pore with the great gift of wet pleasure. I glanced back toward Marty and Doc, but didn't expect to see what was there with them. Marty was lying up against a fallen trunk, Doc was nearby nursing his own legs, which had been ravaged by the tiny bites of thorns and bloodsucking insects. A few yards behind them, a face appeared from the jungle. Black spots littered among a golden coat. Yellow eyes, large whiskers and teeth, with tiny ears at the top of its head, heightened, listening. It had been tracking us for a while and now that we were stopped for a rest, it saw an opportunity.

The jaguar trained its eyes on Doc, seeing an unsuspecting prey with his back turned, and darted with toward him.

"WOOW WOW," it growled as it leapt toward him.

I don't know where I found the energy, but grabbing the sword I had claimed in Atlantis, I hurled it fifty yards with perfect accuracy, striking the beast directly in its is well muscled neck. It collapsed, a few feet behind Doc, who had bound to his feet and recoiled in fear.

It was still alive. Marty joined a stunned Doc as I finished it off.

"Jesus Christ," Marty exclaimed. "That thing almost had Doc. How the hell did you hurl that thing so far?"

"I forgot to tell you that in my younger days, I played for the Tampa Bay Bucs," I joked, trying to lighten the mood.

"He is finally sensing his powers," a familiar deep voice came from behind.

"Thank ya, Daniel," Doc wheezed. "I believe it would have been tha end for me if that jaguar had its way."

"We have lingered here long enough," Prometheus bellowed.

Back into the jungle we went, without a moment to contemplate what had just occurred. After a while, the hours began to merge together in a hot, sticky, painful mess. I didn't have a watch on me, but after a few more miles of endless greenery, I estimated we were getting pretty close to dusk. We would walk for a good three or four hours, then rest, then walk another three hours, then rest, although the rest wasn't refreshing. Our progress seemed to begin to be less and less between each stop. We had reached another clearing when the sky began to turn an orange hue.

"We will stop here for the night. Wait here, I will gather firewood," Prometheus ordered.

It was a good area to stop. Plenty of hollowed out old trees trunks to fall up against, the land was fairly flat, and seemed to be free of rocks and other jagged contraptions that could prevent a good night's sleep. At each rest stop, Marty and Doc sat with their backs against one another to prevent another surprise attack.

"How close do you think we are?" Marty asked, not to anyone in particular.

"I don't know," I replied. "We've traveled pretty far, though."

"Well, I think it's pretty damned disturbing that we haven't bumped into a single soul."

"I guess there's no one left."

Silence... then a cracking of branches behind us, we turned to see Prometheus emerge from the forest with one arm full of firewood, the other steadying the carcass of a wild boar on his back.

"Oh, Promey, you shouldn't have," Marty cracked.

Prometheus glanced over to him, annoyed at his mockery, and sneered.

Marty smiled devilishly, he knew he drove Prometheus crazy and got some kind of weird enjoyment out of antagonizing him. Sort of like the kid near the lion's cage, poking a stick in just enough to piss off the lions.

"How far away are we?" I asked.

"Another two day's journey to an area that will get us close enough that I will be able to levitate us the rest of the way."

I could feel the uneasiness of the group as the words rolled off his lips.

Prometheus stacked the wood and then passed his hand over it, igniting it, as if by thought alone.

"I was able to find a freshwater spring and refilled your canteens," he said, as he used his sword to cut the meat off of the boar. "You all should rest and consume. I have a protective covering over the camp tonight. You will need to stay close, as I do not have the energy to expand the field very far."

"Um, what about our... you know," Marty sheepishly asked. "Our bodily functions?"

"If you need to have a movement, I would not exit the camp – especially at night."

Marty squinted at the blackness of the jungle, and shook his head.

"I can hold it."

We devoured the boar quickly, and the jungle buzzed around us. Growls, howls, and shrieks greeted our ears, as if when the sun set, the milky, bright moon was an alarm clock for every species. Once we were satisfied, Prometheus levitated what remained of the boar's corpse and flung it deep into the brush. The bushes and trees shook as unseen predators pounced on the easy meal.

"The time has come to tell you why we are on this journey." Prometheus calmly said, as he wiped off the boar's blood on some leaves in front of him.

Chapter 15 Rise of the Royalty

As Prometheus' words reached my ears, I once again entered into a transfixion. I felt as if I was a time traveler, pushing twelve thousand years into the past, and arriving over a vast continent in the middle of the Atlantic Ocean. I was floating, like a seagull searching for its meal, swooping across the vast land. Atlantis was enormous. It was no small island; instead it reminded me of the continent of Australia. It seemed to stretch from the Azores to the Bahamas. Hundreds of cities dotted the landscape of the island nation, and each resembled little Roman city-states.

Atlas presented Poseidon with Atlantis shortly after its creation, and he was so pleased he named the continent after its creator. Its humanoid inhabitants were the "Chosen of the Gods". They benefited from technology not even known to us today, except for perhaps the mystics, who have been mocked for the belief in its power – crystals. The entire continent was run from the massive city at its epicenter, Poseidia. There, in Poseidon's temple, the crystal and gold skulls, along with the two Rods of Power created some type of magical energy that spread across the continent, giving the Atlanteans light, heat, and all the comforts of a civilized society.

All the cities of the continent boasted Greco-Roman style of architecture, with triangle shaped topside of the structures, and columns extending to the ground like fingers from a hand. There were circular shaped amphitheaters, large columns that boasted beautifully carved works of art. The people were dressed in Greek-like chitons, and there was a mixture of races; white, black, even Asian, all seemed to reside and work side by side in the community. There was no segregation at all, everyone worked as one, seemingly happy. With the exception of royalty, there were no upper or lower class; everyone was equal. It was a perfect utopia.

Most of the outer cities were harbor, sea-going communities that built vast fishing fleets. The communities closer to the center were mining communities, finding gold, diamonds, rubies, and copper. Any metal deemed precious in the ancient world seemed to be in abundance in Atlantis. There were also large agricultural communities, as the fertile soil seemed to provide a bounty of fruit, vegetables, wine, crops, the land would seemingly never have issues with providing for the populace. Speaking of the people, they were giants. At least it seemed that way, as they were a society of Shaquille O'Neals. Huge, hulking specimens of human beings; they had to be an average of six-five at least. Several tipped to seven, perhaps even eight feet tall. These folks weren't thin, either, they were large, muscular human beings.

In the early days, Poseidon and Zeus ruled the land with an iron fist. Living in Poseidia, they demanded daily tribute, and punished the Atlanteans if they failed to show the proper respect. Soon though, the gods' interest in the tributes of man had waned. Zeus sent the rest of the Dodekatheons across the world to try and build communities similar to Atlantis. They left Atlas and Prometheus in charge of Atlantis, and instructed them to develop a system for the Atlanteans to govern themselves.

Atlas was called the Premier King, he was the ruler of the continent, and resided in Poseidon's temple. Poseidon had chosen a mortal wife named Cleito while he was in Atlantis, and she had bore him nine sons. Prometheus had no interest in becoming a ruler, and instead they chose all nine sons of Poseidon; Eumelus, Ampheres, Evaemon, Mneseus, Autochthon, Elasippus, Mestor, Azaes, and Diaprepes to separate the kingdom into states. The nine kings each garnered a section of Atlantis, each bountiful and as rich as the next. It would be their charge to protect the borders of Atlantis, and thus each built up vast armies that consisted of thousands of armed fighters, warships, and an early version of a chariot.

Eumelus was king of Gadeira, the furthest part of Atlantis, nearest to Gibraltar. He was the spitting image of Atlas and many believed they were related. He had dark hair neatly cut in a Caesarean cut, immense muscles, and a light skin. He had a rock solid, thick jaw line and a cleft chin. Eumelus was a positive ruler, who cared deeply for his subjects. He created a vast navy in the hopes of raiding the primitives in the Mediterranean, protecting Atlantis' interests in the East.

Ampheres ruled a North East portion of Atlantis called Ampherius. Ampherius was accented by one of the ten volcanic peaks in Atlantis. The one in Ampherius was active, and no one could go near it. Ampheres, believing he had drawn the short straw among the kings, was extremely jealous of the lush landscapes his fellow kings owned. Still, he did genuinely care about the welfare of his subjects, and he made great strides in helping the Atlantean scientists develop an early warning system for volcanic eruptions. The world's first seismograph was born, twelve thousand years before today's scientists rediscovered the technology. Ampheres was smaller in stature to the other kings. A shrimp of only six feet, with a thin frame, he looked like a child compared to his fellow royals. With long blond hair, and a fair complexion, he wore eyeliner similar to the Egyptian pharaohs.

Evaemon ruled the Atlantean North Central kingdom of Avalon. A mining community, their temples and homes were lined in enough gold to make a Spanish Conquistador cry. Evaemon was a large-bellied robust man with a huge red beard and balding cranium. He seemed to overcompensate for the lack of foliage up top with hair beneath. Avalon was where much of Atlantis' culture and music would come from.

Mneseus was King of the North Western kingdom of Poseidonis. A deeply religious sea-faring kingdom, there were statues, temples, and portraits of the Gods throughout the kingdom, especially for its namesake. Mneseus dressed as a high priest, with billowing white robes that boasted a large hood covering most of his face. All you could see of the king were his hands, of which each finger boasted a large diamond or ruby. He believed himself to be in communion with the gods, although the only gods he had ever met were Prometheus and Atlas. Poseidon had never spoken to any of the children of Cleito. Mneseus drilled his subjects in preparation for the day that his father Poseidon would arrive to view the kingdom.

Elasippus was King of the Central East Kingdom of Elasidonia. The land gave a bounty of food, as well as mining, and a gorgeous coastline for fishing. Elasippus' dark mocha skin was a contrast from the others, but his gentle soul and kind heart set him apart from all of them. While the other kings showed their love for their people by taking care of their needs, Elasippus eliminated any division of royalty and subject, as he and his court would routinely be seen tilling the dirt, digging in the mines, or pulling in the nets of the day's catch, alongside his people.

Mestor ruled Mestamusia, a lush, beautiful land with large waterfalls, exquisite valleys, stunning mountains, and simply awe-inspiring landscape. It was by far the most beautiful part of Atlantis, aside from the capital itself. Mestor was thin; he looked Asian, and he had a great love for sensuality, often striding around his palace naked. His subjects would present him with the most beautiful of their daughters or sons and they would become part of his concubine. His appetite was insatiable, and he would quickly grow bored with his latest "toy", and was always looking for a new thrill.

Azaes was King of Azaleia, another seafaring community in the Southeast. Azaes also had Asian features, with lightened skin, a thin frame, and dark, short-cropped hair – he looked but the age of seventeen, yet he had already reached the Atlantean middle age of three hundred and twenty-two. The Atlantean lifespan was extended thanks to their advances in medicine. His desire was not for sex like his fellow king Mestor, but for conquest. He built an armada of infantry, naval ships, and war machines, often sending them to ancient Egypt and other parts of what is now northern Africa, looking for conquests and riches. With civilization starting out slowly throughout the rest of the globe, Azaes was frustrated by the lack of challenges that faced him. It was too easy to have his troops rape and pillage Stone

Age humanoids, but he longed for another confrontation worthy of his stature.

Diaprepes, King of Promethia, was also battle-thirsty. Unlike his fellow king to the east, the king of the Central Southern part of Atlantis dreamed of ruling all of Atlantis. He schemed and plotted the downfall of the other kings, trying to come up with a way to eliminate his competition while avoiding the wrath of the gods. Diaprepes, like Ampheres, was smaller than the other kings, standing about six feet. He had large muscles, a dark, Middle Eastern skin tone, and a tight, natty beard.

Autochthon was King of the south western Atlantean kingdom, Sunra. The region was ravaged by war, as they were under constant attack by a warrior race of women from South America, the fabled Amazons. Autochthon's army and his supplies were weathered from the repeated attempts at conquest, but they had successfully repelled the Amazon attacks. He was a brilliant tactician and standing six feet nine, with long black hair, a short, curly beard, and a light complexion, he looked like most of the depictions of Jesus in modern day. A slender frame, he wasn't an opposing figure, but he had a booming voice that seemed to shake the foundation of Sunra's castle.

After the final defeat of the Amazon army, Diaprepes saw a unique opportunity to topple Autochthon and the Kingdom of Sunra, taking it for his own. Before making any moves, he went to Poseidia to ask for permission from King Atlas. Atlas refused of course, but it wouldn't curb Diaprepes' ambition. Despite Atlas' strict orders not to invade, he launched a full out assault on the Kingdom of Sunra. Ten thousand infantry armed with crystal-charged weaponry, two hundred ships, and nearly five thousand battle chariots armed with sabers and spears descended on Atlantis' smallest country. Atlas asked Prometheus to go to the battlefield and assist Autochthon in defending his homeland, and then bring Diaprepes to him for judgment.

Prometheus dropped on a ridge overseeing the two armies as they approached one another. As his eyes scanned the battlefield, he spotted in the front, the young son of Autochthon. Like his father, his hair was dark, flowing like a waterfall over his shoulders. He wore no beard, but his skin was smooth, his dark eyes piercing, his slender, yet muscular frame wore the golden armor of an Atlantean knight. His name – Alosletian, and this was his story.

Chapter 16 Alosletian

"Watch our flank!" Alosletian commanded, as the clash of swords, steel, and armor erupted in a symphony of noise. He didn't speak English but as with my past visions from Prometheus, he transfigured the Atlantean language into something I could comprehend.

Bending down from his steed, he drew his large sword and began slashing at the Promethean invaders. Its thin, yet strong blade was made of the strange Atlantean element that allowed for an iridescent glow. He plowed through the combatants like a farmer tilling his field, dropping one after another. Even with his contribution, the forces of Promethia still began to penetrate the Sunranian defenses. Alosletian would find himself covered in blood, surrounded, and staring at two dozen enemy swords, and crystal weapons.

The crystal weapons were shaped like a rifle, but instead of launching a projectile that emitted from explosive powder – this weapon seemed to blast a short, powerful burst of electricity. One of the Promethean soldiers fired his weapon, striking Alosletian in the chest and sending a charge through his body. He fell from his steed, landing roughly on the rocky terrain below with a horrific thud. They put their swords to the horse, and then trained their blades on the fallen prince.

"It is over for you, Prince of Sunra," one of them croaked. "Surrender – you and what remains of your men will be spared."

Alosletian struggled to regain feeling in his arms and legs. His body ached, and his extremities tingled from the bolt of the lightning gun.

"You should kill me now," he managed to spit out. "Because once I have feeling in my limbs, I will destroy you all."

"Young fool," the battle veteran shook his head and looked toward his men. "End it."

Swords raised and began their drop to end a valiant young prince's life – but they didn't find their mark. Alosletian's body levitated into the air, slipping above the men and floating away from the battle, toward a ridge above it.

"What sorcery is this?" One of them cried out, as they watched their prisoner disappear from sight.

Aloaletian landed next to Prometheus with a thud, feeling some of the air in his lungs escape as his body hit the dirt and rocks beneath him.

"Are you injured?" Prometheus asked quickly, keeping his eyes on the battle.

"What is the meaning of this? Who are you? How dare you interfere-"

"Be silent, boy."

"I will not!" Aloaletian had finally found his extremities and rose to his feet. "I am Prince of Sunra – I command you to identify yourself."

Prometheus glanced to the angered boy and smiled. He liked his passion, his dedication to his people.

"I will ignore your impudence as the passion of war," he said quietly. "I am the god Prometheus and I have chosen to save you from your end. My reasons are my own and I need not explain them to a mortal."

"My Lord!" Aloaletian fell to his knees. "I cannot express the sorrow for my brashness. I should have known you were one of the gods."

"Be silent and at ease," Prometheus commanded. "Your army has lost the battle, your kingdom will likely fall."

"My Lord, can you not help us?"

"I came to see if I could render assistance – but I am afraid the forces of Diaprepes may be too formidable even with my intervention."

"How can this be? Zeus; the gods cannot be happy with his aggression."

"No, Atlas is displeased."

"And the others? Ares?"

"They are not here. It is up to Atlas and I to restore the peace in Atlantis."

"Then you must help us," Alosletian cried out. "You must scourge their evil troops and show them the gods do not favor his attack. If Sunra falls, Diaprepes will not stop. He'll take Azaleia and the other states, working his way to Poseidia. You must stop his aggression."

"No."

"Then you leave us to die." Alosletian looked despondent. "Return me to the campaign, as I wish to fight with my people rather than cower here with an uncaring deity."

Prometheus looked deep into the eyes of the young royal, searching his mind. Alosletian truly loved his people, so much so he would truly wish to die with them if it came to it.

"Issue a full retreat of your men to your country's capital," Prometheus instructed. "I will take care of the rest."

"I will stand and fight these invaders."

"You will do as your god commands, or I will not help you."

Alosletian took a step back, and then dropped to one knee.

"Thank you, my Lord."

"Thank your own bravery," Prometheus sighed. "You are passionate about your people, willing to sacrifice yourself to prevent them from their slavery. It is an admirable quality. You have taken me in, Alosletian, and I will do all that is in my power to assist you."

Prometheus raised his hand and Alosletian again rose into the air. Prometheus deposited him in the front of the battlefield, covered by an invisible shield. Promethean swords would attempt to strike him, but only bounce of his protected skin.

"Retreat to the Castle!" Alosletian called out. "Fall back!"

"No, Sire!" One of his commanders called back. "We cannot give in! We cannot give up the ground to Promethia! We will be finished!"

"I have a plan," Alosletian replied. "Trust your prince."

"Yes, sire. As you say."

The commander then turned and repeated Alosletian's orders. It would spread through the entire legion: "Fall back, the prince has a plan."

Sunra's troops retreated but the rumors of Alosletian's "plan" made the commanding officer of the Promethean troops pause, allowing his vanquished opponent the opportunity to escape, to the great consternation of his fellow officers.

"It is a rouse!" one general cried out. "He was trying to buy them time to get back to the castle and fortify their final position – and you allowed them to do it, General Nalog."

"Silence, Moga," General Nalog retorted, as he stroked his short goatee. "I think there's more to this."

General Moga, a large, light-skinned warrior, didn't seem to accept the decision. He stalked around the commander's tent like a lion waiting for one shot at its trainer. Just one open door that would let him escape and be the animal he was born to be.

Nalog was smaller than Moga, with light skin, short red hair and goatee, but a large muscular build. Then again, in a sea of Arnold Schwarzeneggers, he was puny. It was his military mind that got him to the rank of Commanding General in Promethia's army. He sensed there was something afoot with the rapid retreat; while Promethia was definitely winning the battle, victory wasn't yet assured. Nalog sensed a trap. If they pursued in an effort to finish off the victory, there was a significant chance they could be walking into an ambush. Moga thought more about the glory of a complete victory.

"Stepoh, what is your opinion of this strategy?" Nalog asked the third general in the room.

"I agree with Moga," Stepoh replied, as he stroked his broad mustache. "We had victory within our grasp and we let it escape like grains of sand."

"I believe it was a trap, and as the commander of this operation, my say is final and is not up for discussion." Nalog ended the discussion.

Moga grumbled and stormed out of the tent, into the night sky. The battle had begun during the early morning hours and waged throughout the day. The Sunranian retreat coincided with the setting of the sun. In the pitch-black darkness, it would be impossible to find them now. They would need to assault the castle in the morning, which would cost many more lives. If they had outflanked and finished them off, they would have decimated the remaining Sunranian troops and could have expected the complete surrender of the king. Now, they could be stalled for days because of Nalog's cowardice.

Moga kicked a rock that skidded along the sand, he watched as it pipped and popped into darkness, stopping abruptly at the feet of… what, who? A stranger entered into the light. He had a lion's mane of hair, a frame that looked like it was chiseled out of granite, and golden armor – but he was no Sunranian.

"Who goes there?"

"Greetings, General Moga," the stranger's voice boomed. "I am your god, Prometheus. Take me to General Nalog."

"Prometheus?" Moga laughed. "Prometheus would not waste his time speaking with mortals."

"You should not presume to know what a god wishes to do."

"Why you insolent fool – I will cut you down for -"

Before Moga could finish the sentence, Prometheus waved his hand, tossing the general across the campsite, landing him on a spear. A river of blood gushed out like a collection of geysers, showering nearby soldiers. The army was now awake from its slumber and rushed to get between the stranger and their commanding officer's tent.

"I am Prometheus, if you do not wish to suffer a fate similar to General Moga, stand aside."

Prometheus' name spread through the camp like an un-tamed flame, and several soldiers dropped to their knees in reverence. Nalog and Stepoh exited the tent to see what was causing the commotion, and witnessed their soldiers worshipping a stranger.

"What is the meaning of this?" Stepoh called out to his company.

"Sir," one of the men sheepishly replied, "it's the god – it's him – Prometheus."

"Prometheus?" Nalog questioned and dropped to his knees. Stepoh glanced to his right and saw the draining carcass of Moga impaled on spears, then followed Nalog's example.

"Rise, General Nalog," Prometheus commanded.

Nalog complied, slowly rising to his feet, a hint of fear in his gaze.

"W-what do we owe your visitation to, my Lord?"

"This action you are performing is against the wishes of the gods," Prometheus replied. "If you continue your advance, you will suffer our wrath."

The words send a commotion through the camp.

"Be silent, you fools!" Stepoh called out.

"My Lord," General Nalog timidly replied, "I apologize for any offense to the gods. That is certainly not my intention. But I must do the bidding of my king, Diaprepes."

"I understand your dilemma. However, let it be known to you and your troop, Sunra is under my protection."

"No!" called out one of the men. "We are the people of Promethia, we are your subjects! You cannot favor our enemy over us."

Prometheus flashed to the man, extended his arm, and from it a reddish burst of energy emanated and struck the soldier, turning him instantly into ash. Again, the men began to murmur as if they were all trained to say *bumblebee tuna* over and over.

"I love all of mankind," Prometheus announced to the group. "This aggression will not be permitted. If you advance, you will die."

Prometheus bent a knee toward the ground and, as if he was Neo in *the Matrix*, extended an arm into the air and flew off, leaving the Promethean army to search for their courage.

***

A few days would pass before the Prometheans found the fortitude to advance on the castle. Several thousand of their troops refused to continue, some fled, while others were caught and executed as deserters. Meanwhile, Alosletian and his army fortified the Sunra Castle as much as possible, preparing for the Promethean final onslaught.

Alosletian stood with his father in one of the lookout towers, watching the horizon for a sign of the oncoming forces.

"One of our scouts said they were now on the move," Autochthon said. "It will be a matter of time before our final test."

"Prometheus will not fail us, Father," Alosletian replied confidently.

"Prometheus is the patron God of Promethia," the King sadly replied. "I would not count on his intervention. In fact, getting you to retreat back to the castle may have been a rouse to put us in a more vulnerable position."

"They were winning the battle. I would be dead if not for Prometheus lifting me from their clutches and sparing my life."

"And forever I am grateful, and will offer him sacrifice – if we live, of course."

"He said he favors me – I believed him. Why do you think the Black Army did not pursue us during our withdrawal?"

"I know not, my son, but I do see it approaching on the horizon."

In the distance, the remaining members of the black armor-clad Promethean army climbed over the hilltops. In the Bay of Sunra, their ships began their approach and positioned for an assault.

Alosletian leapt from the tower onto a pile of hay beneath them, slid out of the stack, and ran to his troops waiting near the gate.

"Lower the gate!" he commanded. "Men, we must surround the castle on all four sides. Expect an assault from all flanks."

As his the gate began to descend, a familiar voice halted it.

"Stop!" Prometheus cried out.

Immediately, the drawbridge operator stopped its progression and began returning it to its original upright position.

Prometheus landed next to Alosletian, who dropped to a knee in front of him.

"Rise, young prince." Prometheus smiled.

"I began to wonder if you were coming." Alosletian also smiled.

"I will never abandon you." Prometheus placed his muscular arm around him. "I know now why you are so interesting to me."

"And why is that?"

"I will tell you later. But for now, know that I consider you a brother."

Prometheus bent his knees and in a single bound, found himself on top of the lookout tower.

"For now, brother," he called back, "watch as your elder sibling dispatches your enemies."

Prometheus rose into the air and began firing a barrage of red and green energy blasts from his hands. Each would strike a group of the onrushing army, sending many of its men scurrying in different directions. The ships in Sunra Bay began an onslaught upon Prometheus and the castle, but the God's protective shield prevented any damage.

Prometheus turned his attention to the black-sailed vessels, and with a few blasts from his hands; the ships were on their way to the bottom of the bay. Back to the now panicking army, he again began attacking all flanks, each company losing men with every blast. Their advance stopped and the full retreat began, but Prometheus was not as forgiving as General Nalog. He followed them, killing more and more with each rupture of energy from his hands, until the last man, Nalog himself, was left.

Nalog stood alone, surrounded by a hundred thousand mangled corpses.

Prometheus dropped in and surveyed the damage along with his vanquished opponent.

"I do not fault you in this, Nalog," Prometheus told him. "If you bring me your king, I will spare you."

"I love you, my Lord," Nalog replied as he fell to his knees. "But I will never betray my king."

"I do admire that," Prometheus replied. "I promise your final punishment will be as painless as I can make it."

"Thank you, my Lord."

***

Prometheus returned to the Castle of Sunra and entered the throne room of King Autochthon.

"My Lord," the king began, "the kingdom of Sunra owes the greatest of gratitude to your generosity and intervention. We will praise your name for as long as there is a Sunra. What can we possibly do to glorify you?"

"Thank you, King Autochthon," Prometheus replied. "Sacrifice and tribute is not necessary. I do not desire these things."

"Is there anything we can do to repay you for this great gift you have given us?"

"Yes."

"Name it, my god, anything."

Prometheus glanced to Alosletian, who was stationed at his father's side.

"Your boy," he said, "he has a destiny in the capital city of Poseidia."

"My son…" the King's voice trailed off. "Your grace, please do not ask me to relinquish the only heir to my crown."

"If not for me," the god replied, "you would have no crown or an heir."

"Yes but… please, your highness, anything else. You can have all the gold in our vaults – all the virgins in my court -"

"Father, it is fine," Alosletian replied, "I believe in Prometheus. I will be safe in his care."

"When the time comes," Prometheus continued, "Aosletian will return to claim his rightful place on the throne of Sunra. Until that day, he will be with me, trained by the gods to become the next Premier King of Atlantis."

"Premier King? But Atlas is a god - there will never be another Premier King," Autochthon questioned.

"I know my brother," Prometheus smiled. "He already tires of Terran rule. Soon, it will fall to man to govern Atlantis. I can find no mortal more qualified for this than the son of Hercules."

"Son of Hercules?" Alosletian replied, stunned.

Autochthon looked down to the palace floor.

"Father?"

"I am not your father," Autochthon replied. "You are not of my seed."

"I... I do not understand…"

"In the early days of my rule, your mother and I... we could not conceive a child," the king sighed. "I loved your mother deeply and despite the suggestions of some of my court that I divorce her and find a new queen, I refused. I prayed to Lord Zeus to grant me an heir."

Alosletian began to weep. The king rose from the throne and wrapped his arms around his son.

"The Amazons came in full force," Autochthon continued. "And we were overwhelmed; the kingdom was about to fall. But Lord Zeus sent his son, Hercules, to save us. With his strength we were able to repel the attack. We were so grateful… as we are to Lord Prometheus today…"

Autochthon lifted the head of his son and their eyes met.

"I asked Hercules to take your mother into his bed. Being of nobility, he of course vehemently refused but after privately hearing about our inability to conceive – he finally reluctantly agreed."

"You whored out my mother to Hercules?"

"No… no, it was not like that at all," the King replied. "Your mother loved me with all of her heart. She understood my sacrifice for her and she also understood the importance of providing a prince to our kingdom. If the son of a god could not bring her a child, nothing could."

"And a child was conceived," Prometheus added.

"Yes, you, my beautiful son," Autochthon continued. "No one knew the circumstances of your birth besides your mother and me. You were my son. You are my son. You are the heir to the Kingdom of Sunra. None of this changes that." He turned to Prometheus.

"My Lord?" King Autochthon's voice rose from the chamber.

"Yes?" Prometheus replied.

"I have one more task I need Alosletian to embark upon on behalf of Sunra. Is that permissible?"

"What is it?"

"A diplomatic mission. It should not take long, but it has a direct impact on what happens to Diaprepes' land."

"Once Diaprepes' fate has been decided, I will return Alosletian for this mission. But it will be the last on behalf of Sunra."

"Completely understood, my Lord."

The King and his son embraced, tightly as if it would be the last time they would ever see each other.

"I love you, Alos," the King wept, "I am very proud of you."

"I love you too, Father. With all of my heart, I love you."

"Alosletian, come," Prometheus commanded. "We must deliver Diaprepes to King Atlas for judgment."

"Yes, my Lord."

"Do not call me that," Prometheus replied. "We are equals – you have the blood of a god running through your veins."

Prometheus took hold of Alosletian's arm and together they flew off toward Posedia. King Autochthon wondered if he had seen the boy he raised from birth for the final time.

Chapter 17 Battle for Survival

Prometheus stopped speaking and I was time warped back into our reality. My eyes opened and were greeted by the image of both Doc and Marty sound asleep. I assumed that Prometheus' story didn't have the same impact on them as it had with me. I glanced over toward the Grecian deity. He stared into the fire of our camp like a child who had lost his favorite pet.

"So why tell me this story?" I asked him.

The emerald globes of his eyes seemed to penetrate me.

"The story is not yet complete," he sighed. "And from it, a significant lesson will be learned. Something that will directly impact a decision you will need to make."

"Me?"

"Indeed."

"And when do I need to make this decision?"

"When we reach our destination."

"Which is?"

Prometheus smiled.

"You already know," he smirked.

His response puzzled me. *I knew? How could I know? He had been unusually tightlipped about our trip, as if it was the Holy Grail we were after. But unlike Robert Langdon and the Priory of Scion, I was not on a quest to prove that Jesus and Mary got jiggy with it. So what could he possibly be referring to? We were in the middle of a Mexican jungle…with barely any food, traveling to God knows where, to find who knows what to defeat the gods…*

"K'ak'nab Mam Atot," I said, the name spilling into my frontal lobe.

Prometheus grinned another toothy smile.

"We have a long day ahead of us," he replied. "Try to get some rest."

"AAAAGH!" a voice cried out, startling me. Prometheus reached for his sword as we both glanced toward the source.

Marty was up on his feet, patting his khaki shirt and pants. I grabbed a flashlight we had included in our gear and shined it toward him. The light glistened off Marty's fear-stricken eyes; all over his body were inch-and-a-half-sized spiders with long black front legs, a glossy black torso, and large hindquarters that boasted a red hourglass - Black Widows. Marty's face was covered with reddish marks and swelling. Inside the swelling were side-by-side pinpricks. He writhed in agony and the spiders skittered around his body. There had to be a million of them. Doc had risen to his feet and was approaching him when I heard Prometheus call out.

"No, stay back! He's finished!"

Marty's body twisted and contorted as the spiders continued to feast upon his flesh, and finally he collapsed. Prometheus reached his hand into our campfire, removed one of the logs that bore its flame, and tossed it on to Marty's body.

"He ain't dead yet!" Doc called out as the flames engulfed Marty. His screams were horrific, burning in agony along with the creatures that were killing him.

"The beasts would turn to us next," Prometheus replied, trying to justify his actions.

"Daniel, help me get some water to douse him with!" Doc called out to me.

Marty was moving as the flames licked his flesh, using it as kindling to peel it from his bones.

"Daniel!" Doc called again.

I followed him toward a nearby lake, Doc grabbed a pan we had brought with us from the drug runner's cabin and moved as quickly as his aged legs could take him. Doc plunged the pan into the water, filled it, emerged, and rapidly moved toward the burning carcass that was our friend. Ejecting the water on to the flames, they flickered for a moment but continued.

"Prometheus, ya bastard!" Doc cried out as he fell to his knees in realization that his attempt was pointless, "You killed him!"

I fell to my knees beside him and cradled the old man as he wept.

"Ya killed him, ya bastard…ya killed him," Doc repeated over and over.

"Martin Jackson was dead before the flames hit his body," Prometheus calmly pronounced. "But his mind had not accepted the outcome yet."

"Did you have to burn him alive?" I screamed back.

"He would have died in agony as the poison destroyed his body," he facilely retorted. "And the insects would be upon you as well."

"Gawd damn ya, gawd damn ya to hell, Prometheus," Doc sobbed.

I heard a crack above us, and a huge snake seemed to hurl itself out of the brush and it charged us. I let go of Doc, and the snake went right for him, rising above his sitting posture and plunging its head down on the back of Doc's neck. Doc screamed out in distress.

"HOLY CHRIST!" I exclaimed, as the serpent began to wrap itself around Doc's frame, squeezing.

Prometheus moved quickly toward Doc and with one swipe of his sword, he severed the snake's head from its body. Blood splattered from both ends; the head still had Doc's neck in a death grip, the other end was flooding Doc's body with the snake's cold dark red fluid. I finally overcame the shock of it all, grabbed some sense and my sword, and used the blade to pry open its mouth. The fangs had dug deep into Doc, but popped off like the opening of a zip lock bag. Doc's claret blood began to expel, I applied pressure to the wounds as Prometheus hacked away at the rest of the snake, careful to avoid striking Doc's pale white skin.

"Oh my god…we're in hell, Daniel," Doc rasped, as he collapsed in my arms. "We're in bloody hell."

"Can you fix this?" I looked toward Prometheus, whose healing powers had saved each of us at one point.

Prometheus dropped to one knee and looked at the wounds.

"He has lost a lot of blood," he replied, as he rubbed his hands together. "But I can repair the injuries and stop the bleeding."

"Do it."

"I do not know if I can stop the infection. That may be beyond me."

"Do what you can, Prometheus, please."

I eased Doc to the ground and Prometheus placed his hands on the two holes that used to be part of Doc's neck.

"Don't cha…" Doc wheezed. "Don't cha touch me, ya murderer…"

A bright white glow emitted from Prometheus' hands and the holes were miraculously closed, without even a scar. Prometheus rose to his feet and left Doc on the ground, where I took residence next to him.

"Ares!" Prometheus called out to the stars above. "Ares are you too cowardly to face me? Must you send your pets to distract me? Show yourself! Ares!"

A crackle in the jungle and from behind us appeared a large man, with skin of dark mocha, a deep scar over his right eye, no hair upon his head, and a full, grizzly beard. He wore spiked blue and red battle armor, carrying a large battleaxe in his left hand.

"Do you dare impugn my honor, Prometheus?" his gravelly voice barked.

"Why send all of your beasts to torment me? Why not face me like a true Dodekatheon?"

Prometheus moved between Ares and the two of us.

"Unlike you, rebel, I follow Lord Zeus' commands," Ares replied. "My armies are scouring the planet looking for what remains of the mortals, as are the others, or rest assured your little insurrection would already have been put to an end."

"You know you cannot stop the son of Hercules from going to the portal," Prometheus replied. "It is his destiny."

"Prometheus, you are a fool," Ares croaked. "You always have been. Your caring for these mortals is like me caring for the worms under my boots. Why? Give me the son of Hercules and let us end this nonsense."

"I will not allow you to destroy their race."

"Their race is *already* destroyed," Ares laughed. "We have granted immunity to a handful– those who completely and truly submitted to the will of the gods. The remainder who defy us are being hunted down and eliminated. You have lost, Prometheus. There is no point going on with this foolishness."

"It may be too late to save the billions you have butchered," Prometheus grew angry and more determined, "but if I can save one... two of them – and end Zeus' rule on Terra, then their deaths would have mattered."

Ares shook his head at Prometheus' defiance.

"After all of this time," he chuckled, "you honestly believe that Thoth will give a damn about these mortals?"

"He does... I believe it."

"Then you are a bigger fool than I originally believed," Ares scoffed as he turned to leave. "We are done here. And do not fret. I will send no more of my pets to you tonight. But know this, if you continue on toward the portal – you will face not only me and my armada, but the full force of the remaining Dodekatheons. Zeus will not allow Dan Ryan to set foot in *K'ak'nab Mam Atot*."

In a poof, he vanished and the jungle grew eerily silent.

"I thought we had a protective shield or something?" I asked.

"Somehow he penetrated it," Prometheus replied unapologetically. "I do not know how."

"So we're not safe anymore?"

"We never were."

Chapter 18 Brother Against Brother

"How is Doctor Constantopolus?" Prometheus asked as he placed his hand on my shoulder.

"Well, I'm no physician, but he seems to be alright," I sighed. "He's passed out right now."

Prometheus closed his eyes briefly, and then opened them as if he had just caught a thought.

"He is fine, there was no damage from the constriction, and the wounds on his neck are healed. His heart is working hard to replenish the liquid he lost. He should be able to continue, if he chooses."

"I'm exhausted," I announced; my limbs felt like tree trunks, weighing down the rest of my body.

"You should get some rest, as tomorrow night we will be in K'ak'nab Mam Atot. I will watch over you as you slumber."

"You didn't believe Ares?"

"Honesty…" Prometheus chuckled slightly, "…was never a strength of Ares."

"Well, thanks… for not giving up on us - on me."

"I can only hope when the time comes, you will make the right choice."

"I hope so, too."

"I am going to finish the story," Prometheus added. "But since we are running out of time and you need rest, I am going to go into your mind and present it to you as you sleep."

"In a dream?"

"Yes, but every part of this dream you shall remember, and it will be the complete truth."

"I have to admit, I'm a little uneasy with you implanting things in my subconscious," I replied uneasily. "Our government has experimented with different forms of mind control - subliminal messages and all that. How can I know you won't abuse this and implant into me exactly what you want me to do? I am a free man, you know. I am no slave or a pawn in the Gods' chess match."

"Don't be silly, Daniel," Prometheus scoffed. "Of course you are a pawn. However, the decision you have to make will be yours alone. I cannot tell you what to do. Just the stakes when the time comes. The decision must be of free will for it to work."

I nodded, and lay beside Doc, who was still heavily asleep.

"Now, rest…" Prometheus said calmly. "Let all tension release from your body. Breathe in and out in a steady motion. Let the exhaustion of the day's events overtake you…"

I felt myself drifting, as if in a small dingy between two islands, floating out to sea, deeper and deeper until finally….

***

I was back in Poseidia – the gleaming, beautiful capital of Atlantis. The sky was baby blue, no clouds in the sky. The city was huge. Buildings resembling Roman and Greek architecture spanned for miles, each with the definitive columns and triangle roofing. In addition to the Greco-Roman resemblance, you could also see large, distinct, yellow and white pyramids. Some resembled the Egyptian pyramids in Egypt, while others definitely looked more Mayan or Aztec. Rising in the distance, on the largest pyramid and overlooking the city, sat Poseidon's Temple. It was simply the largest structure of worship you could imagine. The walls and columns were at least twenty stories high, the doors, which from Main Street Poseidia, you could see gleaming in golden amazement, may have been just as large. Rising above the temple was an immense peak. It made Everest look like a molehill, and could be seen a thousand miles away from Atlantis.

Neverpeak. My mind… and I suppose Prometheus told me it was called Neverpeak. And here, I was thinking it was Olympus… but my brain quickly reminded me that Olympus was in Greece – or what would eventually become Greece in this time. The people of Atlantis looked at peace. Warm, tanned skin with dark colored hair, they were attractive. There were no ugly or overweight people here. The men were chiseled out of stone, with rock hard muscular structures, and prominent large facial features. The women, curvaceous bodies accented by large, but not overly unattractive bosoms, smooth, velvety, dark olive skin, and eyes of emerald and blue. Perfection, human perfection. They had different shades, some looked Asian, but all of them were like their gods – beautiful.

I was on the street of a marketplace. Surrounding me were statues of strange beasts, one seemed to have a dragon head, humanoid torso and the wings of a bird. Another was a towering statue of Poseidon, holding his triton. It was the size of the Statue of Liberty, extending stories into the sky and seemed to be the center of the market square. Some of the buildings were stone, but were painted in vibrant colors of turquoise, light green, maroon and darker blues.

Each building had small bluish designs, like miniature waves, accenting the sea-faring culture. While many of the buildings were grey or made of the white iridescent material that seemed to be prevalent on the continent, some were sandy colored, almost Mediterranean in feel. Indeed, many of the buildings extended upward and capped in mosque type domes. A few of the domes were adorned with steeples that resembled serpents, while others boasted elaborate designs and murals, some depicting warriors in battle, others simple fishing or hunting expositions. One peculiar looking building included a water tower but also seemed to double as a windmill, as large sails were attached to a wind catcher device. Small statuettes of goat-like animals seemed to adorn small fountains attached to some of the buildings. One particularly large structure had the image of Zeus, with water pouring out of his mouth and depositing into a pool below.

It was by this fountain that I saw her. She stood out because her skin was light, downright pale, compared to the others. Her lips were pouty; she had emerald eyes, satin skin, and a gorgeous body. Her gown looked ancient Turkish, resembling a bathrobe made of silk. It was light blue and was highlighted by a gold undergarment. She wore a large headdress, bedazzled with diamonds, rubies, and other assorted jewels. It was Mina... but not Mina. Princess Mina?

"Naseha!" a man's voice called from behind her, belonging to someone who seemed familiar, but I couldn't quite place.

"Alosletian!" She smiled broadly and embraced him. They kissed quickly, as if stealing from each other, then looked around to see if anyone had noticed, which of course, everyone had – as all eyes had been on Nashea to begin with.

Alosletian was much older than the young boy I remembered from Prometheus' last story; he had filled out nicely and sported some facial hair.

"Could you possibly have worn anything more extravagant?" Alosletian teased as he pulled his lover into an abandoned alleyway.

"Oh, fine coming from the High Prince of Atlantis, dressed in beggar's clothing," Nashea replied. "I am a Princess of Azaleia for Zeus' sake!"

"Yes... but you know your father does not approve of our coupling." Alosletian was chagrined. "With the spies and the scribes all around us – I warned you to be... discreet."

"Alos, I left my guard at the royal house here in Poseidia – I came naked, alone before you – is it not enough?"

"Naked, eh?"

She smiled, gently sliding her hands along her robe, parting it slightly and exposing her two perfectly proportioned globes; her quarter-sized nipples were already hardened by the anticipation of being in Alos' arms.

"Come... we'll talk later," Alos said, as he took a quick look at their surroundings and proceeded into a nearby house.

***

Prometheus stalked the Temple of Poseidon, furious.

"Where is the prince?" he barked at Prince Alos' servants. They returned blank stares. Prometheus searched their minds for the answer but they honestly had no idea.

"Damn it…" Prometheus cursed. "He knows the importance of this meeting."

"At ease, my brother," a deep voice came from the throne room.

Prometheus followed the voice and found King Atlas sitting on his golden chair. Ares and Hermes were with them.

"Tell him," Atlas commanded Hermes.

"It seems, good Prometheus," Hermes slyly began, "your prodigy has returned to the city below to exchange in coitus with that little vixen from Azaleia."

"Princess Nashea?"

"Yes, that would be the one."

"Damn it all… I told him the ramifications of joining with her. The boy is absolutely stubborn."

"He loves her," Atlas returned. "And what is life without love?"

"Love?" Prometheus looked disgusted. "Love is for the weak."

"But you love him," Atlas smiled. "You love the mortals. If you did not, we would not be here. We would care not about their affairs, only the tributes they provide us."

Prometheus knew that his brother was right. He cared for the mortals deeply, and Alosletian in particular. It wasn't a sexual type of attraction, but a spiritual one. He admired Alos' fire, his passion for life, and the things that were important to him. He admired the intelligence that his young catechumen possessed and the destiny that he could see for him.

"Ah young love," Hermes mocked. "Such a beautiful thing this vexing we call love."

"Silence, you unbearable fool," Prometheus snapped.

Hermes feigned being stabbed in the heart.

"You worshipfulness," Hermes said to King Atlas, "shall I dispense with the rest of the news?"

"No, Hermes, tell him the rest."

Hermes bowed, and then curtsied, in a mockery of Atlas' authority.

"Well, Prometheus the grump," Hermes continued, "it may interest you to know that Lord Zeus and the rest of the Gods will not be in attendance at your little shindig."

"What?"

"Indeed, Lord Zeus believes that the trials of the mortals are not his concern. If they want to destroy themselves and Atlantis, let them."

"Why would he do this? Why would Poseidon allow this? Atlantis, after all, is his."

"Poseidon does Zeus' bidding as we all do. Lord Zeus has forbid any involvement by any deity. And yes, muscle-brain, that includes you."

"We are the custodians of Atlantis – this is our land."

"Uh no, Dense One, it belongs to Lord Zeus – and if he wants to let it go to ruin, he will."

"But why does he want the destruction of Atlantis?"

"There is another land he wants to cultivate, a people he believes he can make even more advanced then the Atlanteans," Ares interjected.

"Who? The Aegeans? They are still primitives. Banging on rocks and playing with fire. Our forces have taken all they have to offer at our leisure."

"*Our* forces?" Ares raised an eyebrow. "Do you not mean *Atlantis'* forces?"

"Yes, of course," Prometheus corrected himself. "I choose no side but Zeus'."

"Ah, but you have been choosing sides," Hermes disagreed. "You have been swaying battles one way or another as you see fit."

"In the interests of peace - Atlantis cannot survive and prosper if it wars upon itself."

"Exactly," Hermes continued, "Zeus believes that the more tranquil, learned nature of the Aegeans could inspire them to more advances in the civilization, while not being burdened by the greed of Atlantis."

"Atlantis and its people are benevolent. They are the rulers of the mortal existence because they have advanced quicker. They take so they can continue their advancement."

"Indeed, at the expense of the advancement of the rest of mortals," Hermes countered. "You said it yourself; they have taken whatever the others had to offer at their leisure. Why do you think other races like the Amazons fight against them?"

"Yes, like any Empire, they enjoy the spoils of their conquests," Prometheus replied. "But additionally they have made their conquered subjects better. They have installed outposts throughout the known world, including the Aegean, teaching them the fundamental elements of mathematics, the written word, how to clothe themselves properly. They did not enslave them… they continued to allow their independence."

"As long as they submitted to Atlantean rule…"

"Of course."

"And this is independence?"

"Enough of the bickering," Atlas commanded. "This is getting us nowhere. What is it that Lord Zeus commands of us?"

"Atlas," Hermes replied, "you are to give up your rule of Atlantis to the mortals. You and Prometheus are to join us at Zeus' new palace above the Aegeans."

"Olympus?"

"Yes, the other Dodekatheons have arrived there. We only await the both of you and Hercules."

"Hercules? Where is Hercules?"

"Even I do not know the answer to that." Hermes sighed.

"Fine," Atlas replied, "go forth and tell Lord Zeus we will arrive as quickly as possible. There will be a short period of transition that we must attend to, to prevent anarchy."

"Zeus understands this," Ares interjected. "But if you do not return within seven cycles of Terra, my armies will come and destroy this place."

"Seven days?" Prometheus replied, stunned. "He honestly expects us to be ready in seven days?"

"He does not care if you will be ready in seven days," Hermes replied. "He wants the gods out of Atlantis by then."

"Thank you, Hermes," Atlas complied. "We will be there in seven days."

Hermes bowed, a quick flash of light and they were gone.

"Prometheus," Atlas said, rising from his throne and throwing his arm around his brother, "are you friend only to Atlantis, or to all of the mortals of this world?"

"All."

"Then why do you look so despondent?"

"Because he is not ready."

Chapter 19 Abandonment

Alos held Nashea tightly against his naked body. Her scent intoxicated him. She slept deeply, content in their act of pleasure and love. They had met as children, the first time in a field of wheat and barley. Alos was playing with his Atlantean warrior dolls, pretending he was a great Sunranian general, leading his armies against the primitives. The Azaleian contingent descended from a hill, overlooking where he was playing. It was a small force, with armed guards surrounding a large royal carrier, buoyed by four muscular slaves. The royal guards of Sunra, the Stagnati, cut off his view of the foreigners approaching. His father, Autochthon, left the castle-like structure that housed their royal dwelling, awaiting the emissary's arrival.

Finally, the caravan arrived, stopping a few yards shy. Alos peeked through the muscular legs of one the Stagnati, and trained his eyes on the royal carrier. A young-looking man with light complexion and Asian features emerged from the protective dome. His robes were adorned with a varied and vast assortment of gold and jewels. Atop his head lay a white gold crown encrusted with immense rubies. Alos' eyes trained on the young girl that followed his highness. Like her father, she was thin, with milky skin. Her dark hair descended beyond the square of her back, and she had already begun to develop what would become her trademark pouty lips.

Alos remembered the feeling of queasiness in his stomach, as if he had swallowed a thousand butterflies and they were panicking in search of a route of escape from their acidic doom. He had seen many young girls in his time, paying them no mind. He was more interested in being the Sunranian general then paying attention to potential wives. But this one… made him feel like he had never felt before. It was a strange, unnatural feeling for him.

"Greetings, Azaes, it has been too long," he heard his father greet the King of Azaleia.

"Indeed, Auto. Indeed, you remember my daughter, do you not?"

"My Gods… is that little Nashea? My, she is sprouting like a tree!"

"Indeed she is, old friend - too fast."

His father looked back toward him and then waved him to come forth.

"And you remember my son, Alosletian."

"Young prince." Azaes bowed to him and as he was instructed during his royal training courses, Alos returned the courtesy.

"Children, go play in the fields, your elders have important business to discuss," King Autochthon commanded.

The two children obeyed, trailed by two guards from each kingdom.

Alos and Nashea played the typical games that children play, running through the fields, giggling and enjoying their time together.

For three days, the children were inseparable… but the moment finally came when Nashea had to return to Azaleia. The guards had to pry them from one another, Alos kicking and screaming while streams of tears poured down Nashea's face. Their bond was established from that point on… and as a good father would, as Alos grew older and diplomacy was needed, it would be Alos that would represent Sunra. Each trip to Azaleia was like a treasure for Alos. While his days would be spent engaging in the monotonous political discussions, his nights would be filled with passionate lovemaking in the Princess' chamber. Everyone in the royal court knew of the relationship, everyone that is, except the King of Azaleia.

Following the defeat and the punishment of Diaprepes for invading Sunra, Promethia was left without a ruler. Diaprepes' son, Dianolactus, was only four years old and the other city-states of Atlantis did not want to leave Promethia in the hands of the same advisors who counseled their ruler to his death. A meeting between Sunra and Azaleia had to be convened to ensure both were on the same page when it came to the position of Promethia.

They weren't; a huge argument arose between Azaes and Alosletian. The Azaleian position was clear – to dissolve the kingdom of Promethia and absorb it into the two countries that bordered it – Azaleia and Sunra. Alos stated the position of king Autochthon: Promethia should remain free and autonomous. Premier King Atlas should select a new family line of royals, and the child of Diaprepes should be absorbed into that family and treated as the first-born. The argument was so vicious that the voices of Azaes and Alosletian could be heard in the village below the Royal Castle.

They adjourned the discussion, deciding to sleep on their positions and resume negotiations in the morning. Alos had no issues with this development, as it guaranteed another night with Nashea. As they retired, Azaleia couldn't help but continue to be troubled by Alosletian's opposition. It seemed so clear to him that the threat of Promethia was too great to ignore. *Even if Dianolactus was spared, would he not want to avenge the failure of his father?* There could be severe consequences down the road for allowing Dianolactus to remain in line for the throne. To ensure it, he would offer his daughter Nashea to Dianolactus, and calm any hostility he may have. He had to convey this point to Alos… and he couldn't sleep on it. He had to tell him now.

The King searched for Alos in the guest quarters but he was nowhere to be found. He searched the dining area and the beautiful royal courtyard - still, nothing. He questioned his servants, but they feigned ignorance. He decided to go see Nashea, as he knew she was close with the Sunranian Prince. Perhaps she knew where he had gone, if he had left the castle, and his motivation for leaving when negotiations were at such a pivotal boiling point.

As the King approached the door to Nashea's chambers, he noticed both his guards and the Stagnati stationed.

"What are you doing here?" he questioned the Sunranian guard but received no response.

He turned to his trusted royal guard, "Dometus, what is the meaning of this."

"The prince has called on the princess, Sire."

"At this hour, how inappropriate behavior for a royal – the scandal it could -"

Then he heard it - his daughter crying out in the throes of passion while the animalistic grunts of the Sunranian Prince seemed to join in a symphony of carnal ecstasy. He burst into the chamber door and saw them, naked, sweat drenching their bodies while he penetrated her, cupping his hands upon her immense young breasts.

"Father!" she shrieked in mortal terror.

"MAFOOKA!" Alos cried out as he withdrew from her and wrapped himself in the blanket covering them, and revealing more of Nashea's completely nude body. Mafooka – for some reason Prometheus couldn't translate that to English – but I assume it's Atlantean for the f-word. *At least that's what I would have said.*

"I will kill you!" Azaes barked.

"Father, no please!"

"You are a dead man!"

The Stagnati poured into the room with weapons drawn, protecting Alosletian, while Azaes' guards got between them and their king.

"Your Highness… I promise you – this is not what you think…"

"Oh it is not? You defile my daughter right before my very eyes!"

"No, sire, you do not understand," Alos said, as he struggled to put on his robes and assisted by a Stagnati soldier, "We love each other. I am going to make Nashea my queen."

"No… Never! You have ruined her, damn you!"

"No, Father… he is my true love. I will be with him forever!"

"You will be with whom I command, child!"

"Your Highness…" Alos spoke gently trying to calm the furious father, "I know you are angry… but please listen. There is something I have not told you."

"Please do not tell me you have given her a bastard!"

"No… Of course not."

"I would command every one of my forces to kill you and your men if you had."

"Your highness, please," Alos pleaded. "Allow me to speak."

"Fine, say your piece."

"The God-King Atlas and the god Prometheus have selected me as the heir to Atlas as Premier King. I am to be the Premier Prince."

"And this gains you what, exactly?"

"What do you mean?"

"Atlas is a GOD – he cannot die. There can be no heir because his reign will never end."

"You are mistaken… and when I am named Premier King – I will take Nashea as my wife."

"Over my corpse!" Azaes screamed. "You will never see her again, do you hear me? Never!"

"Father, please!"

"Be silent, Nashea," he screamed as he backhanded his daughter. "You are nothing but a filthy whore!"

"Do not call her that!" Alos cried out.

"You shut up, be glad I do not order you de-manned where you stand," the King barked back. "And if you ever step foot in Azaleia again, you better come with an army ready to conquer us. Leave…immediately."

Alos collected the remnants of his royal garb, took one last longing look at Nashea and then departed. He returned immediately to Sunra and revealed everything to his father – who wasn't pleased with the outcome.

"This was the final task I asked of you before you left me for Poseidia for good," Autochthon lamented. "And this is how you end your association with Sunra? You defile Azaes' daughter after completely disregarding his plans?"

"I think he was angrier with that than with my relationship with Nashea."

"Bah! You are a young idiot," the king replied. "You are lucky he didn't kill you. If the roles were reversed, I would have never let you leave the castle."

"I am sorry, Father," Alos wept. "It was not my intention to dishonor Sunra. But I love her... and she loves me – one cannot help their heart."

"Mafooka," the King mumbled. "You were always the hopeless romantic, Alos - and always for Nashea. No matter how many beautiful Sunranian maidens I placed before you – she was the only one who captured you."

Autochthon shook his head in disgust; somehow he had known that this day would come.

"Well," the king continued, "I will of course disavow all knowledge of the relationship. Further, you will need to leave immediately. I will contact Prometheus to let him know you are ready."

Prometheus came, and since his arrival in Poseidia, Azaes only spoke with him on matters of state. Whenever Alos inquired about his daughter, Azaes greeted the question with a cold, blank stare. King Atlas agreed with Sunra... and picked a new King of Promethia – Solanus. Solanus was kind, gentle, and had no male heirs, so he could adopt Dianolactus as his own and raise him to be different than his father. At least that was the hope.

As the years passed, Alos and Nashea continued on their relationship, in secret. Her father had offered her to several of the other princes of the realm, but they all feared Alos would take revenge if they complied, refusing by using the excuse that they knew she had been defiled. It only served to increase Azaes' hatred of the Premier Prince. For a time, he plotted Alos' assassination but feared retribution from the gods. He knew Alos was favored among them – but why, the King had no idea. Had he had any inkling the two lovers were continuing their relationship behind his back, he would have them both killed, gods be damned.

And so it went on... year after year. Nashea became a heartbroken spinster, counting the minutes to when she could make another excuse to go to Poseidia, while Alos continued to occupy himself with the massive job of learning how to be a Premier King, not really understanding why an heir would be needed in the first place. For as Azaes had said, Atlas was a god... he would never die. At some point, he always believed that when his father left for Hades' realm of the dead, he would take the crown of Sunra, and then finally take Nashea as his wife... if he could somehow convince Azaes to allow it.

Alos stroked her hair as he held her tight against him. The warmth of her body seemed to seep deep into his soul. He could never see himself with another. He longed to be with her full-time, to protect her from all potential harm. If anything happened to her... he would... he wouldn't know what he would do but he knew he couldn't go on without her.

Suddenly, a knock at the door - loud, angry. *Gods! Had they been discovered?* A chill ran down his spine. She stirred and he placed his hand above her mouth. Fear struck her doe-like eyes.

Another thunderous rap spurred him to his feet and he quickly donned his peasants' clothing.

"Who is it?" Nashea trembled with fear.

"Be silent, woman!" Alos harshly replied.

A quick flash of blinding white light exploded in the room. When it dissipated, a blond, curly-haired young looking male in a white chi ton sat at the foot of the bed.

"Greetings, young king," Hermes said, with a wide smirk on his face.

"How did you... what? Who the hell are you?"

"I did knock before entering... but I did not get a response, although, clearly you are here, sans clothes, but here nonetheless. Whatever are you wearing, my liege?"

Alos finished fastening his belt.

"I command you to identify yourself."

"Ooh, now that's the spirit!" Hermes crowed. "You are such an authoritative brute, aren't you? I totally see what you see in him, my dear. Besides the obvious… physical… attributes."

"I need a name from you."

"And I shall give it… my name is Hermes, herald to almighty Zeus, Himself."

Alos dropped to one knee.

"Forgive me, my Lord. I had no idea…"

"Not an issue, young King. Prometheus sent me to retrieve you."

"Why do you keep calling me *young king*? Has something happened to my father?"

"If you are referring to Autochthon," Hermes glanced toward the naked body of Nashea, who was beginning to dress, "nothing but old age haunts him. He is fine."

"King Atlas?"

"Atlas is a god… and he cannot get sick or die, but you already know this. He can, however, abdicate his throne after being be called upon by Zeus… which has happened. Which is why you must get *your very muscular* buttocks to the castle so Atlas can do all of his decreeing he needs to do before leaving Atlantis."

"Atlas is leaving Atlantis? But why?"

"Because Zeus wishes it to be," Hermes waved his hand. "Come, boy, we must get back to the castle. The others await your arrival."

Alos kissed Nashea one last time and followed Hermes out the door, beginning his journey to destiny.

***

In the main meeting hall, the area was crowded. Twelve seats sat adjacent to a circular table, imagine King Arthur's knights of the round table but with the kings of Atlantis instead of Sir Lancelot and Galahad. The kings' aides, servants, and guards were everywhere. The place was buzzing, gossip had run rampant, and there was much discontent among the royals.

Alosletian entered the meeting hall and all eyes glanced toward him. He was unshaven, and even though he had washed up, he appeared to be disheveled, unprincely.

"Where have you been?" Prometheus whispered into his ear, as he took his place to the right of king Atlas.

"You already know the answer to that."

"I do - and what did I tell you about that?"

"No lectures now, please…"

Prometheus groaned and looked toward Atlas, who rose and commanded the others to take their seats. The royals quickly complied.

Atlas' eyes glanced to each of the Kings of Atlantis.

To his left sat Eumelus, king of Gadeira. He looked more like the brother of Atlas than Prometheus ever did. Seated next to him were Ampheres, Evaemon, and Mneseus. To the right of Alosletian sat Prometheus, Autochthon, Elasippus, Mestor, Azaes, and Solanus, the new king of Promethia. Solanus was an older fellow, almost frail-looking at four-hundred-and-thirty-three years. Wrinkles wrought his skin; a thin, white beard seemed to be pasted on to his skin instead of grown. As the men surrounded the table, Azaes found himself sitting directly across from Alosletian.

"Thank you all for coming on such short notice," King Atlas' voice boomed through the hall. It was deep and gravely. "I have some bad news for Atlantis."

"Whatever it is, Lord Atlas," Eumelus cried out, "I am certain with the help of the gods we can get through it."

"That is just it, good king Eumelus," Atlas continued. "The gods no longer favor Atlantis."

The room exploded in the murmuring clatter of a hundred voices expressing shock, awe, and fear.

"Lord Zeus has called Prometheus and I to Olympus; you will no longer have our protection."

"May I speak, Lord Atlas?" Solanus fraily interjected.

"Yes."

"What have we done to anger the gods in such a way that they want to abandon their creations?"

"Zeus believes the Atlanteans have gone drunk with power and greed. He believes that there is no more to do here and that it is better to focus our efforts on other parts of the world."

"But we cannot exist without the gods," Ampheres cried out. "It is Lord Zeus that prevents Mount Atlantica from destroying us. It is Poseidon who keeps our winds calm. It is Ares who helps us with our battles against our enemies."

"And what of the moral implications?" Mneseus added. "Without the law of the gods, Atlantis will fall into lawlessness, a debauchery of evil and filth. It will be madness. We cannot have a society without the gods."

"You can continue to pay tribute to the gods in the hopes they will cast their favor back to this land," Atlas replied. "But I tell you now, they are not listening. You must show them you are worthy of their love and respect."

"And how do we do that?" Mneseus, the most pious and religious of all the kings said, "Have we not given enough tribute, have we not sacrificed our livelihoods for their glory?"

"Indeed, Poseidonis has shown itself to be god-fearing. It is well noticed by Poseidon. Trust me," Atlas continued. "To beckon the gods' favor once more – you must prove yourselves as a people. Prove you are worthy of their devotion. This does not mean only tribute – but the way you live your lives and obey our directives. Obey the directives of the king I will relinquish my crown as Premier King to."

"And who, pray tell, will this new Premier King be?" Azaes croaked, knowing full well what the answer will be.

"You all know Prince Alosletian of Sunra," Atlas gestured toward Alos. "He graciously accepted an invitation to join me here at the Temple and learn the responsibilities and demands of being the Premier King of Atlantis. For the past six years, the young prince has been at my side while I made my most difficult decisions."

"Lord Atlas," Elasippus piped up, "you cannot possibly be seriously considering turning over the fate of Atlantis to a mere child."

"Indeed, surely one of your kings has proven themselves worthy of accepting the crown," Mestor chimed in.

"Well, it sure as Hade's realm is not you, Mestor," Evaemon retorted.

"Why how dare you! I have every right to…" And so it descended into a great argument among the kings, about who should be Premier King, each stating their case like it was a public election.

"I say we vote on our choice of Premier King," Azaes interjected. "If the gods abandon us, we should have a say in who leads us into our godless future."

"Be silent, Azaes," Atlas angrily replied. "This is not a democracy. The gods are not gone – they just do not favor you. Do you want to incur their wrath by defying them?"

The room grew deathly silent.

"No, my Lord."

"Alosletian is the choice," Atlas continued. "Because he has god's blood running through his veins. You are all royals because I chose you to be such. I have chosen Alosletian, the son of Hercules himself, to be your Premier."

"We are royals because we are the sons of Poseidon," Azaes retorted. "We also have the blood of gods running through our veins."

"But not from the line of Zeus – not Hercules."

"Hercules? But we are the sons of Poseidon!" Mestor cried out.

"Yes," Prometheus nodded. "But Alos is the grandchild of the god of gods."

"I'm sorry, my god," Azaes replied, the anger seeping deeper and deeper into his soul. "I cannot follow his rule. I cannot obey his commands."

"You will, Azaes," Atlas replied. "Or my final act as King of Atlantis will be to order all the armies of the continent to descend upon Azaleia and burn it to the ground."

The room was again silent.

"And what of Prometheus?" Solanus asked.

"I will also be departing for Olympus," Prometheus replied. "But I will have a watchful eye on the events transpiring here."

"My gods," Mneseus began to weep. "We are truly abandoned. We have sinned too much. We are no longer worthy of their favor. What have we done… what have we done…"

"King Alosletian," Atlas turned to his right, "Atlantis is yours, speak to your kings."

All eyes turned on Alos…and a deep chill went up his spine. Atlas removed the golden ten-pointed crown from his head and placed it on Alosletian. He clasped his hands around it and Alos felt a warm sensation on it as it shrunk to his size.

"Gentle Kings," Alos said, as he took a deep breath, "the god Atlas has bestowed upon me the greatest honor any Atlantean can have - the right to govern the most powerful continent in the world – our own continent. I take this challenge not lightly, but with gratitude, humility, and look forward to the trying times ahead. We will get through them, together."

"And what of my land?" Ampheres replied. "Without Zeus' benevolence, Mount Atlantica will surely ignite its flames and reign terror upon us."

"I do not have the power to stop that," Alos replied. "But we can pray to the gods that it will never occur. However, we need to prepare in case those prayers go unheard, we must prepare for the future with contingencies."

"And what of our battle campaigns?" Evaemon interjected. "Without Ares' coordination or Poseidon calming the seas, how long can we last?"

"I say to you, King Evaemon," Alos responded, "do you not have the best navy in the world? Are your seamen not the most highly skilled and trained? Azaes, are your Marines not the most cunning, dynamic the world has ever seen? We may not always have fair weather, but we have what the gods have taught us. It will be enough."

"This is ridiculous," Azaes bellyached. "This cannot be happening. I am taking my daughter, returning to Azaleia, and never dealing with you fools again. We declare our independence from this stupidity."

"No, you are not, Azaes."

"Excuse me?"

"Your armies may well be the strongest of all of us here in Atlantis – but even your mighty army cannot stand up to our combined strength."

"Are you threatening me?"

"Furthermore," Alos smiled, "Princess Nashea will not being going with you. My first act as Premier King is to name her my wife, my queen, until the end of my days."

"Why you… you bastard… You cannot do that!" Azaes exploded and dived over the table in an attempt to get at Alosletian, but the other kings restrained him as Atlas and Prometheus rose from the table.

"Well done," Prometheus whispered sarcastically to Alos, "you have them all eating out of your palm."

"You have made an enemy this day, Alosletian," Azaes barked, "I will destroy you. I swear it."

"And your daughter as well?" Alos retorted.

"If she chooses you over her own blood, then she is no daughter of mine," Azaes replied as he stormed out of the hall.

Alos glanced at his fellow kings and smiled.

"He will come around," he said quietly. "In the meantime, we must prepare ourselves. I have no doubt that the spies have already sent notice of our situation to our enemies. Expect your lands to be attacked soon. But we will not be individual nations defending our own lands; we will fight with each other, side by side, sword in hand."

"One final issue, Premiership," Eumelus interjected.

"Yes?"

"With great humility, I believe I am confident in saying that our court does not feel comfortable with the knowledge that a mortal, even one of divine providence, has control of both Rods of Power and the skulls."

The room erupted into a chorus; full of a series of 'yes' and 'I agree'.

"But the Rods and skulls are what gives Atlantis its power," Alos questioned. "If we dismantle the gods' greatest gift to us, how will we continue to power our machines, our homes, our defenses?"

"Well, my Lord," Evaemon added, "some of our scientists in Avalon have created a power source independent of the crystals. It generates enough energy to light a home. We can place these throughout Atlantis. It will be our gift to you and all of Atlantis in return for our security."

"So be it then," Alos replied. "Prometheus, before you depart, would you please remove the Rods of Power and the skulls, scattering them across the world so they cannot harm anyone ever again."

"Alos, are you sure you want to do that?" Prometheus expressed his concern.

"Yes, if it will promote peace."

"As you wish."

"Anything else, Kings?"

The court grumbled their agreement and Alos adjourned the court, joining Atlas and Prometheus.

"I cannot believe you will not be with us anymore, Prometheus," Alos sadly stated.

"Alos, I will always be with you."

Prometheus and Atlas floated toward the balcony window overlooking Poseidia took one lasting glance at Atlantis and left Alosletian alone.

Alos walked toward the balcony and peered out. The island nation was going dark. There would be panic in the streets. From the very beginning, he would be tested.

Chapter 20 Civil War

For a time, the transition to Alos' reign seemed to go smoothly. Prometheus and Atlas left shortly after the congress of the kings, as the announcement was made to the general populace of Atlantis. At first, there was a lot of fear and anxiety but the smooth words of Alos calmed the masses. While the Atlanteans feared "going it alone", many turned the news into a positive, believing the gods thought they were advanced enough to sustain on their own and no longer required their intervention.

After a few months, cracks began to appear in the confidence. The infrastructure of Poseidonis, without the belief that they were in the good graces of their most revered god, Poseidon, began to deteriorate. Crime against man and property exploded, followed by murders and gang violence. It would come as no surprise that outright rioting in the streets would eventually become commonplace. Alos sent troops from Poseidia to assist King Mneseus, but the uproar in the country couldn't be quelled.

As Poseidonis struggled with its faith, Azaes began to flaunt his military supremacy in the region. He invaded Mestamusia, easily deposing its king, Mestor. After a distinctly one-sided battle, Azaes asked for complete surrender of the country, in return, Mestor would be allowed to live, and could have his pick of the ten finest virgins in Azaes. Mestor agreed as he had always had more of a will to love than fight.

The aggressive move by Azaes infuriated the neighboring kingdoms. With the region unstable, Alosletian was forced to pull his peacekeeping troops out of Poseidonis, and join a coalition force from Elasidonia, Promethia, Avalon, and his father's Sunra. The combined might of the five countries still couldn't match the military power of Azaes' armada. Battle after battle ensued along Mestamusia's borders. The army of Mestamusia, believing that Azaes would be a stronger king than the sex-crazed Mestor, threw their support behind their new ruler, strengthening Azaes' armies.

It was all out civil war, and Atlantis' enemies noticed. With the troops gone, King Mneseus' forces were overrun by a guerilla force. He and all of his family would be butchered. As anarchy reigned in Poseidonis, the Amazon tribe, which typically waged war against Sunra, bypassed Sunra and sailed their armada straight to Poseidonis. Disorganized and ill prepared, it fell easily to the warrior women, giving them their first foothold in Atlantis.

They turned their attention to Sunra, but another tribe, those of the Zurians, had already made their way there. Invaders flooded into the seaside city state and rained hellfire. Autochthon sent a messenger to his troops battling Azaes, but the word would arrive too late. By the time Sunra's troops pulled out of the civil war and returned to their homeland, it was already wrought with the invading scourge. King Autochthon, Alos' father, was put to death. A war between the former Poseidonis and the former Sunra erupted as the two invading forces battled for supremacy in the region.

Meanwhile, not knowing the fate of his father, and with his forces diminished, Alos retreated to Promethia to have his troops regroup. Azaes, believing he had delivered a staggering blow to the young king, had his armies flood into Promethia in an attempt to finish their enemy. On the opposite border, the battle between the Amazons and the Zurians spilled into Promethia as well. Alosletian found himself trapped by Azaes' oncoming forces and the raging battle between two invading armies.

The weary king sat in the throne room of King Solanus, troubled by their predicament.

Solanus entered grimfaced and melancholy. "Premiereship."

"Yes, King Solanus," Alos gravely replied.

"It is confirmed, Sunra has fallen to Zu. Your father is dead."

A deep sadness poured over his soul, a darkness that seemed to consume him. He wanted to cry out but as his generals trained their eyes on him, he knew now was not the time to mourn his father. There would be time for that when this was all over.

"We've lost many... good men this day," Alos whispered.

"Indeed we have, Sire."

Alos' top general of the coalition forces was General Kantok of Gadeira. His strategy wasn't flawed and he provided Alos with several impressive victories, but in the end, despite all of his cunning his forces didn't have the training that the mighty Azaleians possessed. Gadeira had always prided itself on its navy, but in a land war, the navy could offer little support.

"Your Highness," Kantok approached the two despondent kings.

"Speak, Kantok, and do not mince words."

"Yes, Sire." the General looked uneasy as he knelt before his King. "We have sustained heavy losses upon the front lines. Azaleia has penetrated the wall of soldiers. Azaes is coming here. We were able to recover some of the Sunranian armies, but they walked into a battlefield between the Amazons and the Zurians."

"The Amazons!" Alos exclaimed, shocked.

"Aye, they have taken Poseidonis."

"Gods save us," Solanus cried out. "Has the entire continent gone mad?"

"They battle each other for control of Sunra," the General continued. "Once a victor has been determined, they will turn their attention to Promethia."

"So Barbarians to the left of us, Azaleia to the right?"

"Aye."

"Convene the remaining generals; we need to come up with a strategy that will get us out of this mess."

"Yes, Sire, but I must caution you that this may not be a mess we can escape from."

"I am gravely aware of that, General. Thank you."

***

In Olympus, Prometheus could see through the Oracle all that was transpiring in Atlantis. As Sunra and Poseidonis fell, he went to Zeus to plead for his permission to assist the Atlanteans. As he entered the chamber of the Gods, all the major deities were in attendance. Zeus sat on the throne, his golden crown resting comfortably on the top of his head; he looked disinterested. Next to him sat a lovely buxom woman with long red hair, she also wore a crown incrusted with diamonds and gold; Hera – Queen of Zeus. Her sharp features and cool white skin were accented by a multicolored dress made of a material that resembled sequins, similar to the one she wore when I met her before raising Atlantis.

On the throne stage set a step lower than the King and Queen was Poseidon, next to him sat the monstrous Hades. Hermes stood a few steps below to the right of Hera, next to him was Ares, wearing his spiked blue and red battle armor. He was missing the deep scar over his right eye that was so prevalent in our previous encounters, and the beard wasn't quite as full. His skull was still barren of any follicle.

To the left of Zeus, there were three other gods: Apollo, with his trademark bright red hair that spread out all over his head in an unorganized, Einstein-like fashion, and the two others were females, Athena and Diana, both pretty with dark hair, slender frames and dark, deep skin tones.

Seated in a chair just below Poseidon was Aphrodite, simply the most beautiful creature one could ever witness. As she was when I had the pleasure of meeting her, she was completely naked, but her long, blond hair strategically covered her extremely large breasts. Her skin was a creamy white color, without one flaw or imperfection. Her startling blue eyes were hypnotic, all encompassing. You could not take your eyes off of the goddess of love.

These were the Dodekatheons, the rulers of the ancient world.

"Prometheus and Atlas, you may come forth."

As vanquished Titans, the two brothers had to portray themselves as subservient to Zeus, even though they were superior to him in power. It was the order of things. Without the resource of reinforcements from Thoth, there was no way they could challenge the order. Topple Zeus, certainly that could be done... but not all of the Gods at once. Even the lower level Gods, who were not permitted in the throne room, outnumbered the two Titans. Prometheus knew not to challenge the will of Zeus.

"Speak, Prometheus," Zeus's voice thundered throughout the hall.

"My Lord," Prometheus bowed in reverence, "I seek your permission to aid the Atlanteans. They are under siege, both internally and externally. Their society will collapse, and we will lose all we gained with their development."

An uncomfortable pause followed Prometheus' request.

"And Atlas? What say you?"

"I also wish to come to the defense of Atlantis," Atlas quietly added. "They are good people, worthy of our intervention."

Another pregnant pause.

"Ares," Zeus turned to his God of War. "Tell them your opinion of Atlantis."

"The Lord Zeus despises the mortals of Atlantis because they presume themselves to be gods. They have wasted the gifts mighty Zeus and his Dodekatheons have bestowed upon them. They are as insignificant as the rats in the fields. Mighty Zeus wishes for their destruction, and he will send Hermes to the enemies of Atlantis to bring about their demise," Ares proclaimed.

"After all," Hermes added with a smile, "why should we exert energy to bring about their judgment when we can just use the other mortals to do it for us?"

"The Atlanteans have grown powerful." Prometheus' eyes met Zeus. "But you should not fear their development. They are your greatest triumph."

"I fear nothing!" Zeus exploded. "I am forming an even better race here in Aegea – They will know Olympus, they will know their gods and they will not forget to pay us the proper respect."

"The Atlanteans have always done what was asked of them," Atlas interjected.

"I will not be questioned – especially by the likes of you two!" Zeus decreed. "I will hear no more of this. There will be no attempt to save Atlantis - I want their existence removed from the annuals of history. They will not impede our progress with the Aegeans any longer."

"May we be excused," Prometheus replied, emotionless-ly.

"Indeed."

Prometheus and Atlas burst through the doors of the throne room and made for the exit of Zeus' palace. As he watched the Titans depart, Zeus turned to Hermes.

"Keep an eye on them," he whispered. "I do not trust their intentions."

"As you wish." Hermes bowed.

Chapter 21 Betrayal

Prometheus and Atlas left Mount Olympus, resting near a village that bordered the enormous mountain. They passed through several of the brothels, looking for the one soul that could help them. One after another, there was no sign of him. They searched what today would be considered similar to hotel rooms and pubs. Once satisfied that the one wasn't there, they left the town and began to scour what would later become the Grecian countryside. Village after village, they searched the normal haunts, never giving an indication to the mortals of their identity. The trail would finally pick up hundreds of miles from Olympus, in a small village called Niaomi.

He had been seen drinking heavily in a town square, taking two and three girls at a time. They knew his identity, and those foolish to challenge him were quickly disposed of. He had little regard for the status of the women; if they were attractive, he took them, at times right in front of the helpless husband. This created a lot of hatred and animosity. The villagers of Niaomi had no issue with providing the scourge's whereabouts, perhaps hoping that Prometheus and Atlas had come to destroy him. After all, their physique matched his. Surely, they could challenge him.

"The one you seek," said the leader of the village, "is in the Aktos, he took one of our maidens and left for the refuge. We assume he will use her, kill her, and move on to the next village, as he has done several times before. Are you here to save us?"

"No," Prometheus replied, "but once we are done, he will trouble you no longer."

The leader revealed a toothless grin protruding from his almost ape-like face. The males of these folks resembled their Neanderthal ancestors. The females, on the other hand, were as beautiful as any fashion model in today's time. Fully busted, creamy skin – one could see how a powerful being who knew that he couldn't be stopped would want to drink his fill of their pleasures.

The Aktos was a forested area with large mountain ranges. The dense foliage made it difficult to find anyone lost in its greenery. Large predatory animals similar to wolves, tigers, and bears roamed the region, often feasting on our predecessors. The villagers knew enough not to venture there. Atlas and Prometheus had no fear, as they knew no animal could harm them.

It took days searching the area but they finally stumbled upon a rocky ridge that hid a cave. The great hero, Hercules, was inside. The limp body of the maiden he had kidnapped lay motionless nearby. There were bruises around her neck and across her nude body.

"Hercules!" Prometheus called out, turning away slightly in disgust.

Hercules belched, grumbled, and his bulging muscles flexed slightly as he turned over.

"Hercules, rise!" Atlas raised his voice.

Hercules stirred in a second, leapt to his feet, sword drawn, his brow furrowed in fury.

"You?" he growled at the fellow Gods. "What do two servants want with me?"

"Hercules… what has happened to you?" Prometheus reached out his arm to calm the aggressive half-breed.

"Do not judge me, you slave," Hercules belched back, a drip of drool fell from his bearded chin. "Who are you to cast aspersions on my activities?"

"But murder? Rape?" Atlas added. "This is not you."

"Go mafooka yourself, Atlas." Hercules took a swig of his drink. "Mafooka you and that boy-loving brother of yours."

I continued to be amazed that I could understand every word spoken by these deities. Prometheus' power of vision injection continued to wrap the words in ways I could understand them. Who knows if Hercules had actually told Atlas what to do with himself? One thing was certain; he wasn't pleased to see them.

"Gods, you have become an ignorant brute," Prometheus replied. "And you smell like you pissed yourself."

"Watch yourself Prometheus – Titan or not I can put you on your ass – and that smell is the wench," Hercules chuckled sinisterly. "Of course, you would never know that, you don't fancy the females of the species."

"Apparently, neither do you."

Hercules frowned, staring down at the limp carcass that used to be an attractive young girl.

"I… uh… broke her," he said, like a child who had broken his new toy. "I did not mean to… but I was drunk and… Hades' Realm, why should I explain anything to you?"

"What in the world has you in such a wretched state, old friend?" Atlas tried to frame his words kindly.

"My mafooking father… he kicked me out of Olympus for nothing!"

"What happened?" Prometheus asked.

"I defied him, of course," Hercules growled. "As always. But this time he totally over-reacted. Old bastard! Did you forget when I helped you?"

Prometheus' visual memory flashed further into the past, when he was bound by chains and being tormented by an eagle pecking at his flesh. Zeus had punished him for helping a group of mortals who weren't part of the Atlantean experiment, and had commanded the bird to continuously attack him. Hercules killed the menacing bird, and then freed Prometheus from his bonds, allowing him to escape Zeus' continued torture. Zeus was none too happy with Hercules, but didn't return Prometheus to his bondage.

"Of course." Prometheus smiled as he returned to the time at hand.

"You should," Hercules chuckled- "You were so grateful you offered to suck my cock."

"You wish." Prometheus laughed.

Hercules bellowed a deep, vicarious laugh.

"Yeah," Atlas piped in. "Well, you still owe me for that other thing."

"What?" Hercules questioned.

"Come now, Alcides," Atlas smirked. "Did you forget the atmosphere incident?"

"I hate that name. Do not call me that."

"Yes, you were supposed to help me clear the atmosphere after an asteroid struck the planet," Atlas continued. "And you tricked me into doing it all alone; it took me decades, while you were off drinking and fornicating with the mortals."

"You are not blaming me for your stupidity, are you, Atlas?"

"Either way, you still owe me."

"Fair enough," Hercules sighed. "As long as you refrain from calling me Alcides again. What do you want with me?"

"With the departure of the gods, Atlantis has fallen under siege," Prometheus explained. "We look to restore order."

"And am I safe to assume my father does not approve of this escapade?"

"Indeed, he does not," Atlas replied. "He in fact has forbidden it."

"Yet, you both want to defy the god of gods and help your precious Atlanteans?"

"Yes," Prometheus retorted. "We do not want to see all that Atlantis is destroyed."

"You were always soft for them, Prometheus," Hercules chuckled. "But what benefit is it for me to get involved in this caper?"

"Well, you get to stick it to Zeus," Atlas chuckled. "And you have never been afraid of a great fight."

"Afraid? HA!" Hercules bellowed. "Gods, please! As if they could stand up to me. They will probably wet their chi tons when they see the mighty Hercules."

"So you will help us?" Prometheus asked.

"Aye, I enjoy a good betrayal of my father." Hercules laughed as he embraced the other two Gods. "I am just afraid for the two of you once Zeus finds out."

Chapter 22 Reclaimation

After securing the services of the famous champion, Prometheus knew that any excursion to Atlantis couldn't be without the Rods of Power to power the crystal skulls that acted as their conduit throughout the continent. It was amazing to see such an early development in the human race. You could easily see how the Atlanteans were the "fathers of civilization". The power of the crystal skulls powered their lighting systems, they were able to work, build, and advance throughout the night. It not only increased Atlantean productivity, but also helped them rapidly build up their society. While other humanoid species were still hunting, foraging, and discovering fire, the Atlanteans created a complex utopia – the world's first Super Power.

The Rods of Power were central to the grid that acted as the nervous system of the body that was Atlantis. The skulls created a circle of power – the Golden Skull in the center working as the firing pin for the Rods of Power. The power that emanated from the Rods was divine in nature. Created by Zeus, the Rods could only be handled by Gods, or the human bastards of the Gods. Prometheus knew when he was forced to remove them that it would put Atlantis in chaos. All that was light would be dark. He had elected to leave the skulls in their place, not dismantling the entire device.

He would take the Rods and place them in places no human being could go. The energy crystals that powered Atlantean weapons and other devices would be turned into nothing but sharp stone. Once the other countries realized that the Atlantean power was leveled, they would begin to attack en masse. Two groups, the Amazons and the Zurians, were the first to descend on the weakened super power; other tribes were en route. It would only be a matter of time before the society that was Atlantis would be fractured, dismantled, and destroyed.

Prometheus, Atlas, and Hercules raced to a land called Bristonia, what we now call England. Interestingly, England wasn't an island during this time period – it was still connected to the Euro-Asian continent. Prometheus had hidden the Rod of Creation here, in a sea trench just off the coast. The trench was one of the deepest in the world, no human, not even Hercules, and could traverse the journey down as the water pressure would crush a human. As he descended into the water, Prometheus was greeted by the Sea King, Poseidon.

"Greetings, Prometheus." Poseidon smiled as he floated between Prometheus and the trench.

"Greetings, King Poseidon." Prometheus bowed, his hair bellowing in the water.

"What brings you to my realm?"

"I sincerely apologize for not notifying you before entering your kingdom," Prometheus acted with contrition. "I did not wish to trouble you."

"And still you have yet to relay your purpose."

Appearing in the distance were several creatures – shark-like beasts, large whale-like beasts similar to Orca, and gigantic dinosaur-like creatures that resembled Plesiosaurs. They all trained their eyes on Prometheus, taking position behind Poseidon, between Prometheus and the trench.

"Ah, yes, well I am here to retrieve the Atlantean Rod of Creation," Prometheus seemed to nervously spit out. "I fear even though I placed it deep in the trench that it is still vulnerable to being reclaimed by mortals. I want to place it in the fires of a volcano, just to ensure its safety."

"And what of Atlas and Hercules on the surface?"

"Ah – them, well, they were just accompanying me."

"For what purpose?" Poseidon's brow furrowed as he detected Prometheus' deception.

"Well, I am doing the *heavy lifting* by descending into the trench and retrieving the device, they will impart on the next portion of our trek to deposit it into the volcano."

"You know, Prometheus, my kingdom is riddled with several thousand undersea volcanoes."

"Indeed," Prometheus gritted his teeth. "But to be honest, my Lord, I hate the water. I only agreed to do this so I would not have to come back here again."

An uncomfortable silence developed as Poseidon said nothing. *Was he insulted? Did he swallow Prometheus' fish tale?* After what seemed an eternity, the King of the Sea finally spoke.

"I will allow you to retrieve your trinket." Poseidon motioned to his beasts and they swam off in different directions. "But I will have you know that if I find out you aim to use this device for other means than what you have stated here today… I will not be pleased."

"I assure you, my Lord that is not the case."

"Very well, good travels to you then."

Poseidon suddenly disappeared and his pets went about their business – the obstruction was gone. Prometheus descended lower and lower until he finally reached the Rod's resting place. It was hard to miss - long, golden, and phallic. The Rod lacked the inscription that it would possess when we discovered it fourteen thousand years later. The sides were smooth along the trunk and rounded at the ends. Prometheus' immense hand engulfed the Rod and he returned to the surface.

As he surfaced, he noticed an annoyed look on the face of Atlas and Hercules.

"Fornicate with some fish while you were down there, Prometheus?" Hercules bemoaned.

"What the hell took so long? You've been gone for hours," Atlas added.

"Ran into Poseidon and his beasties," Prometheus said, as he emerged from the surf and onto to dry land.

"Did he suspect trouble?"

"I am sure of it. We will need to be more careful in Te-
nochit."

***

Prometheus stayed behind as Atlas "popped out". God
travel was a lot different than human travel. The Gods took
humanoid forms, but they weren't completely matter. They were
ethereal in that while they had the appearance of a complete
humanoid body, they could dissipate their existence in a thought,
or pop in and out, as it were. In contrast, they could make
themselves "hard", to grasp objects, inflict damage on things in
the real world. I still didn't understand where they went when
they "popped out", and Prometheus' dream offered no explanation of the process. Just that it was what it was. Perhaps even he
lacked understanding of its mechanics.

Even though they could pop here and there, there were
apparently limitations to their abilities, especially in water.
Poseidon possessed the power to pop in anywhere in the sea, but
none of the other Gods could. Only a few of the Gods could pop
to any land-based point in the world, Atlas was one of those.
They couldn't take mortals or half-breeds with them. Each time
they traveled, it seemed to sap their power and until they could
feed on the life force of a creature, they would remain in a
weakened state. Thus, only the most powerful of the Gods
continuously used this method for travel.

Prometheus sat with Hercules, awaiting Atlas' return. After a few moments, Prometheus finally spoke up.

"Hercules, why do you always behave in such unbecom-
ing ways?"

"Mafooka you," Hercules responded.

"Exactly my point," Prometheus added. "You're the des-
cendent of a God, yet you act like the worst of humankind."

"The worst of humankind?" Hercules laughed. "For a
God, Prometheus, you are thick."

"Come again?"

"I am the most powerful *mortal* on Terra," Hercules continued. "Of course I am arrogant. A bit abrasive -"

"A bit?"

"Yeah. No woman can satisfy me. No man can challenge me. Yet, I am not a God. I am lonely, Prometheus, and because of that it pisses me off. I am pissed off all the time."

"Surely there is a way to manage your anger."

"Yes. By mafooking, fighting, and calling you a boy lover!" Hercules laughed heartily.

"You've had wives, interests. You used to be a hero to the people."

"And then I began to wonder why?" Hercules smile dissipated. "Why risk my neck for people who in fifty or sixty years will not even be here? I do not know when my eyes will shut for the final time, but I do know that I have lived for three hundred years and have seen wives come and go. I have seen my sons and daughters grow, have full lives, and die off. I do not take wives any longer because of this. I don't even know where my great grandchildren reside."

"So, instead of being a hero, you decide to terrorize the countryside?"

"Nonsense," Hercules interrupted. "I was only having some fun."

"By raping and killing innocents?"

"Innocents?" Hercules laughed. "Hardly. Those bastards have been raiding other villages for the last few years – taking their women and destroying all in their wake. I was giving them a little of their own medicine. Maybe now they'll think twice about doing it to another community. I told them before I left that if they wanted it to stop; they had best not continue their aggressive behavior."

"Still, those young girls did not do anything to anyone."

Hercules grew silent, sad.

"It was not my intention to kill her, or the others. They are just so frail…" his voice trailed off.

"I know one of your sons," Prometheus said.

"What?"

"In Atlantis, Alosletian, the young Premier King, is your son."

"Nonsense."

"He is the son of Nisomoni, Queen of Sunra and wife of Autochthon."

"Oh…" Hercules replied, stunned, remembering the one night in Sunra where he slept with Autochiton's wife. "So she did conceive?"

"Indeed. And he is a fine man. A leader. A true king."

"How is she?"

"Dead," Prometheus replied sadly, "During childbirth. The king raised the boy as his own and never took another wife."

"You have love for the boy?" Hercules asked.

"Great love," Prometheus smiled. "I truly believe he will be the greatest of all the mortals to walk Terra."

"You're not mafooking him, are you?"

"Hercules, I don't know where you got this supposition that I like the males – that is Hermes, not I," Prometheus replied, annoyed at more crassness from the half-breed. "I actually do prefer the females of the species, as does your son. I think of him as my own son."

"Thank the Gods," Hercules sighed.

A bright flash interrupted them. Atlas collapsed before them and they rushed to his side.

"Atlas, are you alright?" Prometheus cried out for his brother.

"The Tenochitans did not believe I was a god," Atlas gasped. "They called on Ares. He and Apollo appeared. It was all I could do to get out of there."

"Did you retrieve the Rod of Destruction?"

"I did, but at a cost."

"What cost?" Hercules asked.

Atlas seemed to slip into unconsciousness.

"Atlas," Prometheus shook his brother. "At what cost?"

"Zeus knows what we are planning. And Hermes has been following us."

"That little son of a bitch!" Hercules exclaimed.

"They know everything… and they're coming," Atlas gasped.

Chapter 23 The Onslaught

Bristonia's skyline suddenly was filled with the gods of Olympus. One by one, they appeared. First Ares, then Athena. I had seen her briefly before when I was on Atlantis with Doc and the rest of the team, but here, she was vastly different. In our previous encounter, she had curly brown, shoulder-length hair and a silk-like gown that covered the contours of her curvaceous body like the wash from the sea caressing the shoreline. Her mocha skin glistened in that dress. But in this time period, her skin was hidden by thick golden body armor, similar to the Atlantean armor worn by Prometheus in my time. Her orbicular locks were besieged by a thick, metallic battle helmet. In her petite hands were not the flowers of my memory, but a thick broadsword that would make any Scotsman proud.

Hades appeared, looking as devilishly demonic as ever. Apollo and Hephaestus popped in shortly after him. Diana, Artemis, and Hermes appeared on the ground, near Hercules and Prometheus. Aphrodite, ravishingly nude as ever, rose out from the sea and knelt next to the unconscious Atlas, stroking his head tenderly, like a mother consoling a sick child.

The nine Gods would soon be joined by the leaders; Poseidon, Queen Hera, and finally, Zeus himself.

Poseidon's face wore the extent of their anger. He was made a fool of by Prometheus and wanted nothing more than to destroy him.

"Prometheus!" Zeus' booming voice called down to him from the heavens. "It is my good will that has allowed you to sustain your existence this long. Yet time and time again, you challenge my will."

"It is not a desire of disobedience, my lord," Prometheus quickly retorted. "But an act of love for all that you have built."

"Silence!" Zeus exploded. "You are not working in concert of my wishes! Do not presume that I, king of the Dodekatheons, can be as easily fooled as my idiot brother!"

Poseidon shot a stare at Zeus that could have killed a man cold, and then trained that wicked gawk back on the rebels.

Perhaps knowing their lives were in peril, Prometheus grew silent. Hercules, on the other hand, became more defiant.

"Ha, Father. There you go again," Hercules mocked. "Your *big booming voice* scares no one. I've told you this countless times, yet you still try to employ it to get your subjects to submit to your will. We are not as dull-witted as your pet, Hermes."

"Why you half-bred -" Hermes began.

"Shut up, Hermes!" Zeus boomed.

Hermes bowed and drew silent.

"You tax me, my son," Zeus replied. "Why do you tax me? I've given you no reason to hate me."

"No reason?" Hercules mockingly laughed- "You banished me from Atlantis. Then you banished me from Olympus. I am a man without a home. I do not belong with the gods, yet I do not belong with the mortals. I am nothing because of you."

"Because of your disobedience," Zeus angrily replied. "You have no one to blame for your situation but yourself."

"Enough of this bickering," Poseidon interjected. "Let us lay waste to them and be done with this."

"You should be down there with them," Zeus replied. "Your ignorance is as much fault as anything they have done."

"I grow tired of you calling me stupid," Poseidon retorted. "The only reason you are the king is because you drew the biggest lot. You treat Hades and me as inferior – but you are no more powerful than either of your brothers… and can be toppled as such."

The twelve Gods suddenly separated to factions of six each. Behind Poseidon floated Ares, Aphrodite, Hades, Diana, and Hephaestus. Zeus' legion consisted of the others, Hera, Hermes, Apollo, Athena, and Artemis.

"Choose your next words carefully, brother," Zeus continued. "As it was I who overthrew our murderous father and destroyed the Titans' power on this world."

"You did not achieve that alone, brother," Hades chimed in, his voice an eerie gravely tone that sent shivers down my spine. "And you tend to forget that."

"Take your swing, if you will, Hades," Zeus barked.

The faces of the other gods were like stone, perhaps fearing what was to come next. In unison, both Hades and Poseidon unleashed an energy surge upon Zeus. The gods by Zeus' side rushed in front of him, like the secret service protecting the President, taking the blows. Almost immediately, the skies filled with explosions and laser-like beams of green, blue, and red, the colors of a civil war erupting above Prometheus, Hercules, and the fallen Atlas.

Prometheus knelt next to his brother and shook him.

"Wake Atlas," he whispered. "Wake, damn you."

Atlas finally stirred and Prometheus placed his hand over his brother's mouth to keep him from speaking, then pointed up to the sky where the gods were colliding.

In the distance, a woman appeared, beckoning them to come forward. Prometheus helped his brother to his feet, tapped Hercules on the shoulder to draw his attention from the battle, and they slunk away together.

As they grew closer to the woman, it grew apparent she was a much younger version of Persephone, with her velvety skin accented by the jet black hair that tangled down her back and across her shoulders to her expansive bosom. Her dark eyes penetrated Prometheus, and they shared a quick embrace.

"Quickly, I will take Hercules to a hidden place," she whispered.

"Finally, Persephone…" Hercules chuckled.

"Be still your loins, hero," Persephone frowned. "You will not have that pleasure."

"Yet."

"Ever."

"Okay, okay," Prometheus interjected. "You will take Hercules, we will go to Atlantis, provide the Rods of Power to Alos, and restore order."

Persephone pulled a boulder aside with a thought, revealing a hidden cave.

She hugged Prometheus once more, whispered, "Be well," and motioned for Hercules to follow. Prometheus watched until their silhouettes disappeared into the darkness, and then replaced the boulder.

"Come." Prometheus turned to his brother. "It won't be long until they figure out their little civil unrest allowed us to escape. Time is fleeting. Hercules cannot help us now but we may need him later."

****

"The barbarians have penetrated the third ring!" General Kantok cried out. "The Zurians and the Amazons have joined their forces. They are overrunning us."

"And Azaleia?" Alosletian asked his top general.

After they had lost Promethia to Azaleia, Alosletian pulled the remaining armies of the Atlantean coalition to the capital city of Poseidia in the hopes that its ringed structure would enable them to better defend the territory.

"They have breached our navy at the second ring from the opposite end; they are approaching the ring of Poseidia."

The fact that the barbarians had successfully navigated the wall of the third ring was definitely troubling for the young premier king. Not only was the most secure section of the city breached, they would lay waste to the factories and shipyards. The war machine that powered Alosletian's forces would be crippled.

Suddenly, the temple of Poseidon shook with violent ferocity.

"Azaes' forces have arrived, Sire," General Kantok solemnly reported.

Alos stroked the slight beard growth he had worked on since the war started, trying to look older, more "kingly".

"What are our chances of surviving the onslaught?" Alos asked, knowing the answer already.

"I am afraid there can be no victory, Sire," Kantok replied. "Azaes' forces are just too strong. Then, with the Amazon/Zurian coalition approaching – even if we were to defeat Azaes, we would have little left for the second fight."

Alos dropped his head, looking down to the floor. His failure was complete. He had failed to lead without the intervention of the gods. He had divided his realm caused a great civil war, making it vulnerable to outside attack.

"Have the remaining kings and generals meet in the Chamber of Rulers, Kantok," Alos said quietly. "And ask for Queen Nashea to join us as well. This decision will affect her as much as anyone."

"Yes sire."

Minutes later, Nashea appeared and embraced Alos.

"It has not gone well, my king?" she asked.

"No, my love, it has not," Alos replied sadly. "I fear we are lost to the will of your father."

Nashea trembled.

"Come." Alos cleared his throat, straightening the golden crown that had fallen to one side. "Let us meet destiny."

Chapter 24 The Stay

The Kingdoms of Sunra and Poseidonis had fallen to the Zurian/Amazon coalition. Mestamusia and Promethia fell to Azaleia, although the coalition was making inroads into Promethia as well. All that remained of Atlantis' independent kingdom-states was Ampherius, which no one wanted because of the active volcanoes and little military advantage, Elaisdonia, Avalon, and Gadeira. Of the nine great kingdoms of Atlantis, only four remained loyal to Poseidia.

The kings and generals of those kingdoms filed into the Chamber of Kings to meet with the Premier King, Alosletian, and his queen.

They all remained standing as Alos and Nashea walked into the chamber. Alos took his seat, the largest, at the long table; Nashea took her place by his side as the others found their seats. Five chairs remained empty.

"My fellow royals, please," Alos began, "provide me the situations in your kingdoms."

"Mount Atlantica has begun to tremble, my lord," Ampheres, King of Ampherius spoke first. "Our scientists believe this could be a massive eruption that could level my kingdom."

"Could there possibly be a worse time?" exclaimed Evaemon, King of Avalon.

"The gods' will be done," Ampheres said, resigned.

"And the other volcanoes?" Alos inquired.

"They too are beginning to tremble with Zeus' wrath," Ampheres replied. "Even Neverpeak has grumbled with dissent. I fear even Poseidia may be in danger. We have begun to consider evacuation. Unfortunately, with the war – we have no place to go."

"Your people can come for refuge here in Galdeira," King Eumelus offered.

"And in Avalon as well," Evaemon added.

"Thank you, brothers," Ampheres replied. "But if my scientists are right, Ampherius is not the only kingdom that will be affected by this tragedy."

The castle shook from another barrage from the oncoming army.

"I am afraid there is a more pressing calamity knocking on our doors right now," Alos interrupted. "King Eumelus, how goes it in Galdeira?"

"While there is natural concern about the aggression of Azaleia and the onrush of barbarians," Eumelus replied, "thus far we have maintained civility. Our military, however, has taken the greatest losses in helping defend Promethia and the capital. I am afraid that if the time does come to defend ourselves, we will have nothing left to defend with."

"And in Avalon, King Evaemon?"

"Thus far, the barbarians have focused on Poseidia," Evaemon replied. "However, we have had to pull our men from the defense of the capital to secure our own borders. Once the Amazons and the Zurians agreed to join forces, they became much more of a threat. Thousands of miles and Azaleia-occupied Mestamusia separated them – but the Amazons have always wanted to have Sunra. When their ships sailed south and they began to battle with the Zurians, I thought for sure they would extinguish each other and we would clean up the mess. Unfortunately, they are a little smarter than we gave them credit for."

"Indeed," Alos replied. "King Elasippus? Elasidonia?"

"Some initial skirmishes with Azaleia," Elasippus replied. "I believe if Azaes is successful in taking the capital, we are next."

The room drew silent, with the exception of the screaming of men and explosions from the outside.

"I cannot understand how we have all come to this," Ampheres broke the silence. "We are all brothers."

"Well, not all of us," Evaemon replied, glancing toward the Premier King.

The Temple of Poseidon thundered and rocked, as a large explosion went off at the bottom. General Kantok rushed into the Chamber and whispered into the ear of Alos.

"It seems that Azaeleia's forces are scaling the pyramid as we speak," Alos grimly reported.

"It is time we fled to our respective kingdoms," Evaemon suggested. "The united kingdoms are no more. We must defend our own borders."

"With what? We have no army to defend ourselves," Ampheres replied. "We have no vast Galdeiran navy to protect us."

"That, my brother, is your own concern," Evaemon replied. "I have my own kingdom to concern myself with."

"Galdeira will not abandon Ampherius," Eumelus interjected.

"Gentlemen, please," Alos attempted to restore order as the kings began to rise from their chairs. "There is another solution to this."

Each king stopped and descended back into their seats.

"Azaes' aggression began with my appointment as Premier King," Alos continued. "If I kneel to his rule, cede my power to him, the fighting can stop. We can band together to vanquish the invaders. Azaes will have the power he craves and we can stop the senseless war that has cost us thousands of Atlantean lives."

"But Azaes has the taste of conquest," Elasippus replied. "What would stop him from toppling our kingdoms?"

"Well, as a condition of my surrender, I can pact that with him in exchange for my life -"

"Alos, no!" Nashea screamed.

"Be silent, woman!" Alos angrily retorted.

Kantok grabbed Nashea and pulled her away from her king.

"In exchange for my life," Alos continued, "he will end his aggression against his brothers and begin the process of uniting Atlantis once again."

"It is a most noble gesture, your highness." Evaemon bowed his head.

"Noble, yet unnecessary," a familiar voice called from the back of the chamber.

From the darkness in the corner of the chamber emerged Prometheus and Atlas.

"My Lords!" Alosletian cried out and immediately rose from his chair, then knelt on one knee before the gods.

"Rise, great Alosletian," Atlas said warmly.

"But – what does this mean?" Elasippus queried. "Do the gods favor us once again?"

"No, mighty Elasippus," Prometheus replied. "They do not."

"Then are you here to bear witness to our final destruction?" Ampheres cried out.

"No," Atlas replied. "We are here to return these."

He handed Alosletian the Rods of Power.

"The Rods!" Eumelus cried out, "We are saved!"

"Kantok!" Alos commanded, "Get these over to the skull room and in place immediately. You know the spell, do you not?"

"Yes, your Highness, we all do."

"Make it occur."

"Yes, Sire."

Within moments, energy erupted from the skull chamber, flowed throughout the Temple of Poseidon, and into the city of Poseidia. Like magic, the crystals that only served as bludgeoning weapons came to life, and their owners were able to use the energy from the crystals to fire powerful blasts of conductivity. The advantage quickly switched to the allied fighters.

Azaes, wanting to give his men the ability to be more agile, had removed the heavy crystal from their weapons and replaced it with a lighter metallic compound. It had given them a distinct advantage in the previous battles against the allied forces, but now that the crystals drew power, it would be their undoing. The power of the crystals would also force back the Amazon/Zurian coalition. Outnumbered nearly four to one, the smaller allied armada began to beat back the coalition forces, forcing them up back over the great wall of Atlantis, and out of Poseidia.

It was supposed to be Azaes' crowning victory but instead it turned into his most crushing defeat. He had sent the majority of his men to capture Poseidia and bring Premier King Alosletian to his knees.

The battle would go on for hours, as wave after wave of Azaleian troops continued to try to press their offensive. As if they were slamming into an invisible wall, each new platoon ended up with the same result - massive casualties and a full retreat, replaced by a new regimen that would follow the same routine.

Alosletian watched the carnage from the royal balcony in the temple. Prometheus, Atlas, and Nashea joined him.

"Thank you, Prometheus," Alos said quietly. "We were at the end of the hook and being reeled in. You freed us to return to the sea."

"You're welcome Alosletian." Prometheus put his arm around his young apprentice. "But you are responsible for the lives lost in this war."

"I know," Alos replied sadly.

"Being Premier King is not as easy as it seems, is it, son?" Atlas added.

"No, my Lord, it is not."

"You did alright, kid," Atlas reassured him, "It would not have mattered who became king. Once the gods left, chaos reigned."

"Yes, but I could have definitely handled things better."

"As you live, you earn experience," Prometheus replied. "You were not quite ready for the responsibility of keeping all ten kingdoms of Atlantis intact. I knew it when Zeus told us what needed to be done."

"And yet you still chose me?"

"Of course," Atlas retorted. "Young and naïve or not, you were still the best choice."

General Kantok came up behind them.

"Your Highness." Kantok looked down, attempting to avoid eye contact with the gods.

"Yes, General?"

"This just came from General Narkomeides," the general continued. "It is Azaleia's unconditional surrender. We have won, Sire!"

An eruption of joy permeated throughout the Chamber of Kings as the four remaining kings began to embrace and cheer. Nashea wept tears of joy and embraced Alos. Atlas and Prometheus smiled broadly.

"What will happen to my father?" Nashea asked as tears darted down her cheeks.

"You know he cannot remain in power," Alos replied carefully. "But I will spare him if you wish it."

"He is not evil, Alos," Nashea replied- "He just has an angry soul. Now that it is over, perhaps his soul can settle and he can retire to the countryside."

"We can only hope, my love."

A loud thunderclap erupted above. Alos and the others looked up to see the blue sky suddenly turn dark and foreboding. Lightning zigzagged across the sky. The wind began to pick up and rip through the city. Rain and hail began to fall.

"Prometheus, what is the meaning of this?" Alos asked.

"As I expected, Zeus has returned to Atlantis."

Chapter 25 Recrudescence

The Chamber of Kings filled with a blinding white light. As their eyes struggled to regain focus, the image of the twelve Dodekatheon Gods appeared before them. At the center was Zeus, the king of the Gods.

"Greetings," Zeus said, more warmly then any of them expected.

"Greetings, your majesty," Alos replied, as he and the other kings knelt before the Gods.

"Prometheus, where is my son?" Zeus trained his eyes on Prometheus like a father eyeing a disobedient child.

"I know not, sire," Prometheus replied. "He fled as you warred with your brother."

Prometheus glanced toward Poseidon, who showed scars of the sibling rivalry that had allowed them to escape.

Zeus growled at the answer, not truly believing the betrayer.

"Prometheus, Atlas, you have betrayed my trust for the last time," Zeus continued calmly. "And your punishment will be fit your crimes."

"My Lord, have mercy on them -" Alos begged.

"Be silent, Alosletian," Zeus commanded. "If you were not of my bloodline I would have already destroyed you for having the audacity to speak in my presence!"

Alos drew quiet and bowed, knowing his next word could potentially be his last.

Poseidon stepped forward and gently touched Zeus' shoulder, leaning forward and whispering into his brother's ear.

"These are my sons," he said, glancing toward the other Kings of Atlantis. "Perhaps we can inflict the most harm upon the two rebels, yet spare Atlantis."

"Go back on my decree to abandon Atlantis?"

"It would not be the first time you changed your mind, brother."

"And what of the Aegeans?"

"We can neuter Atlantis, forbid them from interfering with their progress, and in time, their civilization can rival the power of Atlantis."

Zeus nodded and turned toward the kings.

"Atlas, your betrayal was the most egregious," Zeus spoke authoritatively. "Thus your punishment for your insurrection is to be imprisoned in the center of Terra until your life force has expired - doomed to lay burden upon your shoulders the weight of the world. Hades will take you there."

"No!" Atlas pleaded. "No, my lord, please, no!"

"Ares," Zeus turned to the war god. "Go with him and ensure that the deed is done."

"Yes, Lord Zeus."

"Prometheus." Zeus turned his attention to the other Titan.

Prometheus stood stoically in judgment, awaiting his punishment like a captain going down with the ship.

"Prometheus, your crime is no less that of your brother's," Zeus continued. "However, you have a distinct following among the mortals. To destroy you could bring chaos throughout Terra and interrupt the balance of things. Your sentence is to build a palace for me on Mount Neverpeak."

"But Lord Zeus, Neverpeak is active," Prometheus replied.

"Yes, I am aware of this," Zeus smiled sinisterly. "And as the heat from the blood of Terra scorches your hair and burns your fleshy existence, you will understand what it means to be mortal. I forbid you to use your godly powers for anything other than your own survival. Worry not about Neverpeak. I will calm it enough for you to complete your work. And once you have completed my palace of palaces, you will report to King Alosletian… and be his slave. You will not use your powers to aid him in any way. You will be, for all things, a humanoid servant to a half-breed king."

Prometheus nodded, "Thank you for your kindness, Sire."

"King Alosletian." Zeus trained his eyes on the trembling kneeling frame of Alos.

"Y-yes my… my Lord…" Alos replied sheepishly.

"Atlantis does not deserve the powers of the crystal skulls, or the Rods of Power."

"Yes, my Lord."

"They will be removed."

Zeus looked toward Hermes and motioned for him to make good on the commandment.

"It is your charge," he continued, "to keep the peace in Atlantis and keep the favor of the Gods upon this land. The civil war must be over."

"Yes, Lord Zeus."

"Hermes, give it to him," Zeus commanded. Hermes gaily skipped toward Alos, gave him a strange smirk, and handed him one of the Rods of Power.

"In your hands," Zeus continued, "is the Rod of Destruction. On the sides you will see a new inscription, an incantation that if invoked, would give the speaker immortality."

Alos looked down at the phallic golden piece and could see the inscription written in Atlantean on the side.

"But heed these words carefully, Alosletian," Zeus continued, "The gift of immortality comes at a great price. If you speak these words, and your heart is stopped thereafter, all that you are will cease, and you will become something entirely different."

"Thank you, my Lord."

"To the sons of Poseidon, Kings of Atlantis," Zeus said, turning his attention to the other kings. "Go back to your lands. Inform your people that the Gods have returned to Atlantis and they again favor you."

"Thank you, lord!" they replied in unison.

"Make sure they burn offerings regularly to their gods," Zeus continued. "And we will calm the seas and silence the violence of Terra once again."

Salutations and gratitude erupted from the kings.

"King Alosletian, one final thing," Zeus returned to Alos. "Poseidia is no longer your home. You are also not to return to Sunra. You will take your queen and your child…"

"Child?"

"Did you not know your Queen is with child?"

Alos turned to Nashea and she turned away, embarrassed by her deception.

"I…I did not want to burden your mind in such dire times," Nashea whispered shyly, "But you will have your heir."

Alosletian embraced his love, kissing her and holding her tightly. Strangely, Zeus waited as they expressed their joy.

"King Alosletian," Zeus continued, "You will take your wife and unborn seed to Azaleia, there you will reside as the new king."

"And what of King Azaes?"

"Do with him as you will, but make sure he will not stir trouble in this land again."

"As you wish, Lord Zeus," Alos bowed.

The kings funneled out of the chamber, while Alos held his wife, caressing her face and patting her womb.

Hermes appeared beside Prometheus as he watched them.

"Do you not have work to do, slave?" Hermes mocked.

Prometheus swung at Hermes, who dissipated and reappeared on his opposite side.

"Well, that is not very mortal of you," he cajoled.

"What do you want, worm?" Prometheus growled.

"Oh, the big man forgot to mention that while you are building that fabulous palace to the god of gods, I will be your overseer."

"You?"

"Ah yes, all the birds have come home to roost, Prometheus. Now you are the slime beneath my shoe."

Hermes erupted in laughter and danced around Prometheus like a pompous fool, singing over and over, "*You are the slime beneath my shoe, Oh what will you do, the slime beneath my shoe.*"

Prometheus watched as Alosletian and Nashea left, not even paying attention to the price of his loyalty to them. It saddened him. Prometheus feared for his brother, who was being tortured in the center of the Earth's core. It had been his wish to come back, his desire to disobey and save his beloved boy king. His brother was paying the ultimate price for their treachery.

"Come on now," Hermes called out to him. "Brawn before brains. We are going to have a lot of fun, you and I. In fact, you may find that I do not have the lack of amicableness as you believe."

"Doubtful," Prometheus groaned, as the pair dissipated into the unknown.

Chapter 26 Quietly Into the Night

I awoke suddenly, as if I was ripped off my bed and thrown asunder – but it was no bed, but gravel filled dirt beneath me. It wasn't the silent sanctuary of my bedroom, but the noise of the black Mexican jungle that stirred me.

Doc still slept. His color was gone, his skin beaded with sweat. I was no doctor, but I feared infection was setting in, and maybe some internal bleeding. I scanned the area; Prometheus was nowhere to be found. I edged over to Doc, took a cloth and blotted his forehead. He was in trouble. We needed to end this. Prometheus had done all he could for the external injuries, but the fever and the jungle climate was beginning to take its toll.

"Prometheus!" I called out into the darkness. I was greeted by silence. What was even more disconcerting was the jungle that had just seconds earlier been alive with chirps, growls, and hoots suddenly was absent of sound. The crickets no longer made their mating calls - nothing but the sound of my own breath and the beating of my heart. My hand went to the hilt of the sword I had procured on Atlantis. I didn't like the silence. It unsettled me.

The back of my neck felt the hot, humid moisture of breath upon it. I had felt it once before. A familiar low baritone growl followed it - the growl of a Sacrolite. In one fluid motion, I withdrew my sword, swung it upward and caught the beast at the base of its neck, slicing clean and true through its decayed flesh and bone. It cried out a howl of intense, yet abrupt shrieking and collapsed.

My eyes scanned the jungle looking for the rest of the pack. Sacrolites seemed to be pack hunters, never traveling alone.

"It was a scout," Prometheus' voice came as a reassuring force behind me.

"A scout?"

"Indeed, and now they know our position. They will descend upon us. We must continue our journey."

"Where were you?"

"I was at K'ak'nab Mam Atot. All the gods are assembling there, you have become priority one."

"Why are they not coming at us?" I asked, perplexed by their lack of action.

"They fear you, Daniel."

"Me? I still don't understand. I'm just a mortal. Why would they fear me?"

Prometheus chuckled, maddingly acknowledging that he knew something I didn't.

"Sooner or later, Daniel, you are going to figure out that you are the instrument of their destruction. When the time comes, you will make the choice that will either lead to their ultimate victory, or their completion annihilation."

Prometheus glanced down and saw Doc.

"His condition has worsened. There is nothing more I can do for him."

"I thought you said he would be able to continue?"

"Some things even a god cannot see, Daniel."

I knelt beside him, placed my hand along his cheek and felt the fever burning. There were no hospitals to transport him to. They would be no drugs to cure him. He was finished. His eyes opened, startling me slightly. He coughed and wheezed.

"Dan…" he choked.

"No, no, stay quiet. Conserve your strength."

"Dan," he gagged as he continued. "We both know tha game ends here. I am spent."

"No, don't say that."

"We both know it ta be the truth." He coughed again.

"Doc, I'm… I'm so sorry I brought this on you."

Doc smiled, coughed, and then grinned once again.

"You are nay a harbinger of death, Daniel Ryan," he laughed. "You are a dream catcher. You have given me tha best gift an archaeologist could have. Legitimacy. Those pompous fools that had that audacity ta laugh at my life pursuit have nothin' ta say for themselves."

"That would be because they're all dead, Doc."

"Aye." He coughed and then chuckled. "I guess they are. I can tell ya I'm going ta give them what for when I see them in Tartarus."

Doc reached up and grabbed my arm.

"Ya gave me Atlantis, Daniel," he continued. "Ya fulfilled my greatest ambition. Ya gave me Atlantis."

"It was always there for you, Doc, you just needed to know where to look."

"Now, I got ta ask you two last requests," Doc choked. "First, leave me be in this godforsaken place. I've got no fight left in me and I am just draggin' ya down."

"Doc, no!"

"Daniel, we both know it has ta be this way. I bare ya no ill will for it. In fact, I demand it of ya. I'm tired anyway. It's time for me ta just let go."

"I'm not leaving you here to be devoured like a sick animal."

"Don't cha worry bout that. All they'll get is a meal; I'll be long gone by then."

"Damn it, Doc!" I could feel the tears begin to trickle down my face.

"I won't hear of it any longer," Doc continued. "Now… my second request. It is tha most important you could give me. Please say ya will."

"Anything, Doc. Anything."

"Promise me," he coughed. "Promise me you'll save my Mina."

"With my last dying breath, I will do everything in my power."

Doc smiled and he closed his eyes.

"That's a good lad," he rasped.

"Doc… Doc!" I shook him, but he wouldn't come to.

Prometheus grabbed my shoulder.

"He is leaving this plane," he said. "Let him go."

"I'm… I'm alone." The last human companion from the beginning of my journey was gone.

"Come, Dan. We must move."

I could hear the rustling in the brush. The Sacrolites were coming. We raced down the trail. I could hear their breathing, the gnashing of their teeth, even the drool that expelled from their canines; they were getting closer. The jungle sped by me, as if I was in a car going sixty through the dense vegetation. Prometheus ran in front of me, clearing the way. I was running faster than I had in my entire life. We burst through the jungle, into a clearing, and my eyes trained on a Mayan temple. It jutted into the sky, looking so much like the ancient structures of Poseidia.

Standing in front were the Dodekatheons. All of them. Behind us, I could hear the sound of the Sacrolites. Suddenly, in my mind appeared an aerial visual of the landscape. I could see them coming, thousands – maybe millions. They were throughout the rainforest, encircling the clearing in every direction.

"Abandoned the Doc, huh, Danny-boy?" Hermes taunted as he paraded in front of us. "Here before us is the noble champion of man."

He laughed. Zeus glared at him; he drew silent and returned to the rank and file.

"Right now, the Sacrolites are dining on your comrade's bones," Ares said. "He was wrong, Ryan. You are the harbinger of death. Anyone associated with you has perished, have they not?"

Annie and my child, the Atlantis team, the poor souls on the research vessels that were attacked and destroyed, every life I touched ended.

"I have not," Prometheus replied.

"Oh, your demise is forthcoming, Prometheus," Zeus replied. "I have been too lenient with you. I should have disposed of you the way I did Atlas."

"There is one who is not yet dead, Danny Boy," Hermes added. "And if you surrender yourself, you'll save her."

"He knows the stakes," Prometheus retorted. "And we are going to enter that temple."

"I think not," Zeus smugly replied and then motioned to Ares.

"Dan, protect yourself!" Prometheus commanded.

It was too late; one of the bursts from Ares exploded at my feet and sent me flying into the jungle. I could feel darkness envelop me. I was losing consciousness and I could hear the Sacrolites approaching.

***

I was back in Atlantis, more specifically, Azaleia. Alosletian and his very pregnant Queen, Nashea roamed the halls of the great castle of King Azaes.

"I need a status on the insurrection," Aosletian barked to his generals as they entered a great meeting chamber, "We cannot have this disturbance. It is forbidden by the gods."

"Yes, sire," General Stonus replied. "King Azaes has a loyal following. He has amassed a large army of troops in Sunra and they have engaged several of our legions at the border."

"Damn him," Alos replied. "It was not enough that we spared him and in Sunra? My home, own my people betraying me?"

"I am sorry, my love," Nashea replied. "It is because of me he was allowed to remain free."

"He had us all fooled, Nashea."

"You summoned me, my king?" Prometheus called from behind them.

"Yes, Prometheus," Alos replied. "I need you to put down this insurrection once and for all."

"I am sorry my king, I cannot obey."

"What?"

"Lord Zeus has forbidden me from engaging in such mortal warfare."

"But… you are to do as I say, are you not?"

"Yes."

"Then obey your master and destroy them."

"I cannot."

"Then what good are you to me?" Alos roared angrily as he turned to General Stonus. "Since we have no help from Prometheus, place every legion on course to intercept this rebellion. We must quell this before it disturbs -"

There was a sudden rumble beneath them. It was subtle at first but then rose to a tremendous crescendo, rocking everything with violent tremors.

"Gods! Prometheus! What is happening?" Alos cried out.

"Zeus is displeased, my king," Prometheus replied.

No one could keep their feet as the tremendous earthquake ripped through Azaleia. A fissure developed underneath the men of Azaes and swallowed them all, but it didn't stop there, as it continued its way throughout the kingdom, swallowing Alos' legions as well. Suddenly, a bright light entered the room and as it dissipated, the frame of Hermes materialized.

"King Aloseletian," he proclaimed, "you have been summoned."

***

I came to with the disgusting face of a Sacrolite staring down at me. Like some kind of alien, it glared at me, its carnivorous teeth drooling. I felt around in the brush for my sword and finally found it, using my fingers to pull it into my grasp. *One more second, you bastard. One more…*It lunged at me and I blocked its rampaging teeth with my left arm. It plunged its teeth deep into my flesh and I cried out.

"Do you REEEEEEEEEEMBER me?" it hissed at me.

I was stunned it could speak. I noticed its flesh; burnt and charred. As if it had been in some type of fire.

"It can't be!" I muttered.

"Yessssssss, it CAAAAAN," the beast that was once Grahame Solitaire growled back. "I once begged foooooooooooor death. Now I am consuuuuuuuuumed by revenge and the want… the need to consuuuuuuuuume you."

"Solitaire!" I confirmed. "But how? I saw you burn."

His teeth withdrew from me as he spoke, but his body weight kept me pinned.

"I will dine on your intestines, Daniel Ryan," he hissed.

His jaws went for my head, but I again blocked him with my left arm. His teeth ripped the flesh of my forearm and chomped on the bone. The pain rocketed across my body and I felt myself losing consciousness. With my right arm, I had finally grasped the hilt of my sword and swung wildly, decapitating the beast. As his body fell, his head remained locked on my arm, a death kiss. As I used my sword to cut it off me, I heard the crackling of the branches behind me, and they came at me.

Suddenly, everything stopped. I could see the Sacrolites lunging at me but their motion had ceased. They were suspended in midair, as was all of the debris from the trees they had crunched through, as were the small insects fleeing for respite, everything – except for me. I could move, and I spun decapitating each of the beasts. When the last head was severed, time no longer stood still, the leaves began to move, the bodies collapsed, and all was back to normal.

Another legion attacked, another bullet time freeze frame making my disposal of them child's play. It was as if my body had become superfast, so fast my motion made it seem like the Sacrolites were standing still. One after another they came, froze, and perished.

I backed out of the jungle and into the clearing. I glanced back toward Prometheus, who was engaged in titanic warfare with the other twelve Gods… and he was losing. Without thinking, I sheathed my sword, clasped my hands together and from them came a burst of energy that struck into the melee, knocking Ares on his primordial backside. The anger in his face was priceless. I saw him motion to the sky and instantly, the Sacrolites poured out of the rainforest and into the clearing – toward me. They dived at me, climbing over each other to get to me, and each time they came, my power to freeze them became a little less effective. Whatever power I was using to slay the Sacrolites was waning.

Instinct or maybe self-preservation took control and like Superman, I fired my body into the sky. I looked down at the sea of black decaying flesh as they leapt upward, growling, and scraping at what was out of their reach. Then, with a wave, a power emitted from my hands. Like dominos, the Sacrolites fell, by the thousands, as if a sound wave was toppling them over.

I looked toward Prometheus. He was down on one knee, protecting himself inside an invisible shield as the others railed against him with all of their power. A brilliant fireworks show of explosions impacted his barrier, and with each attack he seemed to draw weaker. I ripped a piece of my clothing and wrapped it around my decimated arm tightly, trying to stop the blood loss.

I arrogantly approached them.

"Hey, you bastards," I called out to them. "The Harbinger of Death wants you!"

Zeus looked back at me.

"Hermes, take care of him."

Hermes bounced toward me.

"So, Danny Boy, it comes to this." He giggled. "I've wanted to do this for a long time."

"Ditto."

I threw a punch and instead of disappearing into thin air, it connected to Hermes' nose, shaking his golden locks as he fell to the ground. I drew my sword once more and plunged it toward him. He span out of its blow and scrambled to his feet.

"You can't beat me with that, you fool!"

"Oh yeah, then why did you avoid the blow?"

He put his hands together; his index fingers met and then separated – between them, a sparkling white light, then the tang of a sword, followed by the quillian, the guard, and finally the grip, which he wrapped his fingers around.

"So, Danny Boy, how would you like to be filleted? Down the middle, spilling out your guts?" Hermes laughed. "Or shall we just lop off your head – it is your most useless part."

"You and I are equals, Hermes," I retorted. "And it frightens you."

"Equals? Hah!"

He lunged clumsily at me; I sidestepped and flashed my blade, tearing into his flesh. He cried out, like a high-pitched woman crying for her lover in the night.

He looked down at the bare part of his torso and saw the wound, oozing something wet, not blood, for gods didn't bleed – but something of him.

"How... how is it possible?" he cried out. "How could you injure me?"

"I am the seed of Hercules," I retorted, believing it for the first time. "Zeus' blood courses through my veins."

"So, you've accepted your lineage and now believe you are a god?"

"One that's more powerful than you."

"Ah, but the one thing you forget, Daniel-san, is that you are still part mortal. And that part will be the end of you!"

Hermes extended his hand and a burst of blue energy erupted, striking me in the chest and flinging me backward. It burned a hole in the camouflage shirt I was wearing and dropped me with a thud of excruciating pain. Thunder cracked above us and the night sky lit up as the lightning danced from cloud to cloud.

"I can't believe how you've screwed this up," Hermes said crassly. "All you had to do was obey me. Listen to me. You would be living with your Missy on Atlantis as a new mortal king - the freer of the Gods."

"King of what?" I replied. "Zeus was exterminating my race."

"Good point," Hermes chuckled. "But you wouldn't be here now."

The rain began to fall; it cooled my skin and soothed the area of the burn. I glanced toward Prometheus. He was nearly finished. The combined powers of the Dodekatheons were too much for him. In the distance, I could see the Sacrolites reemerging along with something else: three colossal beasts with a hundred arms and no head – the Hekatonkheire was joining in the onslaught.

"And now, Daniel," Hermes continued, "the words I've been wanting to utter since I first met you, sniveling in that church over the loss of your wife and child. It's time for you to die."

"I don't think so, bitch," a deep familiar voice came from a distance.

"Who the hell are you?"

"Noah!" I called out to Noah Deauveaux. He wore a black chi ton, exposing his immense mocha muscles and tiny puffs of curly black hair on his chest. When I first met Deauveaux, he was shaved bald, but now he had thick, black locks that seemed to cascade down his head. He seemed transformed.

"I am Noah Deauveaux, a son of Ares."

"What?" Hermes and I both exclaimed simultaneously.

"Persephone revealed the truth."

Persephone had taken Noah back to Atlantis during our escape. We all assumed he died from the extent of the injuries he had suffered.

"Faaking Gods," Hermes exclaimed. "Can you not keep your doodles in your chi tons? Another bastard I have to deal with."

"You are the one that will be dealt with Hermes," Noah replied, as he drew a sword from a scabbard that was strapped to his back. He extended his hand and helped me to my feet.

"Okay now… let's not be hasty here," Hermes sputtered. "We all came a long way to get to this point. We've been through a lot together."

"You are the root of all this pain, Hermes," I replied. "If you had never approached me, my people would still be alive. The gods would still be imprisoned, and you would still be stuck alone watching our television shows and wishing you could be mortal."

"I did as I was commanded by my master," Hermes replied. "He ordered me to kill your wife and chil-"

"What did you say?"

"Come now, Dan," Hermes replied. "Surely you knew this already."

"Say it."

"I killed Annabelle and Jeanie. I diverted that truck to crash into them and end their lives."

"No… it was a drunk driver."

"I added that little spice to it, as well. I thought it would help out Mothers Against Drunk Driving. It had its impact in your local area, lemme tell you."

"You… you motherf-"

"DAN, LOOK OUT!" Noah called out but it wasn't in time. I was hit full blast in the head by a bolt of lightning, it ripped through my body and into the ground. I dropped to my knees, looked at my charred hands, dropped my weapon, and collapsed.

Chapter 27 Atlantean Armageddon

I was back on Atlantis. Alosletian and the other Kings of Atlantis were summoned to the royal palace of Zeus. As they entered, each had a look of terror about them. They remembered the last time the gods were angered – but this was certainly worse. The ground trembled beneath their feet. Mount Never-peak had spurned a few more vents that were expelling lava flows. The area of Ampherius and Mount Atlantica was unstable, and it was passing throughout the island continent. Only the gods could save them.

They all sat silently, awaiting Zeus. Prometheus was at Alos' side.

A bright flash ushered in Zeus, with Hermes and Ares at his side.

"I have grown weary of Atlantis," Zeus said. "You were once left without the love of the gods, yet you defy us by offending us once again."

"My Lord, we did not intend in any way to offend the gods-" Alos attempted to defend them all.

"Silence, Alosletian!" Zeus boomed. "You are the cause of the indiscretion. It was from your loins that Azaes' discontent arose"

Zeus rose up from his chair and approached the young king. He was Goliath to his David, dwarfing him in stature.

"I have had enough of your race's excuses," Zeus continued. "For too long have you sought profit, war, sex and greed. I am sick of these petty squabbles. I will end it."

"But my Lord," Alos sheepishly replied, "Are we not your creations? Do we not exhibit all the characteristics you yourself have given us?"

"Alosletian, be still your tongue!" cried out King Eumelus.

"Yes, you are my creations," Zeus continued. "And as I brought you into this world, I can remove you from it."

"So you brought us here to tell us you will destroy us? Why tell us, why not just do it?" King Ampheres asked.

"No, Ampheres, I did not bring you here to tell you that," Zeus replied. "I brought you here to let you know I will no longer prevent your destruction."

"I do not understand…" Alos replied.

"You would not," Hermes mocked.

"Be silent, Hermes," Zeus commanded.

Zeus placed his large hand on Alosletian's shoulder.

"For the longest time," Zeus continued, "I have held this land together with my power. It was so that your kind would flourish on a land so bountiful - so perfect for your development. I have found the elements and natural order of this planet to continue your progression."

"I am no longer providing this," he continued. "And the land underneath you will rip you asunder."

Zeus returned to his throne and took his seat. His eyes met each of the remaining Kings of Atlantis.

"Your world is over," Zeus replied. "And if you flee this land, you will be met with tempests, monsters, and winds beyond your comprehension. I will not allow your kind to infect the rest of the mortals of this planet. Accept your doom as the price of your villainy. You may leave my presence – and you are never to return."

With that Zeus, Ares, and Hermes vanished.

Alos turned to Prometheus, whose face had gone white, as if all the blood had been drained from it… if he had blood.

"Prometheus, is there anything we can do?"

"Die, my King. Die."

***

The earthquakes and eruptions were subtle at first, isolating in Ampherius. Zeus' castle was blown off of Neverpeak but he used his powers to rest it on top of the largest structure in Poseidia. Mount Atlantica erupted as well, sending soot and ash barreling into the air and on to the terrified Atlanteans below. True to his word, as the mortals began to flee Ampherius, he destroyed them with massive hurricanes and storms the like Earth had never been before. They were forced deeper into Atlantis, where more volcanoes developed and became active, and more earthquakes ripped through the continent. No area was spared devastation.

Alosletian returned to Azaleia, but Prometheus seemed to have deserted him. The abandoned Alos did his best to calm his people, but there was great panic and civil unrest throughout their land. Alos sat in Castle Azaleia's throne room, with no remorse, and waited for the final earthquake or eruption to bring about his end.

Prometheus had been gone for a few months after Zeus' proclamation when Ampehrius tumbled into to the sea, while Gadeira, Avalon, and Poseidonis were being torn apart by earthquakes and tectonic shifts.

Nashea, bracing herself against the trembling walls, entered the throne room. She wasn't far from giving birth to their first child, and the unsteady floor was not assisting her condition.

"So, my King," she said to the melancholy ruler, "have we given up for morbid?"

"Woman, leave me."

"Never."

She joined him on the throne, wrapping her arms around her husband's golden armor, her head resting on the crest, covering the Falcon symbol Alosletian had chosen for his family's coat of arms.

"How can you hold the man who set us to our demise?" he moaned.

"Because he is not the cause of such misery. He is the savior."

"Savior? Are you blind, woman? Look around you. Ampherius has crumbled into the sea, the other northern countries are sure to follow. We cannot flee the land. We are ruined."

"Gods, for a brilliant leader you are thick," Nashea giggled.

"Explain."

"Prometheus."

"The traitorous bastard who abandoned us?" he scoffed.

Nashea began to laugh hysterically.

"You laugh?" Alos replied, puzzled.

"Indeed, my King." Nashea kissed him. "For Prometheus did not abandon you – but sought help."

"Help? But who can help us defy the final judgment of the gods?"

"Perhaps your father," a strange voice called out from behind the door to the throne room.

It swung open and the half man-half god Hercules entered with Prometheus.

Alosletian lifted Nashea off of him, leapt to his feet, raced down the throne's steps, and dropped at the feet of his father.

"Father?" Alos whimpered. "Have you come to see how magnificently your son has failed you?"

Hercules reared back and backhanded him, sending him sliding across the marble-like floors of the throne room.

"Act like a man!" He barked.

Prometheus assisted Alos to his feet. The king massaged the area of his chin where Hercules had struck him.

"So you've come, obviously you have some sort of plan," Alos grumbled.

"Indeed, Alos. We do." From a bag by his feet, Hercules produced the two golden phallics known as the Rods of Power.
                    ***

The plan was simple. Hercules would divert the gods' attention by doing what he did best: causing anarchy. They were to get to the outer rings of Poseidia and find *the tempesta*. In each part of the world, there was one *tempesta*. It was like a doorway to another dimension, the dimension of the Annuna. Alos was going to go to Nibiru and plead with Thoth to send his Angelus to save Atlantis. Hercules did his part, continuously battling the gods at every stretch, assisting mortals through the hurricanes, and reaching the other lands. They would be exterminated by Ares' armies on the other side, but the nuisance was enough to get the gods' full attention.

Prometheus and Alos searched long for *the tempesta* but it wasn't in the outer ring of Poseidia as they originally believed. They left for Sunra, and began the laborious search through the dense foliage of Sunra's upper forest. Alos had played here many times as a child and believed he knew of a mystical place. Deep in the Sunranian black forest, there was a tiny temple.

"This is it!" Alos said to Prometheus, as they broke through the woods into a clearing.

Prometheus closed his eyes, he indeed felt drawn to the temple. There was something pulling him toward it, calling to him like a siren's song. It was a simple structure, only a couple levels high. Instead of the Mayan-like structures, this one appeared more like a miniature Egyptian pyramid, as it was pointed, but grey, almost white in color. As they approached, a priest appeared at the opening near the base of the pyramid. His garments were tattered, old looking, pale grey, almost as light as the pyramid itself, and on its back it sported a hood. The priest had a large white beard and weathered wrinkled skin.

"This is a temple of the gods, you do not belong here," the priest said sternly as he saw the two approached.

"Oh?" Prometheus smiled wryly. "Does a god not get entrance to a temple of their dedication?"

"You purport to be of divinity?" The priest eyed Prometheus, not convinced.

Prometheus waved his arm and the priest was suddenly suspended in air.

"One should not question their gods," Prometheus replied.

"Oh… oh… a thousand pardons, my Lord," the priest begged. "I am a puttering old fool. I have learned to distrust all things not made plain to my sight."

"And is your sight now plain?"

"Yes, my Lord… clearly."

Prometheus smiled and sat the old priest back on solid ground.

"Forgive me, my Lord, of which of the twelve are you?"

"Do you not know Prometheus, the Titan, and the Champion of Man when you see him, old man?" Prometheus replied, clearly toying with the priest now.

"Yes, of course Lord Prometheus… again… pardon my ignorance," the priest stumbled to find words. "I…I have been in the sanctuary of Zeus for several hundreds of years. I have not seen much since my dedication."

"Did he say *hundreds of years*?" Alos asked aloud.

"Yes, young King," the priest replied as he noticed Alosletian's royal armor, "You are the reigning King of Sunra?"

"Not any longer, as there is no Sunra anymore."

"Well, that saddens me. But you will find no weapon of salvation here."

"We seek none," Prometheus replied. "We have the Rods of Power and we seek *the tempesta*."

Alos produced the rods, as the stunned priest looked on in amazement.

"Gods, it's been nearly two hundred years since my eyes have set on such beauty."

The priest turned and they followed him into the pyramid. They walked through various chambers, a labyrinth of turns and circular motions that clearly was created to disorient the traveler so they could never find the true purpose of the structure.

"So, priest, do you know what it is that you guard?"

"I do, my Lord, the God Ares informed me of its relevance," the priest replied.

They turned into a large hallway where there was no door. Prometheus could feel *the tempesta* near. The song ripped through his brain, an evangelical choir of heavenly voices joining into one wondrous sound.

"I am afraid this is the end of the line," the priest said darkly.

"What is this?" Prometheus barked angrily.

Alos drew his sword, preparing for anything.

"You see, my Lord," the priest continued. "Ares warned me that you or your brother would come here, seeking the transition to Nibiru. He told me to stop you at all costs."

"Surely you cannot expect to challenge a god?" Alos retorted.

"Ah, young one, the one thing you lack is knowledge – for I am a son of Ares, and thus I have his power running through my veins!"

Suddenly, the priest tossed off his robe and underneath was dark red and blue body armor, the same as his father, Ares. The priest no longer looked aged; his flowing white mane seemed to dance on his shoulders as he drew his sword.

"Regardless of your lineage, old fool, you are no match for me," Prometheus barked as he pulled his sword from the scabbard and charged the priest. The swords clashed, bright sparks emanating from the joining of the blades as they clanked over and over. The priest was shockingly quick, matching every stroke from Prometheus with a defensive block, and then retorting the attack with one of his own. The two warriors traded volleys but neither seemed able to gain the upper hand. The priest tried to summon his god-like fire-burst powers – but the volleys were weak and did little damage to Prometheus. Prometheus returned with his blue power-burst and it struck the priest, staggering him, but not enough to create a disadvantage.

They would eventually abandon the swords and begin to fire at each other with the godly bursts of power. Each of the priest's strikes seemed to faze Prometheus little, while each of the Titan's blasts seemed to take their toll. Finally, the priest was down to one knee as Prometheus retrieved his sword and placed it on his neck.

"Do you yield?" Prometheus asked.

"No, kill me."

"So be it."

Prometheus slit the priest's throat and a waterfall of blood seemed to gush out of the wound.

"Why did you kill him? We still need him to find the doorway to *the tempesta*!"

"Alos, he was the doorway."

The blood that gushed from the neck of the priest collected in a divot on the ground and slinked its way toward the wall. The blood seemed to go underneath the wall, disappearing instead of collecting as you would expect.

"There it is." Prometheus smiled.

Prometheus walked toward the wall, not stopping, and then went right through it.

Alos trained his eyes, trying to figure out if it was some sort of strange godly trick.

From the other side of the wall, he heard Prometheus' voice.

"Are you coming or not?"

Alos ran toward the wall, closed his eyes and let himself go headlong into it. Instead of feeling the uncomfortable connection with rock, he felt a cool, airy presence around him. He stumbled to a stop.

"Welcome, young king," Prometheus smiled.

"Where are we?"

"*The tempesta* chamber. Can you not hear its song?"

Alos drew quiet for a moment, straining to hear what Prometheus was referring to.

"I am sorry, I hear nothing."

"A shame," Prometheus sighed. "It is beautiful."

Prometheus moved to a large stone that jutted from the floor like a lectern. The stone lectern appeared to have two empty holes, where the Rods of Power were to be inserted. Prometheus took the Rods from Alos and placed Creation on the left, Destruction on the right. He said some strange incantation that wasn't really audible but sounded like something I once heard

Marty speak when he was reading Egyptian back on Akrotiri, so long ago.

"And now, the final piece," Prometheus said, as he pulled a black skull from a satchel he had tied to the bottom of his armor. The skull was small, miniature compared to the crystal skulls in the Atlantean Power chamber. Those skulls were perfect replicas of the human counterparts; this skull looked like the head of a pygmy. Its eyes were like glass portals into darkness.

"Where did that come from?" Alos asked.

"My brother, Atlas," Prometheus replied. "He has been holding onto this for millennia."

"I thought he was…"

"He belched this from the bowels of Terra, through Neverpeak. We arranged it this way so you could take the journey to our salvation."

Prometheus placed the black skull into the center of the stone lectern and suddenly, the ground shook beneath them. Alos took a step back behind Prometheus as the floor suddenly began to glow. There was a light emanating from the indentation in the ground near the center of the room, a humming sound, and then he could hear it as well; the song of Nibiru. The choir seemed to harmonize with the beauty and grace of any church harmonic, with lows and highs, pure as the whitest snow. The light began to spin in a circular fashion, and then separated into millions of tiny dots, like miniature stars. They converged to form a galaxy-like blend of light and motion. It was a tiny galaxy on the floor of the temple.

Alos stared at the bright cyclone, transfixed by the wonder and beauty of what was before him.

"Gods, it is amazing," Alos gasped.

"It is a doorway," Prometheus said. "A path to where the gods came from – the world of the Annuna."

Prometheus came down from the stone lectern and put his hand on Alos' shoulder.

"It is you who must step into the pool of primordial universe and pass to the Nibiru," he continued. "It is you who must save Atlantis and free this world from Zeus' tyranny."

"Will you be coming with me?"

"No, I cannot," Prometheus replied, almost sad regarding the truth. "Only once may the portal be activated, and only one may pass through it – then it ceases to exist."

"But why me?"

"You know why – you are the son of Hercules and you are the King of Atlantis," he continued. "Do not allow your fear of the unknown to overcome your duty to your people."

"What am I to do when I reach the other side?"

"Find the Angelus, specifically the Arch Angelus Gabriel," Prometheus replied. "He is a good, kind Annuna. He will be able to help you."

"Very well, thank you my friend." Alos embraced Prometheus warmly.

He turned toward the galaxy portal, the light from the mini-stars twinkling on him. He took one step forward.

"Stop!" a voice came from behind them.

"Hermes!" Prometheus turned to see the minion of Zeus.

"Before you kill yourself, Alosletian, there is something you need to know," Hermes called out to him.

"What is it?"

"Well, I could tell you, or I can show you."

Hermes waved his arm in a circular motion and a mist appeared. As it dissipated, a large octagonal mirror with an elaborately decorated frame materialized.

"Look," Hermes ordered.

Alos gazed into the mirror, only it did not send back his reflection, but a dark blank nothing. The darkness then began to slowly peel away, revealing a desolate, burnt landscape. As if being beamed directly from a camera, the scene moved and focused on... Hades – the monstrous god of the undead. Hades stepped to his right, revealing a figure on the ground. Alos strained his eyes until he recognized her.

"Nashea?"

"Yes... your wife... mother of your unborn child," Hermes chuckled. "And she is in Hades' realm."

"Damn you – do not harm her!"

"That choice is yours, Alosletian," Hermes replied.

"Alos do not listen to him!" Prometheus pleaded.

"Ah, but he will listen, his ladylove is at stake," Hermes mocked. "Alos, did Prometheus tell you what will happen to you when you step into that pool?"

"No!" Prometheus cried out.

"No he did not – but it does not matter, I will do whatever I need to do to save Atlantis," Alos replied.

"Oh really? Even sacrifice Nashea? Even die?"

"I would die for Atlantis."

"But Nashea? Are you willing to give up her life and your own?"

"I do not understand."

"You see, my boy," Hermes said, as he pushed Prometheus aside and placed his arm around Alos' shoulders, "What Prometheus failed to tell you is as soon as you step into that portal, your body will disintegrate. You will cease to be. You cannot help anyone here because *you will be dead*."

"Prometheus, is he lying?"

"No," Prometheus replied as his gaze caught the ground below.

"Why? Why would you send me to my death?"

"Because, young fool," Hermes interjected, "He does not care about Atlantis or Nashea or you – he cares about overthrowing my master, Zeus."

"That is a lie!" Prometheus protested.

"Is it?" Alos angrily retorted. "You were killing me – right here and now."

"No, you do not comprehend," Prometheus tried to explain. "You cannot take your physical form into Nibiru."

"And there it is!" Hermes catcalled. "So you step into that pool and end up in Nibiru. You are dead. You cannot return. Meanwhile, Hades feeds Nashea to his awful pets. Your wife dies. Your son dies. Oh yes, good king, you would have a male heir to the throne… if only you still had one to bequeath him."

Alos stepped back from the edge of the pool.

"There is another option," Hermes replied. "Give up this fruitless venture and I will show you a way to immortality. You can have Nashea back and your son. You will be spared Zeus' wrath."

"And Atlantis?"

"There is no saving Atlantis."

The ground shook violently beneath them, rattling them and sending Alosletian to the ground.

"The final tremors are coming for Sunra, young King. You must choose," Hermes continued.

Alos looked to Prometheus, who had a blank look on his face.

"You have been my mentor, my guide, my guardian," Alos said to him, as he rose to his feet. "Your betrayal….I could have never expected it. I am broken."

"I have not betrayed you, Alosletian," Prometheus replied warmly. "I have delivered you to this place because it is the only way to save Atlantis. Walk away from this and you cannot go back. Walk away and you desert your people."

The ground rocked violently once more, forcing Alos back to his knees.

"Take another look, Alos," Hermes crowed, as he motioned to the seeing mirror, "Notice in the background – those dark, black creatures that approach her. They will tear her limb from limb. They will tear the fetus from her womb and eat its newborn entrails."

Alos turned away from the mirror.

"Alosletian," Prometheus continued, "I cannot force you to go into the portal. It is your choice. Either you choose the life of one, or the lives of many."

"It would be three lives, not one," Alos replied angrily.

"It is your choice," Prometheus repeated.

Alos clenched his fist, looked back toward the galaxy pool, then back to Hermes and Prometheus.

"What would you have of me, Hermes?"

Hermes disappeared from the edge of the pool, reappeared on the stone lectern and yanked the Rod of Destruction from its lodging. The ground trembled slightly, the sound of power dissipating filling the temple. The pool slowly faded away until all that remained was the indented floor.

"My gift for your obedience is immortality," Hermes smiled sinisterly. "If you speak the incantation written on the side of this rod – you will be invincible."

Alos took the Rod of Destruction from Hermes' hands and read the incantation aloud.

"I accept this gift of the gods, as the will of the gods, and for the gods. If I am struck down, I will rise, born again, and into servitude of the gods."

A bright yellow beam shot out of the rod and directly into Alos' chest, surrounding him with a golden glow that enveloped his entire body. The rod grew extremely hot and he let it fall.

"Excellent, Alos," Hermes lauded.

"Now, take me to Nashea."

"As you command." Hermes smiled as he looked back toward Prometheus.

Prometheus watched as they both departed. The ground shook once more, dust poured down from above. The structure wouldn't withstand another quake.

"*Atlantis is finished, but perhaps mankind can still be saved from the gods.*" the Titan thought as he bent down, retrieved the Rod of Destruction, and then collected the other artifacts, with a tear trailing down his cheek.

Chapter 28 Hercules' Insurrection

Prometheus arrived in Poseidia with the volcanic ash blackening the sky, the lava flows glowing in the darkness, and the panicked populace grabbing whatever belongings they could carry and fleeing to the third ring of the city, where the channel for the seaport resided. He trained his eyes on one small girl seeking her mother, and watched in horror as she was knocked over and trampled by the herd of people who ran in different directions at every tremor and rumble beneath them. The continent had already begun its descent into the ocean. The northern kingdoms of Ampherius, Gadeira, and Poseidonis had been ripped to shreds by volcanic eruptions and earthquakes, causing the ocean to flood into the region. Earthquakes beneath the waves created tsunamis that pelted what remained of the central continent's newly costal locations.

The air was charged with tectonic electricity, and Zeus used that energy to create huge hurricanes that battered and flooded the central and lower parts of the continent. New massive volcanoes burst through the earth's crust in Sunra, Azaleia, and Promethia, sandwiching the remaining central kingdoms in chaos. Anarchy was in rule now.

Prometheus made his way to Nashea and Alos' secret home in the center of Poseidia. It was where they had stolen off to consummate their love while her father ruled Azaleia and he remained only an heir to King Atlas. Prometheus knew this place well, for whenever he needed to find Alos, it would be there - in their sanctuary - where he would be. Prometheus opened the door to the domicile, entering into darkness.

"Are you here?" Prometheus called out to the dark.

"Yes, boy-lover," Hercules replied. "I am here."

Prometheus pointed to a candle in the room and it spontaneously lit, filling the room with light.

"I have what you need," Prometheus continued. "Do you know what to do?"

"Yes, I do."

"You know they will kill you for this."

"Mafooka them. I may be the son of Zeus, but I know I am not immortal – just long lasting."

Prometheus chuckled a little as he gave the Rods of Power and the black skull to Hercules.

"Any sign of Alosletian?"

"None," Prometheus replied sadly.

"Gods, you really did love him, didn't you?"

"Like my own son," Prometheus thought back to all the years of instruction and training for Alosletian.

"Well, if I see him or the girl, I will do my best to help them to safety," Hercules said. "What will you do?"

"I am going to make my way to the outer ring. Help some of the people out there. If you need me, just call out and I will be there."

"Need you?" Hercules arrogantly laughed. "Do you not know who you are speaking to?"

***

Hercules raced up the steps of the structure that was the new home to Zeus' palace. His amazing, inhuman speed enabled him to take hundreds of steps within seconds without tiring. The satchel of artifacts covered the back of his huge muscles. He wore a dark brownish chi ton, exposing part of his bare chest. He wore no armor.

The palace was largely unguarded, empty. Hercules viewed the foundation of the palace and could see a fissure in one of the walls. It had likely ripped open when the palace was blown off of Neverpeak and Zeus rested it at its new location. Hercules quietly eased his way to the wall and peered into the fissure. It went clear through. He had his entry.

**

Prometheus flew above the hysteria below. From his vantage point, he could see the floodwaters inching closer to Poseidia from all four directions. Only the highest peaks still showed through the continent. The low-lying areas had already succumbed to the sea, earthquakes, and volcanic unrest. As he flew over the third ring, he could see Ares' and Poseidon's armies, perched at the outer wall, waiting for the ships to depart so they could crush them. Something shiny caught his eye among the sea of frightened humanity below. It twinkled again and he stopped, focusing his amazing sight on the object. It was a female, pregnant, with priceless jewels, holding a crown and begging to be let aboard one of the few remaining galleons. He recognized her features, even if they had been slightly morphed during her gestation.

"Nashea," he said to himself.

He darted down immediately. The crowd screamed, knowing he was a god and fearing he was there to kill them. They ran in different directions trying to flee him.

"Nashea," he called to her.

She looked toward him; her face was badly bruised, one eye was swollen, and she had wounds to her neck and ears.

"Are you alright?" Prometheus said, as he put his arm around her, shielding her from the others.

"Do I look alright?" she callously retorted.

"What happened to you? Did Hades do this to you?" Prometheus oozed concern.

"No, your king did this to me."

"Alos?"

She nodded.

"But why would he ever hurt you?"

"He believed with his new… powers he could take on the gods and stop this madness – but he wanted me far away from here. Once Hades let me leave his realm, Alos insisted I make for the docks."

She began to weep, but tears only appeared in her good eye.

"I refused, of course," she continued. "And he struck me down. He had a rage in his eyes like I had never seen. He jumped upon me and began…"

"Fine, enough, I see." He embraced her.

"He is not the same man, Prometheus," she sobbed. "My Alos would have never beat me, never bitten me. He is not Alos."

The ground beneath them shook violently and Prometheus braced her against him.

"There is no escape for me; we all know what awaits us in the ocean."

"Let me take care of that," Prometheus consoled her, and then turned to a deckhand of a ship docked in front of them. "You, man. Come."

The deckhand looked down and saw Prometheus. He turned white.

"Fear not, come."

The deckhand did as ordered.

"I want you to bring this woman on to your ship," Prometheus ordered, "Keep her safe. Gods help you if anything happens to her. For this generosity, I will ensure your ship is not disturbed as it flees this forsaken land."

"Thank you, my Lord," the deckhand replied. "But I do not have the authority to bring her on. The captain said no more passengers."

"You know who you speak with, do you not?"

"Aye."

"Then make it so."

"As you wish, Lord."

Nashea grabbed him tightly and he slowly nudged her away.

"Go, child. Save yourself and your offspring," Prometheus continued. "At least the memory of what Alosletian once was can continue on."

"But where will we go?"

"The seas yield other lands, other people," Prometheus smiled. "They are not as developed as your people, but this land is dying. Your people are no more. Make these new lands and new people your own; teach them your ways, and through them, Atlantis will live on."

"Thank you, Prometheus." She wept and grabbed him once more. "Thank you."

Behind them, large golden pillars with strange Atlantean writing were loaded onto the ship.

***

Hercules moved silently through Zeus' palace, careful not to disturb the gods. Each were in their own areas of the palace – some slept, others did whatever it was that gods do when they have nothing to do, awaiting Zeus' call to leave Atlantis once and for all. Not only did Hercules worry about the twelve main gods, but their offspring, the minor Gods, were all over the palace as well. They weren't as fully developed as their parents, and he knew he could likely dispatch them with little trouble, but Hercules knew he didn't have much time – he had to get to the throne room as quickly as possible.

The palace was immense in size, filled with remarkable art and sculptures that would have made the greats blush with envy. Each corner Hercules turned seemed to provide another explosion of culture and space.

He rapidly rounded a corner and nearly crashed into Persephone.

"Persephone, my pet," he purred. "Come back for a little more Herc?"

"The key word is little," she replied coldly. "What happened was a terrible mistake."

"Not from my view," he chuckled.

"Be silent you large idiot," Persephone barked, annoyed. "You've succeeded in infiltrating the palace but you need to move more swiftly. Your father and step-mother sleep comfortably now that Ares and Poseidon have the demolition of Atlantis under control. Hermes is following your son, and the others are idle. The throne room is empty and unprotected."

"And your husband?"

"Hades is with his pets," she replied, annoyed at the insinuation that she was still considered his wife.

"Ah the arrogance of my father and that bitch," Hercules complained. "I cannot believe they sleep while their subjects suffer these terrible atrocities."

"Like you ever cared about them."

"Ha!" Hercules chuckled. "I cared… once. Not so much now, but mafooka it. Can you imagine their faces when I imprison them in this place?"

"Yes… I can… and it will only be in my imagination if you do not get going."

"Yes, yes…. and when I am done, maybe I can stop by your chamber for a little…"

"Uh, no."

"She says no…" Hercules laughed as he walked down the hall.

***

Poseidon's seas, great aquatic beasts, and unforgiving winds battered the large Atlantean galleons as they made their dash from the island continent. The majority of Atlantis had already tumbled into the sea; all that remained was Poseidia. Ares commanded a navy of ships of specially chosen warriors from the Aegeans that attacked any ships not finished by Poseidon's pets.

The warriors were sons of the twelve gods, all specifically trained and honed to serve Ares and their parents. The ships were positioned all around Poseidia, and each galleon would meet the same fate as the last - devoured by a whale or giant squid, capsized by a gigantic wave, or finished off by the cannons of the waiting fleet. Ares and Poseidon floated above Atlantis, watching carefully to make sure none of the Atlanteans escaped.

After ensuring that Nashea was on the ship, Prometheus floated above the third ring and joined the two Dodekatheons.

"Are you here to challenge us, Prometheus?" Ares growled, hoping the answer would be yes.

"No," Prometheus replied, taking slight pleasure in the disappointment in Ares' face. "I have come to warn you."

"Warn us?" Poseidon sounded unconvinced. "Since when do you help us?"

"Since now… as the palace is being attacked on two fronts."

"What are you talking about?" Ares angrily replied as he gazed toward the palace.

"As we speak," Prometheus continued, "Hercules has infiltrated the castle and is preparing to assassinate Zeus. Meanwhile, Alosletian has gained the power of the Rod of Destruction, and his launching his own offensive."

"Hercules? That little bastard!" Poseidon exclaimed. "If I haven't told my brother five million times to dispose of that mistake…"

"How does a half-breed like Hercules presume he could destroy Zeus? No mortal can kill a god." Ares scoffed.

"Hercules has the Rods of Power and a new skull, created by my brother, Atlas in the center of Terra." Prometheus replied, "It gives him the power to destroy all of the Dodekatheons."

"How can we trust you?" Ares queried. "Why would you help us?"

"While I have a definite affinity for the mortals, specifically this group," Prometheus replied, "I do not have the desire to be vanquished and sent to Tartarus. We all know that without Zeus, there is no us."

Beneath them, an explosion rocked the outer portion of Zeus' castle.

"It has begun," Prometheus observed. "Go, I will watch to ensure no ships escape."

"Thank you, Prometheus, Zeus will reward your new act of loyalty, you have finally listened to reason," Poseidon replied.

The two Gods descended to where Alosletian's assault on the castle had begun. Prometheus trained his eyes on Nashea's ship. He dived toward the vessel, and landed on the bridge of the ship.

"Battle stations!" the captain called out.

"Calm yourself, Captain Nasara," Prometheus calmly replied. "I am here to ensure you and my precious cargo escape."

"Prometheus… the champion of man?"

"Indeed, Captain. Now wait, while I cast a shield over your ship so that Poseidon's beasties cannot harm you."

Prometheus closed his eyes and waved his right arm in the air – sparks arose from his fingertips, almost like a fourth of July sparkler, and a golden glow replaced the white iridescence of the hull of the ship.

"You are protected from Poseidon's fury," Prometheus proclaimed. "Now I will clear your way."

Prometheus launched off the bridge and into the air. In seconds, he arrived at the fleet, stationed directly in the path of Captain Nasara's vessel. The crew all trained their eyes on Prometheus, suspicious of his next act. He would sustain their suspicions, as he balled his hands and inside of the ball generated a blue oval. Inside the globe, miniature lightning bolts struck the sides, as if it were one of those novelty lightning globes we see sold at various junk stores.

Prometheus tossed the globe toward one of the ships; it stuck the hull and exploded violently, creating a huge gaping hole in its side. Water poured into the ship and it began to nose down and sink. Prometheus continued to generate the lightning globes, tossing them at the other ships as they scrambled to battle stations and attempted to return fire. It wouldn't matter. None of their weapons would have any effect on a god. Prometheus made quick work of Ares' navy.

He glanced back toward the ongoing battle at the foot of Zeus' palace. All the gods, including Zeus, descended upon Alosletian's insurrection. None noticed what Prometheus was up to. He gazed at the surrounding seas of Poseidia; the other ships were being vanquished by what remained of Ares' navy. Prometheus knew he couldn't help Alos, but maybe he could save some other Atlanteans. He went to work eradicating the remainder of Ares' fleet.

***

Hercules heard the commotion outside and hid as the palace stirred from its slumber. As all the gods darted to defend the palace, Hercules quietly slipped into the throne room, and into the skull chamber in the back where all the power of Atlantis was channeled. Without the Rods of Power, the crystal and gold skulls were dormant, but they wouldn't be for long.

***

"Why are you doing this?" Hermes exclaimed. "This was not part of our deal!"

"Mafooka you, Hermes," Alos growled. "I have one last chance to save Atlantis, and I am taking it. All of my men have invoked the incantation you provided us – we cannot die. If we cannot die, you cannot defeat us."

"You fool," Hermes angrily retorted. "You can die… you just ensure your slavery as an undead member of Hades' army."

Hermes drew a dagger hidden in his white chi ton and stabbed Alos in the back, dark blackened blood began pouring as Alos fell.

"The King has fallen! The King has fallen!" one of the men near them called out.

Explosions rocked the battle zone as the gods used all their power and might to end the uprising. One after another, the men fell and expired. Alos rolled onto his back and stared into the blue sky. There were grey clouds in the distance, the wind kissed his face, the sounds of screams and explosions went away as life drained from his body.

Above them, Ares proclaimed to Zeus, "This battle is over, but we have another issue."

"What is it?" Zeus replied.

"Hercules is in the palace and has set eyes on vanquishing you."

Zeus was stunned by the news. His own son, who he had tolerated for so long, wanted to destroy him.

"Everyone, come," Zeus commanded the Gods. "To the throne room - we must end Hercules' existence once and for all."

"Finally," Hera said, under her breath.

***

Prometheus watched as the gods departed into the palace. He hoped he had given Hercules enough time to complete his mission. Several Atlantean vessels had escaped the destruction of their land, including Nashea's ship. Prometheus had obliterated Ares' navy. Even Poseidon's sea creatures had ceased their attacks, the waters had begun to calm, and Zeus' hurricanes had blown themselves out. All the focus was on Hercules now. Prometheus knew that the gods couldn't be part of this world any more. Even he had to join them in their final resting place. He descended the outer ring. There he found the fleeing remnants of Alosletian's failed attack. They weren't humans any more. They were changing… dead things that were beginning to attack each other and those few inhabitants who remained in the outer ring.

Prometheus entered a house; the owners had already been killed. One had been a soldier in the Poseidian royal guard. He took the warrior's gold and lead armor, an Atlantean claymore-like sword, and proceeded to lop off the heads of any of the Sacrolites he could find.

Chapter 29 Prison of the Gods

"Welcome, Father!" Hercules called out at he heard the Gods enter the throne room.

"Hercules," Zeus returned. "What is the meaning of all this?"

"You know, Father, I have loved you like a prince should love his king, but your time of rule is over."

As the Gods entered the skull chamber, Zeus trained his eyes on his son, at the panel.

"What have you done?" Hera spoke up.

"No one's speaking to you, bitch," Hercules replied coarsely. "Be silent and let the males speak."

"Zeus, are you just going to let him speak to me -"

"HERA, BE SILENT," Zeus commanded.

"How you ever chose her as your mate, I will never know."

"What have you done, Hercules?" Zeus continued, ignoring his comment.

"Well you see, Father," Hercules grinned, "I know I cannot kill you. However, Prometheus and I have devised another solution to your tyranny."

"Ridiculously reckless, even for your level of ignorance, Hercules," Hermes replied.

"Be silent, worm." Hercules barked.

"What do you possibly hope to achieve in the skull room, Hercules?" Ares asked.

"Ah, yes," Hercules continued, "well let me give you the run down, I have placed the Rods here in reverse order. Destruction is in the creation slot. Creation is in Destruction. Get the picture? Now, I've placed this black skull, which has some mystical Terran power that Atlas has cursed into it and it goes in the middle of the center console so it can connect to the rest of the conduit."

"Surely, Atlas has already left for Tartarus by now," Hades exclaimed.

"He has, but as part of his last act, he gave me this," Hercules replied, as the skull clicked into place and the circular wheel that was the Atlantean power source began to hum and spin – but in the opposite direction than it normally did.

"And now," Hercules continued, as he grabbed the Rods like a pair of joysticks, "as you fools all stand there gawking and trying to figure out what the mafooka I am doing. I will say this -

"SACHOOK MAK NELL SAN COFY," Hercules chanted.

"ECKTOCK MANU SENKA MY NOCHA,

"SACHOOK MAK NELL SAN COFY."

As Hercules continued his chant, Hermes slipped away, realizing what was about to occur.

"I do not understand what he is doing?" Poseidon exclaimed, confused.

"He is chanting… but I do not understand what he is saying," Zeus replied.

"AKI MAK NUK SAN ZEUS." Hercules pointed toward Zeus, grinning sinisterly.

The walls of the palace rumbled; beneath them the ground shook as the wheel span wildly, electricity flowing from the Rods, into Hercules, causing him to scream out in pain.

"What… AAARGH… you heard… AAAAAH… was an Annunan…. OOOHAAAH…. binding spell… MAAAAAFOOOKA…"

"KILL HIM!" Zeus ordered Ares.

Ares blasted Hercules with all of his power, knocking him off of the panel and slamming him into the wall of the circle chamber of skulls. Every bone in Hercules' body shattered, he bled internally, and his brain began to swell.

"And now…" Hercules continued as he gasped for breath, "you have ended both me and my lineage. There is no one left to reverse the curse. "

"What? NO!" Zeus exclaimed.

"Black soul envelops Atlantis," Hercules said, as he was losing consciousness. "The gods forever locked, death becomes Atlantis, for it is the final tick that has clocked."

The circle chamber exploded, sending the gods flying back into the throne room. A charge ripped through Poseidia, fissures appearing throughout the rings of the city. The city began to sink into the ocean. Those few mortals who remained in the city began to scream in horror as they saw the mushroom cloud appear above Zeus' palace. Prometheus looked toward the center ring and in his enhanced vision he could see the crystal skulls and Rods flying into different directions. He estimated their destination; they would be separated forever. He smiled, even as the waters rushed into the city and began sweeping away the mortals that remain; Zeus' reign here had ended.

Zeus scrambled to his feet.

"Where is Hermes?" he called out. None of them knew.

"DAMN IT!" Zeus exclaimed as he saw the ocean begin to pour into the throne room. "Quickly, all of us join as one. We must create a protection spell."

"It will not stop us from sinking," Poseidon retorted. "My beasts cannot support Poseidia's weight."

"We will sink," Zeus agreed. "But at least we will survive. We will feed off the lower gods and those mortals who remain. Hades, recreate your realm to harvest the souls here. We will be hungry but we can sustain for at least twelve thousand resolutions of Sol. Hopefully, Hermes escaped and is seeking out a way to free us."

The twelve Dodekatheons joined hands and together created a force shield surrounding the city of Poseidia. As the remainder of the city plunged into the ocean, the water wrapped around the shield. Prometheus and the surviving mortals on the outer ring looked up in awe as the light of the sun disappeared, and the creatures of the sea watched with curiosity as the city plunged further and further down into the abyss.

"For better or worse," Prometheus said to himself, "man is on their own now."

"But what of us?" a young girl near him said aloud. "We cannot fish, we cannot grow, how will we survive?"

"You will not."

Chapter 30 History Repeats

"DAN, WAKE THE HELL UP!" Noah desperately shook my body as he tried to keep Hermes and the Sacrolites at bay.

As I came to, a sharp pain ripped through my body. I looked at my arms and legs; they looked like I had been in an oven for three hours. My head hurt and I was tired of being knocked unconscious – *that had to have caused some brain damage, right?* I heard a growl nearby, spun to my feet, got dizzy, and then focused on the Sacrolite that had trained its eyes on me for an easy pre-cooked meal.

Noah and I were back to back, he was more advanced than I was, and could trade energy blasts with Hermes. I regained my sword and commenced chopping heads like a maniac. One after another, the Sacrolites went to meet their maker. It was almost as if they were sick of living this way and wanted to die. They eventually retreated again and I turned my attention to Hermes. Noah joined me at my side as we approached him. His hands were up, begging for mercy.

"Wait… come now, let's not be rash here," Hermes begged. "Remember all we've been through together, Danny Boy. If it weren't for me, you would have never realized your full potential. Neither of you would have."

"If it weren't for you – my wife, my baby girl would still be alive," I angrily growled back. "Billions of people… would still be alive."

Hermes looked past us and smiled devilishly.

"Oh look there… Prometheus is dead."

Both Noah and I glanced over to where we had last seen Prometheus, he lay on the ground as the other Dodekatheons and Hekatonkheires continued to attack. I glanced back at Hermes, but he was gone.

"Crap!" I exclaimed.

Noah generated a globe of glowing power and fired it at Ares. It struck the god directly in the face. All eleven remaining Gods turned to us.

"Uh… Dan…"

"Yeah."

The gods attack was swift and powerful. I barely had a chance to encompass Noah and I in a protective shield. As I shielded us from the blows, Noah fired globes of power at the gods, but it did little but annoy them. The combined might of Zeus, Poseidon, Hades, Hestia, Hera, Ares, Athena, Apollo, Aphrodite, Artemis, and Hephaestus attacked us from all sides. Each god had their own specialty, and with each assault, my ability to maintain our protective shelter was reduced. The Hekatonkheires got into the act as well, just as powerful as their Dodekatheon cousins, they used their hundreds of arms and hands to pound on the shield.

From Zeus, lightning reigned down. Poseidon used the same energy blasts he had attempted earlier on Prometheus. Hades used ghostly beings that seemed to kamikaze into my shield. Hestia seemed to use some type of telepathic warfare – every once in a while as another one of the Gods would attack, I'd get a quick thought in my head, *"Give up, you can't win. You've put up a valiant effort but you have lost."* It was a woman's voice.

Ares used his enormous battleaxe and slammed it into our shield. Each time he swung, sparks would fly from the contact. Athena also used Zeus' thunderbolts to strike at us. Every strike from the goddess sent electricity throughout the shield and my mind, causing me intense pain. Apollo and Hephaestus, who were both roughed up pretty badly by Prometheus, had found their strength and assaulted us with all they had. Apollo used his arrows, trying desperately to pierce through our shield. Hephaestus surrounded us in fire, tripling the heat inside, making it almost unbearable, and limiting our view of the oncoming attacks. Artemis had her own arrows, and like Apollo, she fired them unmercifully at us, praying one would get through. Hera just seemed to supervise the carnage, not really taking part.

As one of the gods was hit with one of Noah's blasts, she would go over and seemingly heal any of their wounds. And Aphrodite… she had no special power but one. As the others attacked us unmercifully, she lay on the ground, opened her legs, and beckoned us to join her. I told Noah to look away from her, but it was hard for either of his to do so. Her body was so inviting, the beauty she possessed was intoxicating. It almost made you want to just give in, run to her, rip off your clothes and lustfully take her until you were dead. I shook my head, trying to clear the vision of Aphrodite in my brain, and instead, concentrated on the protection of the two of us.

"Noah," I called out, as I winced with pain from another rush, "please tell me you have a plan to get us out of this."

"No," he gasped as he launched another defensive barrage at the gods, blindly through Hephaestus' fire. "I was hoping you did. Aren't you the chosen one?"

"Great," I moaned.

I saw Noah catch a glimpse of Aphrodite. She licked her lips, spread her legs, and put her fingers around her sex, then beckoned him.

"Noah, look away!" I barked.

"God… she is so hot," Noah bemoaned. "She wants it so badly, Dan…"

I smacked him as hard as I could on the back of the head.

"Aaah, what the frig!" he exclaimed.

"Can you please stop thinking about her and figure out a way to get us out of this."

"Hey, you're the expert here," he replied. "I'm just trying to keep them off of us."

Suddenly, one of the arrows pierced the shield, I wasn't sure if it was one of Apollo's or Artemis', but it struck Noah, blasting through his chest and coming out the other side.

"OH… SHIT!" he exclaimed as he collapsed.

"Noah!"

I was alone, my shield was failing, and my fellow bastard of a god had fallen. With my will failing, one of Hestia's thoughts slipped in. *It's over, Daniel Ryan. Your defense has crumbled. Your friend is dead. Lay down your arms and Zeus will spare you.*

"Screw you, bitch! Get out of my head!" I screamed as out of my hands came this bright beam of power that shattered through Hephaestus' flames and struck Hestia dead on. I heard her scream and fall.

"Hestia! Hestia!" I heard Hera call out.

The onslaught stopped as all the Gods looked at their fallen comrade.

"Rise, Hestia," Zeus commanded. She didn't stir.

"Rise, Hestia!" Zeus repeated, louder. Still nothing.

As the Gods surrounded Hestia, I backed away, refocusing all my energy of my protective shield on me. Noah was dead. There was nothing I could do to save him. They all continued to rouse Hestia, preoccupied with her condition, perhaps shocked that I could muster that much power. I took the opportunity to ease across the field and near the opening of the pyramid. Out of the corner of my eye, I noticed that Prometheus' body was no longer there. I kept my eyes trained on the gods as they argued amongst each other.

"How is this possible?" I heard Zeus exclaim. "A mortal cannot kill a God! We cannot even kill each other. She cannot be dead!"

"She's dead, Zeus," Hera replied as she wept. "Her life force has left this body."

"This cannot be!" Ares replied. "This is impossible. Our bodies are not like the mortals. We don't *leave our bodies.*"

"Hestia no longer resides in this body." Hera coldly replied.

I reached the steps of the pyramid and began scaling them as quickly as I could. I was careful to watch my footing, as the stone that constructed the pyramid was loose and near to giving way. I entered the pyramid and raced down its chambers. I didn't know if the gods were still preoccupied with the death of Hestia, or if they were coming after me for revenge. I didn't know where I was going, but I felt pulled down the different corridors. Each turn, I was compelled to go in a direction, as if some unseen force was leading me to my destination.

The pyramid shook violently. My eyes gazed to the ceiling to see if it would come down on top of me. It held. I took the shaking to indicate that the Gods had figured out I had slipped past them. I continued moving down the twists and turns of the pyramid as quickly as I could. With each step, I could hear more attacks on the structure. They were trying to destroy it before I reached my destination. Finally, I could see where I needed to go. Light appearing from an open doorway lit the hallway I was racing down. I was at a sprint now, rushing as fast as I could to get there. As I came closer to the doorway, I slowed as I saw a dark figure blocking the way. It was a Sacrolite - but this one appeared to be different than the others. It wore jewelry, rings, and armor with a crest of a falcon on the breastplate that I had seen once before… where had I seen it? At first, I wasn't sure. Then it spoke.

"Yessssssss, come to the finale…." it hissed at me. "I was onccccce as fooooooolish as you are. I alsooooo believed I could defeat the godsssssss."

It drew its sword, I drew mine, and they clashed in a dramatic spark of contact. Ebbing and flowing, we traded connections, trying to find the vantage point in the small area we had to duel.

"When I run yooooooooou through," it hissed, "I will eat your brain and try to find the sssss-source of your power."

I had only met one Sacrolite with intelligence and that was Graham Solitaire. He was dead, lying headless and twitching in the jungle outside. This couldn't be him. We continued to exchange advances, neither coming to a distinct advantage. My arm still throbbed with pain from Solitaire's earlier attack, thankfully the lightning blast I took had corroded the injury and prevented me from bleeding out but with everything my body had endured, I could feel myself weakening, and my opponent was skilled for being a brain-chewing zombie.

The Sacrolite twirled and his blade sliced my hand, disarming me. I fell to the ground.

"Who the hell are you?" I cried out.

"It does not matter who I am," the thing replied. "Only that I will dine on yoooooooooou tonight."

He raised his sword, preparing to finish me, when I heard the familiar metal ting of a sword being unsheathed. A flash of light exploded over my eyes and the creature dropped to its knees. Its head fell beside its body, and in its place, Prometheus stood, bracing himself against the entryway, a tear trailed down his cheek. I looked at the head; the features were familiar even in its extensive decay.

"Prometheus, you live!" I screamed, as I scrambled to my feet and embraced him.

"Not… enough… time," he gasped.

"Let's get in there and do what we need to do," I replied, bracing his huge frame against me.

Prometheus looked back at the fallen creature.

"Good bye, Alosletian," he whispered.

I nodded and helped him enter the large chamber and around the large indention in the floor. I helped Prometheus to the panel and I concentrated hard, trying to seal the room in a protective casing. I knew I wouldn't be able to hold it for long. I only prayed it would be long enough.

Prometheus had a small satchel that he had kept hidden beneath his armor, never revealing to us what he had. He quickly opened it and as soon as he pulled out its contents, I recognized them - the black skull, and the rods of power. Somehow, Prometheus had recovered them and kept them safely with him. Prometheus had never shared that part of his vision with me, protecting it even from me.

He placed the black skull into the center of the stone lectern, then the rods in their respective places and suddenly, beneath us the ground shook and the floor began to glow. There was a light emanating from the indentation in the ground near the center of the room, a humming sound, and then, just like in my previous vision, I could hear the song of Nibiru. The choir filled the chamber, one female voice permeating throughout. The light began to spin in a circular fashion, and then separated into millions of miniature stars. They converged to form the galaxy blend of light and motion. Just as I had seen before, a small galaxy formed on the floor of the Mayan temple.

"There is not much time, Daniel," Prometheus gasped. "You must go now."

"And what will happen to you?"

"I am finished, Daniel, do not worry about me. Save your people."

"I will – but where will I go, how do I see Thoth?"

"Find Gabriel - He will get you an audience with the hierarchy of the Annuna. Only they can make the decision on whether or not to save Terra," Prometheus wheezed. "Please, hurry. You must convince them or all is lost."

I took a step toward the edge of the indention. The pool swirled beneath my feet making a strange whooshing sound.

"I wouldn't do that if I were you," a familiar voice came from behind me.

I turned and saw Hermes, an arrogant smile on lips.

"Save it, Hermes," I replied. "I know the consequences of what I am doing."

"Do you?" Hermes retorted. "Oh well, Mr. Know-it-All, I guess this will not interest you then."

Hermes made a circular motion with his hand and in the center of the circle, a mist appeared, as it dissipated a mirror appeared, similar to the one that I had seen in my vision. When the darkness cleared, I could see a nude Mina, beaten, bruised, and unconscious. Hades was beside her, a huge sword held by her jugular.

"Do you love her, Ryan?"

"Yeah, I love her." I confessed. I did; seeing her so vulnerable at Hades' mercy tore me apart inside.

"You can still save her."

"Daniel, NO!" Prometheus pleaded. "Remember the vision! Remember Alos!"

"Oh shut up, Prometheus," Hermes barked, a blaze of flame blasting from his other hand, striking Prometheus in the chest, and flinging him away from the stone lectern.

"If you loved her," Hermes continued, "you would give anything to save her."

"And what do you suggest?"

"Give up, right here, right now," Hermes replied. "You will pay for your crimes – but she will be spared and Zeus will end the war against your people. That's what you want, is it not?"

"Yeah," I wearily replied.

"All you have to do is step away from that portal. Step away from two senseless deaths instead of one. Haven't enough died for your cause? Doc Constant? Noah? Marty? The fat man?"

"Yeah," I agreed.

"Did you not promise Doc while he sucked down his last dying breath that you'd save Mina?"

"Yeah."

"Then are you to break your word to Doc? Are you to seal her fate by committing suicide? And the fate of the child she carries in her womb."

"A child? My god… No… I won't break my word."

Hermes smiled devilishly.

"Yes… there, there, come away from the portal," Hermes continued. "I'll tell Hades that he can release her and she will be made a queen in the new world order. Your child will be a prince of New Terra."

"You don't understand," I continued, "the only way I know how to save her… to save the baby - is to go to Nibiru and bring back the Annuna to finish you bastards off once and for all."

I turned away from him and leapt into the vortex. I heard Hermes shrill scream as my body sank. I could feel the atomic particles that made up my body disintegrate. It wasn't pain, but a strange, soothing warmth. My torso descended and I could feel my heart stop and my breath go away. My mouth ceased to be, and then my nose, finally, all I could see was a brilliant white light. I was no more.

BOOK III

RISE OF THE ANNUNA

Chapter 1 Tartarus

Bright light - engulfing me, surrounding me, enveloping every pore of my soul. I wasn't breathing, for I had no lungs. I wasn't seeing – no eyes. I had no heart beating or a chest for it to beat in. As the light subsided, I looked down at my limbs. They were transparent visions of their former selves. I was a ghost, floating in the abyss of nothing. I looked around my surroundings. There was nothing but white iridescence. There was no ground for me to walk on, no sky above me. I was nowhere.

"Peace be with you," a voice said from behind me.

I turned and saw a man with olive-colored skin and dark curly hair that cascaded down to his shoulders. He wore the brown eyes of eons of experience, and his blocky chin sported a full, but shortly cropped beard that had a slight tinge of grey mixed in with the dark brownish circular wisps. The Middle Eastern man sported a simple, light brown robe with a rope acting as a belt around his waist. In his hand, he held a walking stick.

"Greetings," I replied and smiled warmly, at least I thought I was smiling. As a ghost, you're not really sure.

"You have come a long way, Daniel Ryan," the man said.

"You know my name?"

"Indeed, we all know it."

"And you are?"

"I am called Yeshua MiN'zaret," the man replied.

"What is this place?" I asked.

"Ah, now there is an interesting question," Yeshua chuckled. "You are in the space between the kingdom of the one

God and the world of which you come from. Some call it Tartarus, others call it Purgatory."

"So I am dead then?"

"Death is relative, Daniel Ryan," Yeshua replied. "You have been born into a new existence."

"Right, well with all due respect, Mr. Minnazet-"

"Min'zaret."

"Whatever," I continued, "I know about the Annuna. I know what happens here. I know those who are chosen can join the Annuna at Nibiru, while those who are not are devoured by them. Their life force consumed to feed the Annuna."

"You know a lot, that is certain," Yeshua replied. "But not as much as you think."

"I know everything I believed before I met the god Hermes was a lie."

"Oh?"

"There was no Jesus Christ, there was no God or Angels – it was all bullshit."

Yeshua erupted in rip-roaring laughter.

"I'm sorry?" I was confused by his levity when I was bearing my soul.

"I… I apparently gave you too much credit." Yeshua tried to contain himself. "Because you know nothing."

"Well, enlighten me then."

"Come." Yeshua extended his arm toward the white nothingness.

We walked for a little while, or floated if that's the proper terminology. Yeshua was silent as we walked through the area. I could feel the ground, or whatever it was we were walking on, dip downward and in the distance I could see shapes. As we advanced closer, the shapes transformed into people. Lost, searching. At first, there were only a few, then more, until we were surrounded by more people than on the streets of New York.

"These are those who have recently perished on Terra," Yeshua said sadly, scanning the millions of souls that had now appeared. "This is the result of your releasing Zeus and his minions."

There were millions, billions, just wandering aimlessly. Not knowing where they were or what had happened to them.

"God…" I muttered.

"None of them will join the Annuna," Yeshua continued.

"Why not?"

"Because there are too many. It is an unnatural order, and the Annuna do not have the resources to allow even the most pious in when we are dealing with this many souls."

"So you'll have yourself a buffet then," I replied, slightly annoyed.

Yeshua didn't respond, he continued walking through the masses. Some reached for him, while others simply parted as he passed. One old woman grabbed my arm.

"Harold," she said, a confused look on her face. "Have you seen my Harold?"

"No, lady, sorry…"

Her face turned from the kind elderly lady to a hideous, zombie-like creature and she screeched a horrific sound, and then disappeared.

"Jesus Christ!" I exclaimed.

"Yes," Yeshua replied. "They tend to be a little frightened."

"Them? What about me?"

"You, Daniel, have nothing to worry about. They cannot harm you."

I continued to follow him through the billions of souls until we had passed through. There was a newer area, one which held the level of structures. They weren't built with human hands.

"We call them the hallows," Yeshua said. "They are built with the imagination of those souls who have accepted their existence in Tartarus. They make an existence for themselves until they are either culled or called."

"Culled or called?"

"If they are culled, their life force is absorbed into the Annuna. If they are called, they join the Annuna."

"And will these people be culled?"

"Some will. Even the most penitent soul will never go directly to Heaven."

"Why are you showing me all of this?" I asked.

"Come," he repeated.

We walked by the structures. They appeared as if made of stone, with wooden roofs. I placed my hand on one, but it slipped through as if it was a projection. We weeded through the structures. As we passed, I could see more figures but these were different than the rest. They wore light brown robes tied with rope; similar to the one Yeshua wore. One man approached. He was also Middle Eastern, but had a much larger build than Yeshua.

"Master," he called Yeshua as they embraced.

"Shimon Kefa," Yeshua called him. "It is so good to see you."

"And you, Master," Shimon replied. "Who is this that is with you?"

"Daniel Ryan."

"Oh, the freer of Zeus?"

I felt like my name had been brandished all over the Annunan tabloids.

Others brown robes approached. All of different shapes and sizes. Each greeted Yeshua with the title of *Master*.

"Daniel," Yeshua called out to me, "I would like you to meet my brothers. This is Yahqov, Yahuda, and Shimon."

"Greetings."

"Peace be with you," they all greeted.

One final robed man approached.

"And this is my closest friend," Yeshua added. "Yahuda Sicarius."

"It's been a long time since we have seen you, Master," Yahuda Sicarius greeted him with a hug. "We've missed you."

"Yes, I know, I apologize," Yeshua retorted. "How goes the calling?"

"As you predicted," Yahuda Sicarius replied.

Yeshua made some type of hmmph sound and looked toward me, sadly.

"I thought you said that you weren't calling anyone anymore?"

"Come, Daniel, my friends have more work to do," he continued. "And there is someone I'd like for you to meet." He turned to the others.

"Men, I'll see you in Nibiru."

"Yes, Master."

We walked for a little while longer until my curiosity couldn't be contained any longer.

"Yeshua," I asked, "why do they call you master?"

"Oh!" He smiled slightly. "It's a term of endearment. I hold a high office with the Annuna and those men have been in my service for quite some time."

"I see."

We reached one of the dwellings, and Yeshua knocked on the door, or at least it seemed like he knocked.

The door flew open, there was no was there... or so I thought before I gazed downward.

"Je... Jeanie?" I recognized the tiny nine-year-old face of the one female I would give anything for.

"DADDY!" she cried out and darted toward me. We embraced and I could feel an electrical charge spark between our souls, creating the sensation of warmth.

My world had come rushing back into my arms. My Jeanie – my little girl. Instantly I was transported back to our times playing with her Barbies while watching *Dora the Explorer* and her favorite Disney movie, *Beauty and the Beast*. If I had tear ducts, there would have been no doubt the waterworks would have been on. The pain of her loss hit me as well as it crystallized just how much I missed her.

"Danny?" I heard a familiar voice.

"Annie!" I cried as my wife rushed past Yeshua and embraced me. We were together, the three of us. Finally, after all this time – so many years of pain and suffering – we were together.

My wife was beautiful; her fire engine mane trickled down her shoulders and accented her creamy complexion. Her hourglass figure seemed to burst out of the white-colored clothing she was wearing. I didn't recall ever seeing her wear white, and it became her.

"Danny, I missed you so much," she said as we kissed, between our lips a little spark flew.

"Annie, I need to tell you -"

"I know about Mina." She smiled. "It's fine. I understand. You had to move on... she is a lovely girl."

"You do?"

"Yes... in this world we can observe the living."

"Oh..." I replied, as an uncomfortable feeling rose over me.

"While I was a little surprised at her age," Annie continued, "I can definitely understand your interest in her."

"Annie, this is my new friend, Yeshua?" I asked, desperately wanting to change the subject.

Her eyes met Yeshua's.

"Oh my god!" she exclaimed and dropped to her knees before him, bowing in reverence.

"Annie, what the hell?"

"Don't curse, Danny!" she gasped, "Don't you know who he is?"

Yeshua grinned, amused by the comedy in front of him.

"He's my guide through Tartarus."

"Your guide... oh my God," she gasped again.

"Daddy, that's Jesus." Jeanie giggled.

"No, honey, his name is..." It hit me like a ton of bricks. Yeshua MiN'zaret - *Jesus of Nazareth* in Aramaic. I felt like an idiot. I had researched the historical Jesus for my novels, and knew the names of Jesus and his apostles in Aramaic. I had met Simon Peter (Shimon Kefa), his brothers; James (Yahqov), Jude (Yahuda) and Simon (Shimon), and of course, Judas Iscariot (Yahuda Sacarius) without even realizing it.

I had been walking with Jesus, the Son of God himself.

Chapter 2 Yeshua's Story

I fell to my knees in reverence of the Son of God. He laughed at me. The Son of God laughed at my ignorance.

"Get up, Daniel," Yeshua said jovially. "I am the same man you were walking with."

"My Lord," I stammered for words. "I am so sorry... I blasphemed in your presence. I... I doubted you... I'm so so sorry."

"Daniel," Yeshua replied warmly, "you have been writing about me your entire life. I know your soul and I know you did not mean those words. Remember, my own disciples denied me."

"I know... I'm sorry."

"Stop apologizing."

"Yes, my Lord."

"And stop calling me that."

We joined Annie and Jeanie inside her home, and we re-hashed all that had happened on Earth. It troubled Yeshua greatly.

"I commend Prometheus' dedication to man," Yeshua said. "But he was wrong to send you here."

"I don't understand."

"Our God, some call him Allah, others Yahweh, some call him Jehovah. We call him Thoth or simply, the Father," Yeshua replied. "He does not have an interest in your cause."

"How can you say that? He created Heaven and Earth. He created man in his image."

"Yes, he did," Yeshua replied. "Let me try to explain it to you. Consider on Earth the automobile manufacturer -"

"You know about cars?"

"*Son of God*," he mocked.

"Sorry."

"Right," Yeshua continued. "Anyway an automobile manufacturer makes his creation and sends it on its way. He is not obligated to continue to check on his creation, he just creates the next one and the next one. He knows the auto may have its flaws, but he hopes that in his best wisdom he created the machine the best he could."

"So basically, he just creates... he doesn't intervene."

"Sorry, Daniel. That is the way it is."

"And all the prayers to you and to God? Are they pointless?"

"No, no of course not," Yeshua replied. "We hear the prayers. We take into account all that has been requested. But you have to understand, Daniel. Things are different."

"How?"

"When God was primarily in everyone's life, they could appreciate a miracle," Yeshua continued. "When I came to Earth, they believed in healing the sick, curing the blind. When God was in everyone's life – his acts made a difference. Sodom and Gomorrah. Jericho. Egypt. Time and time again, his miracles made an impact. It was not science, it was miracles."

"But we've progressed, we've enhanced our knowledge."

"Indeed," Yeshua continued. "But what was once miracles, are now commonplace. We are no longer needed... and we moved on to other worlds."

"But war, famine, global warming," I interjected. "We pray for peace and your return."

"Do you really? It has always been the nature of man to fight. I do not believe you could exist without it."

I contemplated his words for a while. He was absolutely right, of course. Even in times of peace, there were still diplomatic squabbles and arguments over senseless things like land and sea. Which people had the right to settle where, whose God was the right god. In the end, everyone was wrong.

"So we just allow Zeus to destroy the human race?"

"No, of course not."

"Yeshua," I continued, "I have another question."

"I am sure you have many, Daniel," Yeshua chuckled.

"Hermes told me you were a fraud, that your disciples stole off your body in the middle of the night, and made up the tale of the resurrection."

"Search your heart and your faith," Yeshua replied. "I believe you know the answer to that."

"Hermes is a liar."

"But yet you have questions about where I fit in to all of this."

"Yes."

"What Prometheus showed you is basically accurate," Yeshua continued. "Thoth commissioned Cronus and Rhea to create life in your solar system. Uranus and Gaea interjected themselves and there was a great war, which resulted in the destruction of Eden. Cronus and Rhea created life on Terra, and their love created their offspring, the Titans. The Titans eventually transformed into the Dodekatheons, and a great war exploded. You know who won."

Yeshua went on to tell me after the fall of Atlantis, the survivors of the calamity went to the different ends of Earth, relaying the story of Atlantis' destruction. Their culture and history would eventually be lost to time but their influence on the advancement of civilization would trickle down throughout the ages. Still, without the Gods' presence, man went into chaos. At first, they attributed any celestial object in the sky to be a sign from God (or the gods). They told the stories of Zeus and made up their own mythology around it, continuing on the traditions of praying to the gods for guidance, and using any coincidental element as confirmation of their devotion.

Thoth had the Angelus, servants to him alone, come to Terra and try to set the record straight. Only a small group believed; the Israelites. They became Thoth's chosen. Unfortunately, they were constantly persecuted, and interred in slavery under the Egyptian rule. Thoth sent the Archangel Gabriel to free them from their bondage and give the world a clear signal that the gods of the Egyptians were false gods. Eons passed and the

Hebrews grew in stature and power. They dedicated and made offerings to one god, and Thoth believed that their work had been done.

As the Romans rose and the Macedonians fell under their thumb, a new power rose in the known world. The Romans brought back polytheism. The people cried out for a redeemer, and deliverance from the persecution of Rome. Thoth had seen enough, he felt that he had troubled himself enough with the affairs of Terra. He would give the world one more chance at understanding their place in the universe, and the opportunity to join the Annuna.

Thoth impregnated Maryam, the mother of Yeshua, and the Messiah was born. His mission wasn't to deliver the Jews from Roman oppression, but to show them the way to Nibiru. He did everything he could, but the Jews rejected him, and the Romans, fearing an uprising, put him down like a dog. Those early Christians who chose his way were made Annuna. Those who rejected them were food for the Annuna.

Through the years, the Christians were persecuted in Rome. They knew to finally avoid death and eventually transcend the current status as a fringe Jewish sect; they would need to convert the Romans. To make Christianity more appealing to the Romans, they changed the religion to include pagan holidays. They knew the Roman Empire would never follow Yeshua, the Jewish rabbi who dared to claim he was a king.

Instead, they associated Yeshua with Zeus, using the Greek name Iesous. This made it easier for the Romans to associate with Iesous, the son of a god, the redeemer, and the deliverer to Heaven. They basically got his goal right, but changed his name and incorporated pagan holidays to placate the Romans. Eventually, Rome took to Christianity, and the rise of the Roman Catholic Church began.

"Somewhere," Yeshua said, "my message got lost in the greed of man. Still, even with that, it is good that my words are still known to many, even if there were some embellishment to add the mystical to my teaching."

"So you didn't really walk on water?"

"No," he chuckled, "but I did heal the sick and the dying, I did cure the blind, I did teach of peace and love. I did take it upon myself to be the vessel of all goodness in the world; I endured terrible torture at the hands of the Romans… for you, Dan."

"Did you really rise from the dead?"

"In a manner of speaking," Yeshua replied. "Much like you are here, I was freed from my mortal bondage and but instead of coming here I was transported into Hell, Satan's realm."

"There's a real Satan?"

"I'm afraid so. I spent three Earth days there, and then returned to my disciples so that their faith could be restored."

"How did you escape?"

"Thoth sent the Angelus to free me…Satan resisted but in the end, he had to give up my soul."

"I don't understand – why did you go into Hell?"

"Thoth willed it. It was the final act to purge man of original sin. My final sacrifice."

"So you came back to Earth…and your body?"

"I re-inhabited it, spoke with my disciples, made peace with my wife-"

"Your wife?"

"Mariamne," Yeshua continued. "The Romans have not been kind to her memory. Of that I am very displeased."

"Mary of Magdalene."

"Yes, I believe that is her name in your language," Yeshua continued. "So I made peace with all of them, and then stepped into a tempesta, very much like you did. Only, I was transported directly to Nibiru, or as you know it, Heaven."

"Yeshua, I can't tell you how much it means to me that you are real," I blabbered on, "That it's all true."

"No, thank you, Daniel for having faith in me, even in the darkest of times."

"And so, what now?" I asked.

"Annabelle would you like to tell him, or shall I?"

"Tell me what?"

"Danny, I don't know how to tell you this," Annie said, "but children aren't allowed to become Annuna. Judas Iscariot gave me the option to go to Nibiru, but I declined."

"But…"

"I can't leave Jeanie here alone. I have chosen to be absorbed along with her."

"So you have a choice," Yeshua said to me. "You can return with Yahuda Sicarius and I to Nibiru, where you may or may not get an audience with Gabriel, the leader of the Arch Angelus. Or, you can remain here with your wife and child for your remaining time in existence, until your energies are culled back into the universe."

"What about a third option?" I asked. "I stay with Jeanie, and Annie goes to Nibiru and becomes Annuna."

"Danny, no!"

"You deserve it more than I do," I replied. "If anyone deserves to be there, it's you."

"If that is your desire," Yeshua interjected, "but understand your choice well, Daniel. If you stay with Jeanie, man on Earth will be no more."

"Damn it," I grew angry, "How can you put that all on me? I'm just a man. You're the son of Thoth. Why is it my job to convince a God that has no interest in us that we matter?"

"I asked myself the same question once," Yeshua said. "And the answer was that I was to be the deliverer of man. You, Dan Ryan, are the new champion of man. If you choose to only be a man, be with your family, and return to the universe, no one would think any less of you. However, if you chose the more difficult path, the path to Nibiru, to Thoth, and to champion the cause of your people, and their right to exist, then maybe you will be the savior your world has been longing for."

Prometheus' successor - Dan Ryan, the champion of man, the savior of mankind. *How could one mortal, even one with the bloodlines of a god, handle such a responsibility?*

Chapter 3 The Trial

I chose to go. It was extremely difficult, considering the beaming little face staring back at me, delighted that she was seeing her daddy again. I didn't do it for man as we have been a plague on the planet ever since Hercules imprisoned the gods in Atlantis. No, it had nothing to do with man. I sought redemption. Redemption for making the mistake of believing Hermes' lies, for freeing the gods, and causing the premature expiration of billions.

In all the evil that is man, there has always been some kindness. Some good people that cared for others, lived to help those in need, and dreamed of peace. I cost them a chance at their just reward; admittance into Nibiru. I didn't know whether those who survived were good people, evil, or a little of both, but I owed it to them to at least try.

So, Yeshua took me to the place of the calling, a tempesta to Nibiru. There were a few souls there, brought to the portal by Yeshua's disciples. They followed them into the tempesta, and in moments, their essences disappeared. Yahuda Sicarius awaited us and greeted Yeshua with an embrace.

"See, I don't get that," I finally piped up.

"Get what, Daniel?" Yeshua turned and asked.

"Your relationship with Yahuda."

"What do you mean?" Yeshua looked confused.

"He means, Master, how can you embrace the great betrayer?" Yahuda smiled.

"Ah… of course," Yeshua understood. "Thank the Romans once again."

"Oh?"

"There was much confusion among the disciples when Yeshua was seized by the guards and I identified him," Yahuda continued. "Many believed I betrayed him."

"You didn't?"

"No," Yeshua answered. "Yahuda is my closest friend. The only one I could trust with the greatest of burdens and not waver."

"Wait a minute…" The picture had become clear to me. "You wanted to be seized?"

"Yes," Yeshua continued- "The time had come to take my ministry to the next level – to have those who were with me understand the gravity of the task in front of them."

"So Yeshua bestowed upon me the greatest of honors," Yahuda continued. "He trusted me, among all others, to have the strength to do his will."

"Then why did you commit suicide?"

Yahuda looked to the ground and didn't say anything. Yeshua looked annoyed at me, his face contorted into a frown.

"I'm… I'm sorry," I stumbled.

"No, no," Yahuda replied. "It is fine. It is a fair question. I killed myself because when I saw the torture the damn Romans inflicted on him – because of me - I… I could not live with it. He was my master but he was also my closest friend. I loved him as such."

"Now, Daniel," Yeshua said, "stay close to Yahuda and I as we walk through the tempesta. Clear your mind. Be at peace. You must let go of Tartarus, of your loved ones here. You must be ready to go to Nibiru."

I took a deep breath and nodded that I was ready. I let all my fears, doubts, and concerns wash away. Yeshua stepped into the portal and disappeared. I followed. Even though it was visually identical to the one on Earth, this *tempesta* had a different feel than the last.

I didn't feel any pain, or the strange sensation of my atomic particles disintegrating beneath me. I stepped in, the white light hit me, and before I knew it, it was over, and I was in a strange, new and wondrous world. A world called Nibiru.

***

Heaven wasn't as I had imagined. There were no pearly white or golden gates in the clouds. In fact, the terrain of the world was similar to that of Earth's. There was land, air that I at least felt like I was breathing, and wind caressing my face. While I had gotten a brief glimpse of the world in Prometheus' visions, I never had been able to focus on the surroundings. I was standing in an amazing, technological metropolis. Skyscrapers ripped into the sky, the Annunan people buzzed about. Some walked; others had angel-like wings and flew. There were strange-looking, non-human beings that walked on two legs and had two arms, but facially looked like bugs. Huge, gigantic insect-looking eyes adorned their smallish heads and a small "snout" extended from between the eyes.

"NEW ARRIVAL!" a voice to my right called out suddenly.

"New arrival! New arrival!" The words seemed to explode across Nibiru's inhabitants until they all chanted it.

"They greet all new Annuna in this way," Yahuda said, as he placed his large hands on my shoulders, a tiny spark shooting up from their contact.

We went through a sea of Annuna, all extended welcomes and well wishes for me. As we walked down a street, I glanced up toward the starry night. The stars looked different, foreign. Their moon was larger than ours, and it was accompanied by a sister. I followed Yeshua and Yahuda into a building. It was strange; it was clearly a technologically advanced society, with modern conveniences and gadgetry. It even had its own form of television, which currently showed a picture of me with a subheading stating, "New Arrival from Terra – the Freer of Zeus". Yet none of it was real. It was all in my conscious imagination. Beings of energy had no need of inanimate objects – of buildings or vehicles or anything but a power source to feed upon. Yet, here we were in the lobby of a towering skyscraper. It was *the Matrix* and this time I was Neo.

We entered an elevator and began to ascend.

"Not what you had imagined, Dan?" Yahuda asked, slicing the silence.

"Not at all."

"Imagine how it was for me," Yahuda chuckled.

"I honestly can't believe this," I continued. "I mean to have the Greek mythology combine with Judaism and Christianity? I never thought it would be possible."

"All of your world's religions are steeped in some truth," Yeshua replied. "The Muslims are right in their belief in the prophet. He was touched by an Annuna, but a fallen one. The Christians had both the pagan rituals and the belief in me. The Jews still believe in the Law of Moses. Each believes in the one true God. They are remarkably similar, with just simple differences."

"And the Buddhists? The Hindus? Vastly different than the mono-theistic religions."

"Indeed, but there is some *veritas* in their beliefs as well," Yeshua replied. "It truly amazed us to see the progress of your world without the gods. You were like orphan children, needing to invent parents to help ease your mind that you were not abandoned."

"But we were, weren't we?"

"I can see your point, Daniel," Yeshua replied. "But it is the grand question, is it not? If God is real, why does He not stop the hurricane or the tornado or an earthquake from killing innocents? If God is all-powerful, why does He not end war, famine, and pestilence? If He cared enough to create life in the universe, why does he allow it to be senselessly destroyed?"

"Yeah, exactly."

"It is a question that has even puzzled the Annuna," Yeshua replied. "Even as we speak now and you understand my words in your native tongue, you cannot comprehend the magnificent plan of Thoth. None of us can."

"He is just the creator," I conceded. "It is up to us to assign our own destiny."

"Indeed," Yeshua replied. "For it is our destiny that determines what happens to our souls."

"So why the Annuna? Why did he choose you to be his messenger?"

"*Us*, Daniel," Yahuda corrected. "You are one of us now."

"It is written," Yeshua replied, "that Thoth created the Annuna to be his messengers, his warriors, and his servants. We live in servitude of him. We love it, simply because it is what we were created to do. We exist to exalt him. We exist to create life throughout the universe at his behest. It is for him we carefully choose the members of our society."

"So, who created Thoth?" I asked.

"Thoth was not created, he just is."

"How do you know you don't have it all wrong, too?" I continued. "Just like we did. We thought we were the chosen ones, and God, or Thoth if you like, preferred us over all creatures in the universe. How do you know it's the Annuna whom he prefers?"

"Because, Daniel, he lives with us. He exists, we can be in His presence – if we are summoned," Yeshua replied. "As some of your fellow Terrans like to say, seeing is believing. We are the reason you exist, how all life in your reality exists. He is the reason we exist."

"I guess there's just some things we'll never get a handle on, huh?"

"As an Annuna, you will gain knowledge of the universe like you have never imagined," Yeshua continued. "But the one thing you will never understand is Thoth's plan. He alone knows why things are as they are. Not even I, his own son, know anything about the design."

The doors slid open to reveal a large spacious area that resembled a court room.

"We are here," Yeshua said.

"But where is here?"

"The Justice."

There was a bench where a judge would preside, but instead of a jury, above us was a coliseum of sorts, almost like an auditorium or a theater. Seated and peering down upon us were beings that neither appeared to be male or female. Some had wings, others had pig-snouts for noses, and some had antlers like a deer.

There was a strange silence. As my eyes cascaded around the room, the wooden paneling struck me as a curious effect. I knew none of these seats, walls, or even the building we were in were real but as we moved toward a chair and I placed my hand on it, it felt as real as if I was in a real courtroom in downtown Tampa, getting ready to see a judge about a parking ticket - except this particular ticket held the fate of mankind riding upon the outcome.

I heard a door to the left open and an individual in a long white robe and white feathered wings entered. His (or maybe her) face was absent of any features that would help you deduce if you were looking at a male or female. He had long, straight blond hair that cascaded down his shoulders and back. His eyes were dark, absent of pupils. There was a dark blackness where his eyes would normally be. He took the position where the judge would normally sit.

"Be seated," he said in an ethereal voice. The sound from his vocal cords were as if spoken by three different people.

I sat next to Yeshua, while Yahuda retreated out of the area.

"I am Archangel Raguel," the judge said, training his dark orbs upon me. "We will discuss your matter now."

"Grand Archangelus," Yeshua rose. "I bring before you the new champion of the Terrans. He freed our brother Zeus from his prison on Terra, but like his father before him, Zeus has abandoned the ways of the Annuna."

"Greetings, Prince Yeshua," Raguel replied. "What is it you seek of us?"

"We ask for the will of Thoth to end the genocide occurring on Terra."

"Terra has abandoned the way of the Annuna," Raguel replied. "Thoth has no interest in their world except for a special few."

"Yes, but Thoth has always favored Terra over all others," Yeshua countered. "It is why I was created to save them."

"And yet here they are anyway – at the brink of extinction."

"Uh, that's my fault," I shyly interjected.

There was a murmuring of chatter among those in attendance.

"I do not believe you were invited to speak," Raguel replied.

"Sorry, but I typically beg for forgiveness rather than ask for permission," I retorted. "And you are speaking of the end of my species here."

"Be that as it may, you need to be silent."

I did as commanded.

"Your Highness, please continue," Raguel instructed.

"Yes, well, as my young colleague here said – it is the responsibility of the Annuna to act because it is the Annuna's mistakes with this world that has put their species on the brink."

An explosion of conversation lifted up to the rafters.

"Silence!" Raguel called out and the room complied.

"The Annuna do not make mistakes, Yeshua. Please explain your reasoning," Raguel continued.

"Two Annuna, Uranus and Gaea, allowed their personal ambition to interfere with Thoth's will -"

Another explosion of murmuring and another call for silence from the judge.

"Their greed for the spotlight enabled a young Annuna, Cronus," Yeshua continued, "to stray from our ways and destroy a perfectly good world that would have produced not only more worthy candidates to join the Annuna, but a sustainable source for Tartarus for quite some time. Now, the offspring of Cronus are about to do the same to Terra. They have already nearly succeeded. Tartarus overflows with immature souls that will not sustain us."

"And what is it you ask of us?"

"To have the Archangelus, with the will of Thoth, commence in waging war on Zeus and his new race of Dodekatheons," Yeshua replied. "Eliminate their rule and return it to that of Man."

"And to what purpose would this serve the Annuna? Man has been a pestilence to this world far greater than any of Cronus' seed."

"Think about it!" I cried out. "Our species would be enlightened by our voyage to the edge of the precipice. If the Annuna intervene on our behalf and destroy the Dodekatheons, we not only would have the confirmation of our beliefs, but a new outlook on our existence, our place in the universe – everything."

"Daniel, you have yet to earn the right to speak at these proceedings," Raguel replied. "You need to be silent or be removed."

"I came here, gave up my life on Terra, to speak on our behalf," I replied. "I deserve the right to be heard."

"You deserve nothing!" Raguel cried out, the voices converging all at once to one deep angry tone.

I drew silent again.

"Michael, come forward," Raguel called out to the audience.

From above us, another winged, asexual being descended from the balcony and took his place to our left. He wore white, but instead of long blonde hair like Raguel, he sported short curly locks that perfectly framed his beautiful face.

"Thank you, Raguel," he said quickly. "I have studied this case for some time and I believe I can add some arguments against our participation in liberating Terra from the Dodekatheons."

I leaned over to Yeshua.

"I need to get to Gabriel," I whispered, "Only he-"

"She."

"She?"

"Well, they do not really have a gender but she considers herself a female."

"Okay, she can help us," I continued. "Prometheus told me to specifically seek her out."

"Gabriel is bound by the will of the Archangelus' judgment," Yeshua whispered back. "She will only act if all the Archangelus have agreed to it."

"May I ask all the others to reveal themselves to the Justice?" Michael requested.

I knew them as soon as they appeared. Raphael had a kind face; like the others he didn't have any eyes, he sported wings, and wore a white robe. He had dark, brown skin, and short curled black hair. Uriel looked older, sporting a long white beard and bushy hair. Gabriel, like Raguel, had long blonde hair, I could see some female features, longer eyelashes, poutier lips, but basically she was indistinguishable from the others, with the exception of the hair type and color. They were all nearly identical with that being the lone difference. Chamuel had short blonde curls and looked an awful lot like Hermes, more than the other Archs. Finally, Jophiel was the last to arrive. He also was identical to the others, with the only difference being short, spiked, dirty blond hair and a short, well-kept beard.

"Thank you for coming," Michael greeted his other angelus. "I know you all take great concern with the matter before us."

The Archs all nodded as they took their seat behind the bench with Raguel.

"So, Daniel comes before us seeking the deliverance of Man from the rule of the Dodekatheons," Michael continued. "But we have to wonder, do we not, whether they are worthy of such interference? I would submit to you that Man does not deserve this reprieve from their extinction – simply because of what they have become. We have all been to Terra. We all have tried to guide them on the path to Nibiru. But their true nature has been to destroy, not create. They are everything the Annuna are not. Greedy, self-absorbed, vengeful, aggressive. These are not traits that the Annuna subscribe to. Further, there is the delicate situation that we would be facing our brothers in combat. We all know how that last turned out."

"Yes," Raguel replied. "None of us can forget the Great War."

"When Satan rebelled against us," Michael continued, "he took a third of the Annuna with him into hell - it was over Man. Thoth wanted to elevate Man above us, the Annuna. Satan could not accept this and he tried to overthrow Thoth. We lost a great many Annuna on the account of Man, yet Man decided to abandon Thoth. To rebel against their custodians, the Dodekatheons, who are our brothers?"

"The Dodekatheons are not Annuna," I interjected. "They don't follow the Annuna's code of beliefs. They seek only their own glorification. How are they your brothers if they are the antithesis of all you believe?"

"How is it you are here for a few minutes and already believe you know all there is to know about the Annuna?" Michael countered. "This, my fellow Archs, is the arrogance I speak of. When their custodians were disposed of, Man was left to their own devices. We all remember when Cronus and Rhea returned – and we remember the sentencing and his punishment. Rather than enjoy their independence, Man wasted it and we were forced to go to Terra multiple times to put them back on the path. Even you, Prince Yeshua, were created for the sole purpose to help Man find their way to Nibiru."

Yeshua looked down at the table in front of him, not wanting to meet Michael's gaze as he worked the Justice.

"And how did Man repay your message of love and peace? By torturing you, mutilating your body in such a horrific fashion that all of Nibiru shook with the news. Further, man carries trinkets that represent and immortalize your torture."

"No, that's not true," I replied. "They are there to remind us of the price Jesus... Yeshua paid to deliver us from evil."

"Yes, your kind got the message," Michael countered. "So much so, they left Thoth behind and harnessed the power of the atom, creating even more destruction and devastation to Terra. Thoth turned his back on Terra a long time ago. I do not see any reason to change that now."

"Look," I replied, "I'm not saying we're perfect - far from it. But Thoth once loved us so much that he gave us Yeshua to save us from ourselves. We deserve the right to continue to get to that place. Cronus and Rhea should have created Earth, I mean Terra, and left. Instead, they stayed and created offspring who brought about their demise. My God, these beings have murdered other Annuna without any consequence. Do you not have law? We are taught that one of Thoth's primary rules is Thou Shalt Not Kill. Does this not apply to the Annuna?"

"Yes but…"

"Zeus and his new race killed billions of souls on Terra," I continued. "They killed the Annuna to gain power of the world, and they have ruined the Annuna's food supply by prematurely terminating those souls who have yet reached a point to provide a power infusion. Their act significantly impacts the Annuna now and for the future."

"What would you have us do?" Gabriel interjected.

"Gabriel, Prometheus told me to seek you out," I replied. "Because he believed so strongly that once you heard our plight, you would take upon our charge and deliver us from the evil of Zeus' rule."

"He asks us to go to war against our own!" Michael cried out. "To have a second Great War."

"It would not be that dramatic," Yeshua replied. "You are not seeing anyone attempt to overthrow Thoth, only to defy Thoth by ruling a world instead of creating life there."

"Michael, take your place on the panel," Raguel ordered, and Michael fluttered his wings, floating to a chair next to the others.

Raguel rose, as did Yeshua. I followed suit.

"We have one last witness to speak," Raguel announced.

The doors opened and an older female Annuna I recognized as Rhea strode into the room.

"Rhea," Raguel ordered, "Please speak to Terra."

"Zeus is my son." She began, "But I know his thirst for power is like his father's. He will grow tired of his life on Terra and will eventually, once he is powerful enough, turn his attention to Nibiru."

Once again the room exploded into murmuring.

"Silence!" Raguel repeated.

"As a mother, I cannot tell you to decide to destroy my son," Rhea continued, "As an Annuna, I do not see an alternative."

"Thank you, Rhea," Raguel replied, "You may go."

She turned and quickly exited.

"The time has come to vote on the matter of Zeus' extermination of Man on Terra," Raguel continued, "Indicate your choice with yea or nay for whether we are to intervene on Man's behalf. Vote as I call out your name."

"Michael."

"Nay."

"Uriel."

"Nay."

"Gabriel."

Our eyes met… or at least my eyes met where her eyes would typically be.

"Yea."

I mouthed a thank you to her.

"Chamuel"

"Yea."

"Raphael."

"Yea."

"Jophiel."

"Nay."

We were deadlocked at three apiece. Raguel would have to make the final choice.

"As we are without a majority," Raguel said, "it falls on to me to decide the fate of Man and the Dodekatheons."

He paused for a moment. I could feel every inch of my essence tense up.

"While I agree with Michael's fears regarding another Great War," Raguel continued, "I cannot help but think that Thoth has a plan for Man. I believe that is why we have been so involved in Terran's development. We have not done this for any other world. After we create worlds, we leave them to their own devices. If they advance and become Annuna, great. If they destroy themselves, it is typically not something we concern ourselves with. But Man is different. They always have been. Further, with the extermination of Man, not all of their souls are bound for Tartarus, but to Hades' realm and the consumption by Zeus and his subjects, giving them significantly more power; making them dangerous to us. Thoth has left the decision up to his Archs, and the decision has fallen to me."

I held my breath.

"My decision is Yea. We will go to war with the Dode-katheons and preserve the race of Man on Terra."

"YES!" I exclaimed, and embraced Yeshua.

"Well done, Daniel," he replied. "But now the hard part begins."

"What do you mean?"

"We must convince Satan to assist us."

Chapter 4 Better To Reign in Hell

Hell wasn't what I expected, either. There was no fire, and brimstone wasn't visible. There weren't lost souls enduring horrible torture. There was just darkness, similar to what I experienced in Hades' realm. There was the rub – I didn't think there was a Satan – I believed that Hades was the Lord of the Dead. On Earth, he was – but in the grand scheme of the Universe, Hades was small potatoes.

All the dead souls in the universe who were lost and couldn't find their way to Tartarus ended up in Hell. There, they would be devoured by Satan and his rebellious *Fallen*. Once Hades and the other gods were imprisoned on Atlantis, Satan had taken his domain to Earth…and basically squatted on the realm of the dead Hades had built.

The Fallen had no power against Yeshua, but the Archs Gabriel and Michael went with us anyway. We arrived in Hell the same way most of the transportation happens in Nibiru, via a tempesta.

We were led by one of Satan's minions to the Red Palace. It lived up to the name, as the metal and concrete-like substances that sustained it were different shades of red, some dark, others lighter, nearly pink. As we walked through the gates, we passed through rooms with no furniture or decoration, just vast emptiness. As we followed the demon, a small nearly dwarf-like creature with large puffy lips and cheeks, we passed into the royal chambers of Satan.

"Ah, the bastard returns," I heard a deep, sinister voice. I glanced around the chamber and trained on an immense throne I had failed to notice before. Seated on this red-colored, ruby-

jeweled throne was a man, very human looking – nothing like the
demons and angelus that surrounded us. He had long dark hair
that trickled down his back like a bubbling brook. His skin was
extremely light, nearly ghost white, and his goatee curled neatly
under his nose, encircling his lips. He wore black material with
red sprinkled in parts, similar to Victorian royal garb, and he held
a red, ruby-encrusted scepter.

"Greetings, Satan," Yeshua replied.

"To what do I owe this unexpected pleasure?" Satan
growled, as another dwarf demon stood beside him and trained
its red eyes on us, the same piercing red eyes that Satan now
trained on me. "And who is this Terran?"

"He is Annuna," Yeshua replied. "A special Annuna."

"Oh, please don't tell me Thoth knocked up another
meat bag on Terra."

"You will watch your tongue when you speak his name!"
Gabriel exclaimed.

"Ah, Gabriel," Satan snarled. "I see... still cupping
Thoth's massive testicles with your mouth...."

"Enough!" Michael cried out and grabbed the scabbard
of his sword.

"Better to reign in hell then suckle testi-"

"Shut your mouth!" Michael exclaimed as he drew his
sword.

"Stop it," Yeshua said calmly to Michael, whose head
bowed in reverence.

Satan erupted in a dreadfully sinister laughter.

"So what do you fools want with little ole me?" Satan
asked.

"We require your assistance-"

"Haha!" Satan erupted, "Hahahahahahahaha. Are you serious? Hahahaha."

"Very," Yeshua replied coldly.

"Haha-ehem," Satan composed himself. "And why in the
universe would I ever help you, meat bag?"

"Terra."

Satan erupted in hilarity once again.

"I own Terra," Satan countered. "Most of my lost souls here are from that pitiful little spec of space rock that Thoth turned his back on."

"Not anymore," I said.

Satan's eyes shot to me. The red pupils seemed to pierce through my soul and into the darkness deep inside of me. It frightened me and I looked away.

"What does this young one mean, Yeshua?" he croaked.

"Zeus and his fellow Dodekatheons have been freed. Hades is taking your souls again," Yeshua replied.

Satan rose from the throne and tossed his scepter aside violently, storming down the steps of the throne toward Yeshua. Michael and Gabriel jumped in front of Yeshua like two secret service men protecting the president.

"What the hell do you mean they are free? How the hell could that have happened?"

"I did it," I said.

Satan instantly reached out his large hand and took hold of my throat. His large, daggered fingernails dug into my energized epidermis, burring into it. If I had blood, it would have come gushing out.

"Release him," Yeshua commanded.

Even though I didn't require air to survive, I found myself gasping for it.

"Release him," Yeshua repeated more forcefully.

"Very well," Satan said grudgingly.

"So then you now understand the predicament we find ourselves in," Yeshua continued. "The Arch council has voted to intervene and end Zeus' rule on Terra, but we need the assistance of the Fallen."

"Why?"

"Zeus has exterminated most of the species on Terra," Yeshua continued. "He and his fellow Dodekatheons have gotten extremely powerful. It was a miracle that Dan got out to warn us."

"Why did you free him?" Satan asked me.

"I was tricked by Hermes."

Satan looked away in disgust.

"This?" he growled. "This is your champion?"

"Indeed."

"No wonder you need my help."

"Do we have it?" Yeshua asked.

"No." Satan grinned evilly, revealing his dagger-like teeth. "I have conditions."

"Of course you do," Michael mocked.

"We must be allowed to return to Nibiru -"

"Out of the question," Yeshua quickly replied. Satan looked like a kid who was told by a parent he couldn't have that new toy in the store.

"Fine," Satan continued. "No Nibiru – then I must have Hades. I must devour his energy source so he can never prevent me from receiving my lost souls again, and I must take his new Erebus."

"Done."

"And him." Satan pointed one of his pointed fingers directly at me.

Yeshua looked at me, large puppy dog eyes greeting me with sadness.

"I get him or there is no deal," Satan repeated.

"Forget it," Michael interjected. "We don't need them, we can take Zeus ourselves."

"He knows that's not true," Satan replied. "Or you wouldn't be here. Zeus has grown too powerful for the Archs, for the Fallen – for *Thoth* himself."

"No, Thoth could put him down," Yeshua replied.

"In fact, instead of joining you to put down Zeus," Satan grinned, "maybe I'll just recruit Zeus into my fold and finish what I began eons ago…"

"You can have my soul," I said quickly, without thinking.

"Daniel, NO!" Yeshua cried out.

"He can have me… I don't care, I just want to save what's left of my world," I continued. "I don't want to see millions more trapped in Tartarus with no chance at ever reaching Nibiru, or stuck in Hades' realm."

"Wow, courageous there, Daniel," Satan laughed. "I think we have ourselves a binding agreement."

We left quickly, feeling sickly about what had just occurred. None of us spoke, perhaps not believing that Yeshua and the Arch Angelus had just made a deal with the Devil, with my soul as the clincher in the deal.

Chapter 5 The Return

It took a few days for all of the preparations to be finalized by the Arch Angelus and the Fallen but in Annuna time, days were years. The attack would be two-pronged, emerging from different hemispheres. Yeshua, the Archs and I would come back through the Mexico tempesta, while the Fallen would erupt from one that was hidden deep in the mountains of the Himalayas. They would converge on Zeus' forces and if it all went according to plan, annihilate them.

During our down time, Yeshua told me more about Satan's fall. As had been written before, Satan had a falling out with Thoth once Eden was created. As Uranus and Gaea were doing some of their best work, Thoth had taken a great interest in the fruits of their labor. He had grown to favor Man, even above the Annuna. Satan, of course, believed that was unacceptable. He wouldn't allow Thoth to replace the Annuna in the natural order of things, and a great war erupted in Nibiru. Many of the Annuna went with Satan, believing that Thoth was betraying their obedience by favoring Uranus' new creation. The war lasted for weeks in Annuna, which for us would be millions of years. While the battle continued, Cronus' insurrection went unchecked. When Eden was destroyed and both Gaea and Uranus were murdered by their son, the reason for fighting changed. It was no longer about Man, for Man on Eden was no more. Instead, now it was for ultimate supremacy in the universe. The battle waged on as Zeus overthrew Cronus and the Dodekatheons took their place as rulers of Terra.

Eventually, Satan and his crew would be stopped. While Satan's original goal of stopping Man from replacing the Annuna succeeded, in the end he lost the war. Thoth, in a rare public appearance, decreed that Satan and the Fallen were to be expelled from Nibiru, never to return. Satan's group was to feed off of the energy of lost souls who didn't find their way to Tartarus, and if there weren't enough to sustain them, so be it. Satan made his own version of Nibiru in the netherworld, Hell, and ruled there. Satan and his minions then culled the lost souls, tricking them into losing their way to Tartarus.

With the war over, Thoth turned his attention back to Terra. Zeus and the immortals had already been imprisoned in Atlantis, and the mortals were on their own to develop as they will. Without the guidance of the Dodekatheons, the animal of Man would be dependent on themselves. Thoth wanted to help along their development, sending his Archs to assist here and there, but eventually the evil of Man began to take shape. Some were so evil that they would have no place even in Tartarus… Satan searched long and hard for these misguided souls and feasted upon them.

Thoth decided to attempt one more reclamation project for Man, and created Yeshua. Try as Satan might, he couldn't corrupt or cajole Yeshua into giving up Thoth's plan for redemption. The wicked, the spiteful, even the hated tax collectors all could find salvation in Yeshua's message. Eventually, Yeshua would be rejected and put to death, descending into Satan's realm.

"What happened there," Yeshua said to me, "cannot be said."

"Why?" I asked.

"I choose not to tell you."

He would be released from Satan's grip, returned to Earth, and then ascended into Nibiru. Man, meanwhile, went along truckin'. Satan changed his tact. Instead of imploring Man to do evil, disrupting their souls and making them lost on their final journey to Tartarus, he would go one better - convince man that Thoth, the Archs, Nibiru, all of it – didn't exist – that it was all myth and legend created by simple-minded people who didn't have an explanation for what they were seeing around them.

Man went more toward science and away from religion. Oh, religion still prevailed on Earth, as it did before I released the Gods from Atlantis, but it was more out of tradition than outright belief that God truly did exist. As Man withdrew from Thoth, He withdrew from them. He went on to his next creation, interest or whatever it is that the Supreme Being in the universe did – not even Yeshua truly knew. He stopped, for all intents and purposes, caring about those who didn't care for him. Yeshua took it upon himself to look over Terra and make sure that those who were worthy became Annuna. He made it the mission of his disciples and the Archs to try and keep the message of God alive for those who chose to accept it. While he tolerated the misinformation campaign of the Romans, and the Greek nickname of Jesus imposed upon him, he cared that there were some that still believed in his message.

"So, Thoth has moved on but you haven't?" I said to him.

"I cannot," Yeshua smiled. "They're my kind. I do not possess power like Thoth to prevent bad things from happening to people. I do not have the strength to divert hurricanes, end wars, or provide miracles. On Earth, I could do miracles… but those miracles are now done every day by your doctors and scientists. It is amazing to me how far you have come, even without knowing or understanding your order in the universe."

"So with Zeus back in charge, has Thoth taken interest again?" I asked.

"He… well," Yeshua uneasily replied, "…He knows what has happened and what is happening now. He has no issues with our course of action – other than working with Satan, of course."

"But he won't assist?"

"No," Yeshua frowned sadly. "His interest in Terra is no more, I am afraid. He does not really care if Man blows itself up or if Zeus exterminates you all. He only cares that we, as you say, nip any potential rebellion by Zeus in the bud."

"But isn't he amazed at our advancement? I mean, before Zeus and all of his supernatural power – we ruled Earth unchallenged."

"Yes, it does please him."

"But not enough to get interested in us again…"

"No, he is otherwise engaged."

"With what?"

"A new species he has taken great interest in."

"Oh no," I gasped. "Man is no longer the chosen of God."

"I am afraid so."

***

The Archs and lower level angels had geared up to the hilt with swords, arrows, and a variety of armaments that would have made any ruler proud. This wasn't only an invasion force, but an annihilation force. Having seen what Zeus could do before I left, I was confident in the outcome. After all, Zeus couldn't stop one Titan, how would he fare against hundreds of Annuna and Demons?

As we approached the tempesta that would return us to Terra, I thought about Jeanie and Annie.

"Yeshua, may I ask a favor?" I asked him.

"Consider it done." He smiled.

I felt content that even while I would be devoured by Satan and his minions in Hell, Annabelle and Jeanie would be in Nibiru. I was at peace with that.

"How long have we been gone in Earth time?" I asked, just now noticing that Yeshua also wore the golden battle armor similar to what Prometheus wore on Atlantis.

"Actually, Thoth has given you a gift." He smiled. "We will return at the exact moment you left."

"Really?" I replied excitedly, "Fantastic!"

"Michael and Gabriel will lead the charge against the Dodekatheons," Yeshua continued. "You and I will go to Hades' realm to save your new wife."

"We're uh… not married…" I sheepishly replied.

"But you consummated, did you not?" Yeshua asked.

"I… ah… yeah… uh…"

"Different times…" Yeshua sighed.

"Yeah, definitely."

"Daniel, you should know that once we get there, you will not be the same," Yeshua continued. "Flesh will be on your body, blood will flow through your veins, you will breath air, and you will be whole – but you will also be Annuna. You will have powers like you never imagined. You will be like -"

"Like Prometheus."

"But stronger."

I drew silent for a moment. The other Angelus around me were all gritting their teeth, readying themselves for the battle about to ensue.

"It is time," Yeshua said, and almost on cue, the tempesta on the floor began spinning. One by one, they stepped through until only I and Yeshua were left. I stepped forward and into the pool, I immediately felt my energy be broken down into little bits, only this time, it was a vastly different sensation. As I passed through the white light, I could sense mass to my body, I could feel skin and muscle reattaching to bone, I could sense my heart begin its drum roll, and the seas of my blood begin to flow. I could feel the tinge of the hair on my arm, and the flow of air descending into my lungs. I was alive again, and standing in the same Mayan ruin that had ended my previous existence.

"Oh shit…" I heard the voice of Hermes, turned and saw him vanish.

Chapter 6 Saving Mina

I darted toward the stone lectern and found Prometheus, falling in and out of consciousness, his humanoid form badly scarred and burned. I could sense his life force fading.

"Prometheus," I called to him warmly. "Prometheus, wake up."

"Daniel... you did not... go?" he weakly replied.

An explosion rocked the top of the Mayan temple, sending the entire complex trembling. Dirt, dust, and debris trickled upon us.

"Look at me," I said, "and ask your question again."

"You have returned." He smiled weakly.

"We must get to Atlantis, Daniel," Yeshua said behind me.

Prometheus grabbed my arm.

"Was it... beautiful?"

"Yes, it was amazing." I smiled, realizing that the vision of Nibiru given to me by Prometheus wasn't how he remembered, but how he had imagined it.

"Raphael," I heard Yeshua command, "help him."

The Arch Raphael came beside me and placed his hand on my shoulder.

"Fear not about Prometheus," he calmly said. "He will be healed."

"Stay calm, my friend," I said to Prometheus. "The Calvary has arrived."

I rose quickly and turned to Yeshua.

"I am ready."

We both closed our eyes, but even with them closed I could see a white flash. Suddenly, I could smell a fishy, seafaring smell as if I was back on our Atlantean ship. As I opened my eyes, I could see we weren't on the boat, but in Atlantis.

"Hades' realm is at the bottom of Atlantis," Yeshua said. "We must hurry."

Another eye close, I guess we can call it God Zipping, and we were in Hades' realm, the new Erebus. Dark, black, evil. If you ever had a vision of hell, this would be it. I could see through my newly formed god-like eyes all that my mortal eyes wouldn't be able to see in the darkness. There were bones, disfigured, tortured bodies strewn across the dark chamber we were in. It was like being in a cavern or a cave. The thick smell of death seemed to permeate throughout. Then I could see them, the souls, the lost souls of those who refused to go to Tartarus, but had no other place to reside. They were like a depository for Zeus and his ilk to feed, meandering about as they waited for their final destruction.

"Yeshua," I called out to him, as he passed quickly through them.

"Yes, I see them."

"We can't just leave them," I replied.

"They belong to Satan now."

"We can't do anything?"

"Not without breaking our deal with him," he replied.

"That's right," a sinister deep voice said from behind me.

"Jesus Christ!" I exclaimed, startled by Satan's sudden appearance directly behind me.

"Guess again." He chuckled.

Yeshua stopped and joined us.

"We have subdued most of Hades' minions," Satan reported. "But Hades himself and that worm Hermes have your lovely morsel Mina Constantopolus held up in Hades' under-world palace. If you offer me her soul, we'd be happy to -"

"No!" I cried out.

Satan laughed.

"Oh, Daniel," Satan continued. "You are so easy to push. I can't tell you how much I will enjoy feasting on your essence. I'm going to take time with it. Savor it. Like a fine wine or a superb steak."

"Silence, Satan," Yeshua replied. "Finish taking Atlantis for the Archs or you will not get any of your just rewards."

"Atlantis is just about ours," Satan replied.

"It is not until it is."

"So be it," Satan grudgingly replied, then cast a longing eye toward me, sending shivers down my spine.

In an instant, he was gone.

"Come, Daniel," Yeshua sadly replied.

We rushed to the foot of Hades' underworld palace; a large, dark medieval-looking castle. Its ancient walls held moss, saw grass, and evidence of significant age with what seemed to be a billion steps led to the palace entrance. To be able to god-zip, we have to be able to visualize where we were going, since neither of us had ever been inside Hade's palace, we couldn't just zip to where we wanted to go. For a mortal, impossible to climb, but for two gods, it was a single leap. In an instant, we both were hurling through the air and landing on the top step.

The doors were immense, like Hades himself, going up at least ten stories. No mortal could open these doors. I cupped my hands together, created an energy oval, and fired on the doors, blowing a hole large enough for us to proceed.

The inside of the castle didn't look much different from the outside; it was dark, dank, and depressing. We moved into a large ballroom area that led to Hades' throne room.

"It is not often I have visitors," Hades' deep harmonic voice shook through the ballroom.

Yeshua and I both scanned the area but couldn't see where the voice originated.

"I know one of you," Hades continued. "But I know not the other."

"Come out and I will properly introduce myself," Yeshua courageously replied.

Without warning, a large, hulking dark mass came barreling into view, and swung a gigantic red sword toward Yeshua. I didn't think, I just reacted and in a moment, just before the blade reached Yeshua's neck, mine blocked it, sending a cavalcade of sparks lighting the area. Yeshua tumbled away from the blow, while Hades and I began a furious ballet of clashing metal. Hades' strength was immeasurable. Even in my heightened state of power, it was everything I had just to keep him off of me.

As we exchanged volleys, we would also fire at each other with the primordial goo that constituted "God weapons", so with each attack, we would have to dodge a blade and a power blast. We continued to battle, one after another, neither getting the advantage over the other. After a furious exchange, we both stopped for a second, and stared at our opponent.

"You have ascended to the 'Annuna," Hades suddenly acknowledged. "Yet, you do not yet know your power."

"I am Annuna," I replied. "And I know I am more powerful than you."

We exchanged another furious combination of acrobatics and sword play. His sword was proportionate to his gargantuan frame, making each strike difficult to get past. While there was a lot more of a target, it was nigh impossible to get past his defenses.

"ARRRRRRGHEEEEE!!!" Hades erupted in a terrifying explosion of pain, and fell with a large thud to his knees.

I took the opportunity to drive my sword deep through his armor and into his torso. I heard him groan loudly and then collapse. Behind him, Yeshua stood, his hands cupped with a white power ball between them. He fired once again, striking the limp body of Hades.

"He is done," Yeshua said. "We must get to the throne room."

We raced into the throne room, and sitting on Hades' throne was Hermes, beneath him, the semi-conscious nude body of Mina. The throne looked like it was made of dark black charred bone. Embedded into its sides were large swords; Hades' personal collection I supposed.

"Well done, wonder boy," Hermes mocked. "I expected you to be back, Daniel, but I had no idea I would be facing the dynamic duo."

Hermes rose from the throne, bent down, and traced his arm along the milky white skin of Mina's nude body.

"She is something, let me tell ya," Hermes continued, as his hand traced around one of her breasts. "If I wasn't so keen on the males of your species, I could just… yes, something indeed."

"Let her go, Hermes," I commanded.

"Oh, now you are giving the orders?" Hermes continued. "I see, the new world order."

Hermes drew a sword from behind Hades' throne and placed it by Mina's neck.

"You know, Danny boy," Hermes continued, "all you had to do was free my master, Lord Zeus, and then freaking die. That's all you needed to do."

"I couldn't just do that, Hermes."

"Yes, I know. You were too much of a boy scout," he replied. "I didn't quite see that quality of yours at first, with all your crying and carrying on in that miserable little church I found you in."

"Things have changed, and now you need to let her go."

"And who is this with you?" Hermes asked.

"This is Jesus."

"Oh yes!" Hermes exclaimed. "I knew I recognized you. It has been two thousand years, after all."

"Hermes, you have lost," Yeshua continued. "Even as we speak, the Annuna are finishing off the Dodekatheons. Satan and his demons are taking control of Atlantis. It is over; no one else needs to die."

"Ah, but there you are wrong, Mr. Christ," Hermes replied. "I inadvertently began this by finishing off two of our friend Daniel's most important women in his life. Now, we've come full circle – and while it may be my last act here on Terra, I'm going to end this the same way I started it – by killing the woman he loves!"

Hermes fired two quick energy bursts from his left hand, knocking us both backward, then swung the sword but before it could strike, he was impaled on a blade from behind. As the edge blade of the sword exploded from his chest, he looked down in shock, behind him stood Persephone, holding the last of Hades' throne swords.

"I cannot tell you how long I've waited to do that," she said, as she pushed him off of the blade and he collapsed to his side.

"You... you... BITCH!" Hermes gasped.

Persephone helped Mina to her feet, but Mina was still in a trance-like state.

I raced toward them and braced Mina in my arms.

"Dan..." she said as she cracked her eyes open slightly.

"Yeah, baby. It's me, I'm here," I soothed.

"Am I... dreaming?"

"No, honey, I'm here."

"AH, FAK!" I heard Hermes scream out in agony.

"Hold her a sec, there's something I need to take care of."

Persephone nodded, smiling gently as she held Mina close.

"Come, young one," she said softly. "Let's find you some suitable clothing."

I moved toward the fallen carcass of Hermes. He was writhing in pain.

"Does it hurt?" I asked mockingly, and then shoved my thumb into his wound.

"AAAAAH- you son of a – you bast- AAAAAAH Muthaf-" he cried out.

"It's good to know that you've learned all of our curse words, Hermes," I chuckled...

"Daniel," I heard Yeshua say from behind me. "It is not the way of the Annuna to take revenge. We war only to defend our way of life, not for personal gain."

"Yeah but..." I knew he was right.

"Ah, yes," Satan's voiced boomed from behind us. "The contrite way of the Annuna. Surely, Daniel, you see how weak it is. It is like choosing the good side of the Force over the power of the Dark Side."

"Yeah, but in the end, Vader is defeated."

"Damn it, I never watched the last one, you just ruined it for me."

"Sorry."

"Well, all is fair," Satan chuckled. "But what have we here?"

"Dan was going to finish Hermes and send him to Tartarus," Yeshua replied. "Just like the others of his kind."

"All but Hades, who's already on his way to Hell," Satan corrected. "Just like the rest of the lost souls who rightfully belong to me."

"Good riddance."

"So here's the thing, I'm thinking of amending the deal," Satan continued.

"Oh?" Yeshua questioned.

"Yes." He looked toward the fallen Hermes, who suddenly grew terrified.

"I want all of the Dodekatheons… especially that one," Satan continued, as he pointed to Hermes.

"And why would we ever agree to that?" I replied.

"Well, for one, even with the power of the Archs and the other Annuna, the battle in Mexico is at a stalemate. You need my Fallen to seal the deal," Satan replied. "Further, as much as it pains me to do this, I am willing to give up you in exchange for the rest of the Dodekatheons."

"If you took all the Dodekatheons, you would have an abundance of power," Yeshua observed.

"Yes, my dear holy meat bag that is the point."

"Well, sorry, a deal's a deal," I said. "We're not giving you anything."

"Is that your final answer?" He turned to Yeshua.

"No," Yeshua replied. "We accept your terms."

"What?" I gasped. "Yeshua, you can't give him that kind of power!"

"Sorry, no take backsies," Satan crowed, as he fired an energy blast knocking me away from Hermes.

"NO! Gods, No! Dan, you can't let him take me!" Hermes screamed in horror. "I know we've had our differences but I don't deserve this – PLEASE, DAN, HELP ME!"

"Shhhh," Satan soothed Hermes. "Dan wants you to burn in Hell and become my dinner."

"Dan, you can stop him - please!" Hermes cried out. "Please save me!"

"Actually, Hermes," I replied as I came to my feet, "he's right. I hope he takes his time and burns you for all eternity."

"NOOOOOOOOOOOOOOOOOO!" Hermes cried out… and then they were gone, only the echo of Hermes' voice permeated the throne room.

"Why did you do that?" I asked as I turned to Yeshua.

"Satan thinks that with all the power of the Dodekatheons, he will be unstoppable," Yeshua replied. "But what he doesn't realize is he just gave up the only power in the universe that would have allowed him to challenge Thoth – you."

"Me?"

"Yes, you," Yeshua continued. "I knew once the battle began and Satan saw the power of the Dodekatheons, he would get greedy and want them all. I knew he would offer you back to us, believing you were just a simple new Annuna."

"I'm not?"

"Dan," Yeshua chuckled, "by now you should know that you are not like all the others."

"I just don't understand -"

"No you don't," Yeshua continued. "But the time will come when you will. For now, we have a final battle to wage."

"And Mina?"

"Persephone will take care of her and when it is over, she will join with you."

"Okay then, let's roll."

Chapter 7 Endgame

We were back in Mexico at the site of the Mayan temple only there was no Mayan temple left; it was in ruins. Above us, a fireworks display of explosions and a rainbow of energy blasts were being exchanged in a symphony of violence and chaos. Outnumbered by Thoth's Archs and Satan's Fallen, the remaining Dodekatheons were fighting for their lives.

It was a fruitless battle for the Dodekatheons; Satan's army numbered in the hundreds, and while they weren't as powerful as their Arch allies, their strength in numbers, and their love for war definitely seemed to be the difference. Zeus faced off against Michael, Gabriel, along with the demons Belial and Beelzebub. He wasn't doing well. Poseidon was challenged by Uriel and the demons Astraroth and Leviathan. For Ares, as the most powerful of warriors among the Dodekatheons, he also got the most attention – facing Archs Raphael, Metatron, and Raguel, as well as the demons Asmodeus and Behemoth. The other lesser Dodekatheons; Hera, Demeter, Hephaestus, Apollo, and Hestia battled other angels and demons called by the two converging forces. The remaining Sacrolites and Hekatonkheires had already been wiped out.

One by one, the Dodekatheons fell, until only Hera, Zeus, Poseidon, and Ares remained. For a moment, the warring between the three armies stopped as they all attempted to recover.

Yeshua stood and watched as, like boxers, each side went to different areas of the courtyard.

"War sure is somethin' ain't it?" a dark familiar voice appeared behind us.

"War is horrible," I replied.

"Yes, fantastically horrible," Satan replied. "I love it."

"Who knew Lucifer could love?" I waxed.

"Don't ever call me that!" Satan suddenly shot back. "That name no longer applies to me."

"That was Satan's name in heaven," Yeshua explained. "Before he rebelled against us."

"Lucifer died when he fell, Satan is king of Hell," Satan continued.

I had not noticed the dark haired, emerald-eyed beauty next to him. She wore a black, slinky, almost dominatrix-like dress that hugged her incredible figure, not leaving much to the imagination.

"Ah, I see you have taken an interest in my wife, Lilith." Satan grinned. "You know, I do believe that is one of the big ones in regards to commandments."

Suddenly, the fighting broke out once again, as the demons and angelus converged on the final four. As the explosions lit up the night sky once again, I could see in the distance the fallen body of Prometheus, and I darted across the battlefield toward him, ignoring the chaos happening above me. As I got to him, I could see he was once more close to the end.

"Prometheus… what happened?" I gasped as I finally reached him.

"I… I was told not to join the battle…" Prometheus wheezed. "You know how I like to follow orders."

"You fool!" I exclaimed. "We had saved you – why did you do this?"

"Daniel, I don't belong on this world… neither do they." He winced and glanced at the eruptions above. "This world belongs to you now."

"But you're a god," I replied. "You can't die!"

"Gods can die, Daniel, look around you," he replied. "You've killed them yourself since you've… reached your potential."

"Yeah but…."

"No, no," he wheezed. "I'm fine – this is my desire. I need to go to Tartarus… and if they let me – Nibiru."

"No, but I need you here! We have to complete my training."

"No, you have completed…you have completed your training…you don't need me anymore," Prometheus coughed his reply. "The war here is over, but another is on the… CAHAAK… on the horizon, the war of wars. I… I need to be ready… and in my Terran form I am at my weakest."

"Prometheus!"

"Good-bye… Daniel," he gasped. "We will see each other again."

His body went limp. He was gone; the solid mass that housed his essence was barren and began to disintegrate.

"Thank you…" I sobbed as I shut his eyes.

I could hear in the distance Yeshua and Satan arguing. I rushed back over just in time to hear Satan say, "He's one of them – I get him!"

"No, Prometheus is not one of them," I angrily retorted. "He is a Titan – a different order."

"Titan-schmitan – he's here, he's one of them. He's mine!" Satan replied.

"NO!" I screamed, and without any thought, I exploded with all my force and power into Satan and Lilith, sending them both backward and into the woods.

A scream ripped across the sky above us, a deep bellowing, "Noooooo." I looked skyward and saw Hera fall, and as they were distracted, both Poseidon and Ares were struck down as well. Zeus was alone. Just as suddenly, the forest in front of me was obliterated by a blinding red light. The charred remains of the trees seemed to encompass Satan and Lilith as they moved toward us.

"Uh oh," I heard Yeshua whisper.

"You dare strike *me*?" Satan angrily barked. "You dare attack the King of Hell, the Prince of Darkness, the Deceiver himself?"

"You will not have Prometheus," I restated.

"Oh, you've done it now, Danny-boy," Satan angrily retorted. "Mark my words; I will get my revenge for your insolence!"

"Consider them marked."

"Fallen!" Satan called to the combatants above, "IT'S TIME TO GO."

Red flashes began to pop all over the sky, and in seconds, all that remained were the Archs, the other Annuna, and Zeus.

Zeus descended from the sky and took foot on the ground, he knelt before us.

"My children, my wife, all dead," he said. "I have no strength to go on. Finish me so I can take my rightful place beside them in Hell."

I drew my sword and prepared to gladly fulfill his request when Yeshua grabbed my arm.

"Wait," he said.

"Why?"

"Because I am not willing to hand him over to Satan so quickly," Yeshua continued. "He means more to us in his current state than in Satan's service."

"He put my race at the brink of extinction! He should pay for his crimes!" I replied angrily.

"He will," Yeshua replied, "in slavery – to Thoth. He will be stripped of all of his power. He will be shipped to another, barren world where he cannot hurt anyone."

"No… no, no way!"

"It is the only way to protect the Annuna," Yeshua continued. "And the new world you will build here."

I stood in shock – after all of this – Zeus would remain.

"As his power continues to subside," Yeshua continued, "long after you decide to end your rule on Earth and join us in Nibiru, he will be gone – and Satan can have whatever remains."

"Prison… for all eternity," Michael added, as he placed his hand on my shoulder. "It is the right way."

"So be it," I replied. I didn't have to like it. There wasn't going to be a choice in the matter.

Epilogue New Terra

Yeshua and I returned to Atlantis, where thousands of mortals awaited the outcome of the battle. As we arrived at Zeus' palace, I found Mina, who was badly scraped up but as beautiful as ever. Her luscious, bulbous lips beckoned my kiss and I obliged, a deep, long, toe-curling moment of pleasure and ecstasy. Her arms enveloped me and I could feel her heart pound against me. We kissed once more, our tongues swirling around like ballerinas.

"God, I missed you…" I said.

"Me too." She smiled. "And the others – Marty? My grandfather?"

"Mina, I'm sorry…"

She grabbed me tight and held me close, choking back her tears.

"All your grandfather wanted was for me to protect you."

"And you did… thank you, Dan."

Yeshua placed his hand on my shoulder, I looked back and smiled.

"Mina, I'd like for you to meet someone." I motioned toward him. "This is Yeshua MiN'zaret."

"Jesus of Nazareth?" she gasped, annoying me that she knew instantly while it had taken me a little longer – and I was supposed to be the biblical scholar. She dropped to her knees in reverence.

"Come, child, rise," Yeshua replied, as he helped her to her feet. "There is no call for that."

"Lord, I prayed you'd come to deliver us," Mina said. "And here you are."

"Thank you for your faith, my child," he continued. "But your faith should be in Dan – as he championed your cause."

She glanced over to me, flashing her warm, light eyes that beamed pride.

"So what now?" I asked him.

"What now?" He chuckled. "Now you must rebuild your world, your civilization. Your race has received a fourth chance, Daniel. As their king, you must guide them through rebuilding their lives…"

"Their King?"

"Of course," he laughed. "A civilization needs order, a hierarchy. And after all, you are a God."

"I have no idea how to lead a people."

"You'll find your way."

"Yeah – but I don't want this."

"It doesn't matter what you want," Yeshua continued. "It is your destiny. And your world will need your strength to rebuild it to an even greater height. And at some point – we will need it for our defense against Satan."

"You still believe a war is coming?"

"War is inevitable," Yeshua sighed. "But we will face that challenge when it comes."

"Yeah," I agreed, "But this King stuff…"

"A King needs his Queen."

I looked over to Mina, she blushed a little.

"I can't do this alone." I said.

"You won't be alone, Dan," Yeshua smiled, "She'll be with you…as will I."

"You're staying?"

"For as long as I can," Yeshua replied, "But at some point Satan will figure out our deception and I will need to join the Angelus."

"If you need me -" I began.

"Yes, I know," Yeshua smiled, "We know where to find you but I think we'll survive without Dan Ryan – for now. You'll have your hands full here. Just always remember-"

"Please don't give me the '*with great power comes great responsibility*' line." I grinned.

"Haha, so you know it."

"Anyone who has seen Spiderman knows it."

"Spiderman?" Yeshua looked puzzled.

"You've been gone a long time, Yeshua," I chuckled. "Let me tell you a story about a young kid named Peter Parker…"

As we walked off, I could see Mina move out to the balcony and look over Atlantis. The thralls of people below called out her name, and mine, desperate for any kind of news. The news would be good… Zeus and the Gods were gone. Yeshua was among us, and we, as a people, had another chance to make things right. It would all begin here – in Atlantis.

About the Author

Speculative Fiction author JC De La Torre was born on September 4th, 1973 in Tampa, Florida. Author of the critically acclaimed underground success Ancient Rising, De La Torre continues to press on to provide his fans the best in Speculative Fiction today.

De La Torre has a special relationship with his fans, whom the author says he "loves dearly", and makes himself available to them via his website and email.

De La Torre has a passionate interest in Speculative fiction - including Sci-Fi, Fantasy, Horror, the Occult, Alternative History, and strange, amazing worlds. His writing will include all of these sub-genres and other interesting excursions. De La Torre also has a keen love for sports including American football (both professional and collegiate), NHL hockey, Major League Baseball, and college basketball.

De La Torre currently resides in Wesley Chapel, Florida with his loving wife Rita, their new Yorkshire Terrier, Lestat (aka Mr. Poopenstein) and their two cats, Marius (aka Blackie) and Artemis (aka Arty). Rita and JC were married on November 17, 2001 and in 2006 Rita completed her own work of Fantasy fiction, Dark Dragon, which should be re-released soon.

Fans can visit JC at his website
http://www.jcdelatorre.com.

DLT Atlantis Publishing

http://www.dltatlantispub.com

- Home of JC and Rita De La Torre's works
- Offers services and other benefits for authors
- Get ISBNs, Covers, Interior Book Work, or all other publishing needs from us.